Money Game 2

Smoove Dolla

Lock Down Publications and Ca$h Presents
Money Game 2
A Novel by *Smoove Dolla*

Smoove Dolla

Lock Down Publications
P.O. Box 944
Stockbridge, Ga 30281
www.lockdownpublications.com

Copyright 2021 by Smoove Dolla
Money Game 2

Lock Down Publications
Like our page on Facebook: Lock Down Publications @
www.facebook.com/lockdownpublications.ldp
Book interior design by: **Shawn Walker**
Edited by: **Tamira Butler**

Stay Connected with Us!

Text **LOCKDOWN** to 22828 to stay up-to-date with new releases, sneak peaks, contests and more…

Thank you!

Smoove Dolla

Submission Guideline.

Submit the first three chapters of your completed manuscript to ldpsubmissions@gmail.com, subject line: Your book's title. The manuscript must be in a .doc file and sent as an attachment. Document should be in Times New Roman, double spaced and in size 12 font. Also, provide your synopsis and full contact information. If sending multiple submissions, they must each be in a separate email.

Have a story but no way to send it electronically? You can still submit to LDP/Ca$h Presents. Send in the first three chapters, written or typed, of your completed manuscript to:

LDP: Submissions Dept
P.O. Box 944
Stockbridge, Ga 30281

DO NOT send original manuscript. Must be a duplicate.

Provide your synopsis and a cover letter containing your full contact information.

Thanks for considering LDP and Ca$h Presents.

Acknowledgements

Thanks to Ebony, my mother, and Anajhia, my daughter, for your help. I appreciate you, Ca$h, for waiting on me to finish writing this book. Thanks to all the people who have helped me in any way in the process of writing part two. You know who you are. Shout out to Bell, J More, YC, Big South Dallas, Boosie, Elexis, Mavis, Zsa Zsa, Erica Bailey, Brent, Chase, Peter Mann, Big D, Bankroll Bubba, Qana, Circle, Jasmine Johnson out the Grove. Sorry how things ended for you. Continue to fight and stay strong. Keep ya head up, baby girl.

Shout out to all the real pimps, macks, and queens who are playing the Game the way it is properly played.

Smoove Dolla

Chapter 1
Square Business
Masonic Meeting - 06:54 P.M.
Monopoly

Not knowing what to expect at this late-evening Masonic meeting at this closed barbershop had me a bit uneasy. I'd missed the last seven meetings we had on Mondays or Tuesdays, for no apparent reason. I'd been in the streets pimpin' hard. I knew my brothers would say something about my absence. On top of that, I knew something would be said about what happened with Tight Game and what took place in Houston, Texas with Jerry. Even though they weren't going to ride down on me for my actions, I was prepared for all that might come against me.

There were six cars that belonged to my Masonic brothers who were already inside, that were parked in the shopping center's big parking lot. I got out my Rolls Royce and headed towards the entrance of the nice but small barber shop. I counted eleven brothers after passing the two deacons that guarded the front door. Five of them were sitting in plastic chairs up against the wall, six in the barber chairs. Tight Game, Jerry, Mark, and Timothy were included in that group. There were no outsiders. Everyone in the spot were Masons, and we were all dressed in black, two-piece suits with white shirts.

I greeted all the brothers here in our Masonic handgrip. Jerry acted like everything was normal and fine between us two, like we had talked since our confrontation. We hadn't. I didn't know how to take that, so I went along with it for the time being. I really didn't want it to be any beef between us in the first place, because we were brothers and we both were caught up in our feelings about Tight Game being in a coma. If any shit was to take place, it was all good. I knew how to conduct myself. This was my first time seeing Tight Game in person other than Facetiming with him since he had been out of the hospital. Other than the fact he lost about 15 pounds, he still looked good and his tall, normal self. He told me not to worry about anything, just play it cool at the meeting. I sat down in one of the chairs that was backed up to the wall. They resumed their conversation before I respectfully interrupted their discussion about giving charity to our communities, mainly South Dallas. About ten minutes later, two more brothers walked in separately, who also attended our lodge. Our lodge secretary started talking about Masonic things that helped us on our journey, to strengthen our loyalty and determination to our deeds as Masons.

The secretary spoke for almost two hours before he passed it to our Worshipful Master Tony to discuss any issues we might have in our lives. That was when I was brought into the picture. He gave the floor to Jerry, our Lodge Warden.

"Damion, there's two issues that I want to bring to the table here, that involve you." He stood up out the barber client's chair and walked towards me slowly in a non-threatening way. After I stood from the chair I sat in, he then extended his arm for a handshake that I accepted. We held hands as he spoke, "Young brother, I apologize for getting out of character at the park in Houston. You're a good brother. I have much love and respect for you. That was all my fault. That should have never happened. Forgive me, brother," Jerry said with meaning in his face and eyes.

I peeped Tony looking in Tight Game's direction, so immediately, I thought they had something to do with Jerry apologizing, other than the fact he was being himself by apologizing when he was in the wrong.

I accepted his apology. "I'm not trippin' on that. I understand, it doesn't have to be explained. I forgive you. I apologize for acting in that manner as well."

After we unlocked our Masonic handgrip, we returned to our chairs. "Well, Damion, you haven't violated any Masonic laws, but you've been absent for eight weeks now. Can you give us a good reason why you haven't been attending meetings?" asked Tony.

"No. I don't have a good enough reason why I haven't been coming. Well, I was in the hospital for three of those weeks. I've been on the road since I discharged out the hospital the first time. Although, I did check in both lodges in Austin and Houston upon my arrival in those two cities like I'm supposed to. And the reason why I missed the last two meetings is because I checked in the hospital again. I had gotten myself into a little mess, but I fixed the problem."

Honesty beats a fuck-up. Especially when dealing with family, friends, and the group you're a fellow member of. Being honest might cause a person to leave you and feel some type of way depending on the situation, but it brings respect from them. "About any other lodge, you would probably be going through the process of being expelled. But because we have love for you and we know that you're a good brother in spite of what you do on your own time, we're not going to put you through that, Damion. You need to start using your Gravel, Chisel, Square more than you do. It will really do some good, because you're heading for self-destruction."

He was talking about chipping away my bad habits as well as reminding me that I must strive for order and harmony in my behavior and my dealings with others. He was right, no doubt. "I know you've gotten yourself arrested last month, similar to the same charge that sent you to prison the first time around. What's that about?"

The only person that could have told them that was our Masonic brother, Mark, who worked the Human Trafficking Unit in the FBI. Mark was one of the ones that was here at the barber shop before I pulled up. It was cool, though, because I knew I couldn't keep anything away from them too long if I wanted to. They knew damn near everything about me and could find out anything they wanted to know about me if they wanted to.

Really, there was no need to explain myself, even though I got set up by that bitch, Christie. I wasn't going to tell them that, especially not without telling Tight Game first. I planned to keep that between me, Tight Game, my lawyer, Jennifer, and Christie. If he decided to tell the brothers, it was cool with me. I knew I didn't gorilla no hoe to prostitute.

"Yes, that's true. It's a bogus case, 70 percent of what's said about me is false. I guarantee you that I will beat that case."

"That's good to know, Damion. Look, brother, this is your last straw with us. If there are any more incidents involving another brother or catching another criminal case, you will be expelled from being an active Master Mason. You need to choose whether you want to be a pimp or a Mason. You can't be both anymore. Do I make myself clear, Mr. Johnson?"

"Yes, Master, you made yourself clear," I told him. See, I had to respect what he had said. As a Master Mason, I was supposed to be living more righteously than I was. The way he was thinking was the longer I lived my life as a pimp, I couldn't progress in life nor Masonry. And that was true. I couldn't fully see myself not pimpin'. Fighting that pimpin' disease was going to be one of the hardest things that I had to do in my life. I had to let go of that lifestyle sooner or later, because I did love being a Mason. I wasn't giving that up for anything.

To distinguish myself as a Free and Accepted Mason U under the Most Worshipped Prince Hall Grand Lodge of Texas (MWPHGLOT) was something I had wanted to be able to do for years, ever since I'd been knowing and hanging around Tight Game. I loved and wanted the power he had in his life and the connections he had, for myself. It didn't take until I was in the feds that I wanted to know more about Tight Game's involvement in the culture of Masonry. I asked him about it on a phone conversation. He didn't want to talk about it over the phone, but two weeks later, he made time to come see me in the feds in Beaumont, Texas.

That's where he broke it down to me in depth. While in prison, I strived to know all I could about Masonry. A month later, after my release, I went to the lodge where Tight Game attended on my "Free

Will" and was officially raised to the sublime level of Enter Apprentice. I've been raised twice since then.

Being a part of one of the biggest fraternities in the world, I had Brothers in every city and state. I had Brothers in every hood from the ghetto to the upper class. I had Brothers of every race and religion, I even had brothers in politics. Yes, I had a lot of connections and an abundance of power that I did my best to not abuse. As the youngest member of my lodge, I had gained so much wisdom, knowledge, and understanding from my elders and from striving on my own. When I did attend our weekly meetings, the peace that I got carried me through the remainder of the week. As a Mason, I was a builder, an architect.

Even though pimpin' was what I did, I still considered myself a good standing man, no matter what anybody said. I had learned how to use the Tools I was given to fashion, shape, and mold my mind into a success-oriented machine.

My outlook on life had been defined by not only my relationship with the Pimp Game and to the Supreme Architect of the Universe, but by Mathematics and Science of Self. At times, I felt Invincible. I was proud to be a Prince Hall Freemason.

After the meeting, I pulled Tight Game to the side and told him that it was urgent that we talked inside my car.

When we got into my Rolls Royce, I got straight to the point. "Before I get into what I want to tell you, I want to show you this." I took the manilla envelope out of the glove compartment. The same envelope Shae got from Big Country's house that contained the photos of me, Shae, and my mother as well as our addresses. Big Country's flip phone was inside of it too.

I could tell he was wondering what was inside when he looked at the bulge in the envelope. He bent the small, flappy metal part that locked the contents inside the envelope to open it. He pulled out the documents, leaving the phone inside.

After looking at every document and the photos, Tight Game asked me, "What's going on, Tunke? What is this about?"

"Hand me the phone, and I'll show you."

Tight Game flipped the envelope upside down, and the phone fell on top of the documents. After he handed me the phone, I went straight to the text conversation Big Country and Christie had with each other, and then gave it back to him.

He was a quick reader, so I let him read every text between them before I said anything.

"Tight Game, I love you, bro. I'll never do anything to jeopardize our bond of friendship and brotherhood. I look up to you bro. I cherish our friendship," I told him while looking at him dead in the eyes. "While you were in a coma, some foul shit took place, as you can see. Man, Christie has been trying to take me down because of you being in a coma. While you were in the hospital, Christie called me, offering to pay me to do this freaky shit to her. I let her suck my dick. I would've fucked her too if I didn't find out she was the reason why a detective called my phone. Plus, she had one of my hoes set me up on that charge I caught last month. She really tried to fuck over me."

I looked in his eyes and then his facial expression to see if he felt any way about what I just told him. He just had a curious look on his face, like he was trying to understand everything that happened.

"Why would Christie have a detective call your phone?"

"She said that she was trying to find who was responsible for shooting you, not knowing I had taken care of that already."

"Timothy was telling me that you did, except for the one who is locked up. Don't worry, we're gonna handle that soon. Anyway, back to Christie. I don't give a fuck about what you did with her. You're my brother and a pimp that I brought into the life. I'll never bring harm to you, and especially, not over a bitch. I understand you and I understand her, so I'm not trippin' on that. But I will get on her ass for doing that punk ass shit by getting that bitch to set you up. I don't get down like that, and a bitch of mine won't neither," Tight Game said.

"I'm not done yet, Tight Game. There's more, bro."

"Spit that shit out, nephew. Don't hold back from me," Tight Game said with curiosity and warning.

"After I bailed out, some kind of way, I got kidnapped by Big Country's ass. This nigga had my mouth, hands, and legs all taped up. Put slabs of meat all in my clothes, and had fuckin' dogs bite the fuck out of me, bro." My suit jacket was off hanging up in the window, so it was easy to take my dress shirt out of my pants. I lifted it up to show him my bite marks on my waistline. "I got bite marks all on my ass and shit too. If it wasn't for Shae, I probably wouldn't be here right now talking with you. I'd be dead, all because of Christie being fucked up at me for you being in a coma."

"Is that so? What happened to Country? Where is he?

"I had to kill him, bro," I lied. I believed he wouldn't harm Shae for killing Big Country, but I still had to protect her, no matter if she was my baby's mother or not. I loved her for real, it was a must that I protected her by any means necessary. "I'm sorry, big bro."

"It's okay, you had to do what you had to do. Where is his body?"

"In the back of his house. Probably ate by wild hogs by now."

He shook his head. "Alright, man, I'll go there to check it out to see if it needs my clean-up crew."

"Oh, you will need them. It's too much evidence," I told him.

"Alright. Anyway, Damion, you need to really think about your future and where you're headed. Man, sometimes, I be regretting that I introduced you to the Game. I should have given you a job, lil' bro." I could hear it in his voice that he really meant what he said. "Promise me something, Tunke."

"What is it?"

"I know it will be hard on your end but promise me you will chisel the Game out of your life before the Game destroys your life."

I wasn't going to be fast at answering that question. Changing my lifestyle was going to be one of the hardest things I ever had to do in my life. It was really a disease for a real pimp. I was a motherfucking addict to the Game, but I was going to fight it. "I promise, I will take the steps to get out." I knew he really cared about me like his own son, and I did see him as a father and big brother. I knew he wished the best for me. "Thanks for caring Tight Game, I love you, big bro."

We shook a firm Masonic handshake and hugged each other. "I love you too, nephew. Don't get yourself caught up in no more mess, Damion. I mean that shit, Tunke."

"I won't," I said as we unlocked our embrace.

"In a couple of months, I'm going to Dubai. You got time to join me?"

"Of course, but I don't know if I gotta go to court or not at that time. I'll tell my lawyer to reschedule it for a later date."

"Okay, do that. Yeah, I have to close a business deal in person. I want to show you how real business is done between men. Me and a brother of ours will be discussing details on a skyscraper that will be built in Dubai. I'll call you in a month to let you know when we are leaving."

"Alright. I'll be looking forward to that," I mentioned.

After he left, I sat in my Double R, thinking about the steps I had to take towards getting out the Game. Like I said before, I couldn't fully imagine myself fully out of the game. I wanted women to work for me in some kind of way. I didn't want to own an escort service. I didn't want to go through the shit it took to own a strip club. Plus, I went to prison for pimpin', so that wouldn't look too good at all. My mind kept going back to owning a modelling agency.

Chapter 2
Not Making the Same Mistake
Tight Game

"Boss, we have a problem," Jon Jon said when I answered the phone.

"What's the problem?" I asked curiously while taking my reading glasses off. I sat them and the *Dallas Morning Newspaper* down on the walnut wood desk in my office at home.

"It's a kid here, what you want us to do with him?"

"I know that ain't Elijah. He's not supposed to be there," I said to myself. Elijah was Big Country's 17-year-old son. "Look here, Jon Jon, don't lay a finger on him."

I had a three-man cleaning crew: Jon Jon, Darias, and Lonny. They were all about that business. Just in case I had a problem arrive at the scene while working, they took care of it. I didn't have any weenies on my cleaning crew. They had to be about some murder shit and no snitch shit, just in case they got caught up on a charge. "Put him on the phone."

I heard shuffling on the phone, and after five seconds I said, "Hello." There was no answer, but I knew Elijah was on the phone being quiet because I heard Jon Jon tell him to get the phone. He probably was fucked up about his father being dead. I felt his pain. My dad was shot down by the police for resisting arrest and running a police officer over when I was nine. I was 58 years old now, and I still suffered from that hellified blow.

"This Tight Game, I'm sorry for your loss, youngin'. I'm on my way over to get you."

I was glad Christie wasn't home. There was a big chance I would have let my anger get the best of me and exposed myself. Her head had gotten too big for her own good. When a bitch made a big move like that to take out family, she was dangerous and couldn't be trusted. I really loved Christie a lot, but I couldn't forgive her for what she had done. I had to get rid of Christie some way somehow.

The bitch deserved murder for what she did. Her sucking my nephew up wasn't included in the list. I didn't give a fuck about that. What I was fucked up about was she was the cause of Big Country dying, putting a hit out on my nephew, and setting him up on a felony charge by his own ho. That shit boiled the blood up inside of me.

I was already dressed in my casual golf gear from going out golfing this morning. I grabbed my tan Kangol hat, put it over my long-permed hair, and then headed out the front door to my late-year Bentley truck.

The whole way to Big Country's house, I was thinking what I was going to do with Elijah. His mother was my ex-ho from 17 years back. Back then I was letting Big Country bust her up sometimes when he used to stand guard for my hoes for me at their rooms. He liked the black ho a lot, she gave him the best treatment. After five months of that, he knocked her up. They liked each other and Big Country asked me for her, wanting a relationship with her. He wasn't a pimp or anything close to it, but I gave the ho to him. They ended up splitting up after being together for two years. Denise and Elijah moved to Oklahoma with family, leaving Big Country in Dallas. Sometimes twice a year but for sure every summer, Elijah would visit his dad. It's the end of July, so he should have been in Oklahoma because of the new school year.

I turned my Bentley onto the road that led to his home on 10 acres of land. I parked next to Jon Jon's white van. A pond was 20 feet in front of us with five ducks trailing behind each other. After getting out of my truck, I swiped at two flies while heading towards Jon Jon, Lonny, Darias, and the half-cleaned corpse. My sense of smell was still completely gone, but I knew from being present while they cleaned up the mess before that the smell was unbearable. The smell of bleach, acid, and dead flesh had to be lingering in the air. That was another reason why they wore face masks. Also, they wore a plastic body suit to protect their hair particles, body fluids, and fingerprints from getting on something that could be used as evidence. From the looks of it, wild hogs did get a hold of his body out here. They ate his flesh like someone does a chickenn leg or squirrel.

Jon Jon walked up to me, leaving Lonny to finish up the cleaning about ten feet away. "What's the news, Jon Jon?"

"We'll be done in about 20 minutes, Boss. The kid is in the house."

Jon Jon attempted to follow me, but I stopped him. "Stay here and help Lonny finish." I headed straight to the house without saying anything else.

Elijah and Darias were sitting at the rectangle-shaped table, opposite sides, longways. Elijah looked like a split image of Big Country. Big, black, and tall. It's like he gained 5 to 10 pounds every time I saw him, which was every summer. He weighed about 200 at 17 years old, but I could see the youth in his face when he looked at me.

I saw he had a swollen lip with ice in a washcloth in his hand. "Darias, who hit him?"

Darias didn't say anything, so I went to the back door and then stepped onto the back porch. "Bring y'all muthafuckin' asses here!" When they made it inside, I pointed to Elijah. "Jon Jon, you didn't hear me when I said don't lay a finger on him?"

"You did, Boss, but that was before you said that, Boss."

"Which one of y'all did the shit?" I asked.

Lonny spoke up. "I did, Tight Game. He was trying to buck so I punched him."

"Since you punched him, I'm firing you," I said, lying. I just wanted to be hard on him. I'd talk to him later on tonight.

"Come on, Boss," Lonny pleaded.

"It's over, holla at me later. You can finish this job, tho', since I gotta pay you the other half. Eli, come with me, you going to my place."

While walking to my truck, I asked Elijah, "Have you told your mother what happened yet?"

"No, sir, not yet," he said sadly.

"I'll call her and break the news to her. I thought you were supposed to be in Oklahoma for school. Why you still in Texas?" I asked as we got into the Bentley.

"I didn't spend the summer with my dad this year, I spent it with my mama. I moved to Texas. I transferred to Cedar Hill High for my last year."

"How long have you been here?"

"Since yesterday."

"Elijah, you'll be staying with me for now. I'ma take care of your dad's funeral and tombstone."

When we made it home, I got his mother's number and called her up. "Hey, Denise, this Herbert, Tight Game. How are you?"

"I know who you is, Herbert," she said happily. "I'm great. How you been?"

Denise was my ho for five months, until I gave her to Big Country. She was a good little ho back then, one who didn't give a pimp too many problems. "I been great as well. You know me, just been achieving greatness, that's about it. Anyway, the reason I called is to give you some bad news."

"Oh, Herbert, it's not about Elijah is it? Where is Big Country?"

"It's about Big Country. He was murdered a couple weeks back."

"Murdered? How that happened?" she asked, shocked. She knew Big Country's lifestyle and knew what he was about. I knew she was wondering how the hell he let himself get killed.

"I don't know any details. All I know is he was shot and killed at his house."

"Ain't that a bitch. Herbert, put Elijah on a bus for me, please. Send my baby home," she said, worried.

"I was thinking, you should let him stay with me. You know he needs a father figure in his life. I'll take care of him. You know he's in good hands, anything he needs and more, will be provided."

She was quiet for some seconds and then said, "Alright, Herbert, I'm trusting you to not let nothing happen to my child. Take care of my baby."

"I will, you know I got him. And don't worry about the funeral, Big Country is family. I'll take care of it all. It's going to be a closed casket. I'll let you know when the funeral will be. Do you need or want anything?"

"Nall, I'm good. Just take care of my child."

I was glad that she let Elijah stay with me. I was sterile from birth, so I couldn't have babies. That's why I treated Tunke, Mack Tre, and Solo like my sons. With Elijah, I wasn't making the same mistakes I did with them. I should have put them on another hustle other than bringing them into the Game, but they really had the heart to pimp.

After talking with Elijah for about three hours straight, I learned that he was a highly educated kid. This 17-year-old kid had already completed the 11th grade. He knew Spanish, Chinese, and French fluently. He was an A and B honor roll student. He really didn't know what he wanted to go to college for, but then mentioned, "I like fashion, I'm into designing men and women's clothing." Even though he was dressed in designer clothes, look wise, he didn't appear to be a person into fashion. He looked like a young Biggie Smalls.

Looks could be deceiving. I chuckled. He favored his pops, the hit man. "Youngin' you don't have to go to college. I can help you jump that off now."

He got excited about what I said, but I wasn't going to help Elijah that easy. He was going to have to show me something. "Success is not going to be easy. There's going to be obstacles. Do you have any sketches that you've drawn up yet?"

"No, sir."

"If you can bring me some sketches, let me look at them, then we can talk about jumping it off.

"Bet that," he said, smiling.

"You have some money?" I asked him.

"I have a hundred and 17 dollars."

I took $500 out my wallet and took my late-model Bentley truck key off my keychain, and then gave it to him. "You can drive my Bentley for now. Go get whatever you need to draw them sketches. I'm ready whenever you ready."

"Thanks, Herbert. I really do appreciate it."

"You're welcome, youngin'. This is the least I can do. Big Country helped me out a lot, and plus, we were childhood friends." Saying that made me think of Tina, Big Country's mother, to tell her what happened. I knew she was going to be devastated. Damn.

I had to be there for Elijah. I felt bad and hated other shit black males, really black people, went through. That's why I helped out so much like I did. I used the pimpin' as a steppingstone to build my platform. In my hood, The Bonton and The Turner Courts Projects, I was labeled as an OG. I was almost considered as a godfather in South Dallas for how much I'd given back to the hood. I'd given back over a million dollars. All the block parties, the Christmas gifts, the free events, the giveaways, the help I'd given single mothers, and the bail out for all of South Dallas. I was proud of myself because I did it all without selling a sack or brick of dope to the hood. There were few that could say that. I wasn't talking down on who had sold dope. I had best friends that were big-time dope dealing, I just didn't participate in that Game. That's why my sons, Mack Dre, Tunke, and Solo, were the way they were. Pimpin' our black women was bad enough, selling drugs to our hoods was messing them up even worse. I stressed that to them. But I understood that hustle, so I couldn't look down on it. That's the way some of our people ate and took care of themselves and their family. Because of that, I was here for support, providing everything that Elijah needed to be successful in this world. Plus, Big Country worked for me, was there whenever I wanted him to be. He wasn't just my hit man and hoes' security; he was family and a good friend also.

Every time I thought about Christie being the reason Big Country got killed, I got heated. That bitch had to go for that. I believed any prostitute that had been down with a pimp for more than six months should be repaid for her effort of being a down hoe. Getting what I wanted without repaying her in some way that she deserved wasn't my style The way I saw it, a pimp must make sure his truest hoes are pursuing their dreams in life. Other than the luxury lifestyle, being treated fairly, and good, they deserved that too. A pimp looks out for his truest hoes.

Smoove Dolla

I just gotta ask you, what you need
What you need from me, oh you wanna be a star
Oh, you messing with the right one
I can take you there, I can make sure
You've got all the finest things
Let me be your manager
—"Overnight" by Twista

Chapter 3
Setting Things Up for the Come Up
Monopoly

One of my duties to my queens as their pimp was to help them all pursue their dreams and inspirations in life. Most of my hoes had paid their way. That was what was due to them. Thing about that was, four of my hoes didn't want nothing out of life concerning a professional career. My bottom bitch, Rosemary, would be running her own pole dancing class and dancing career. In my eyes, I saw Erika pursuing an acting career. Naturally, to me, every woman could be good actresses, but Erika really had a gift for it. I would be putting her in performing arts school soon. Syn would be pursuing singing. Claire would pursue being a professional dancer. As for Heather, Sarah, Bre, and Jazz, they didn't have any legal goals. From being around them, I hadn't seen any gifts, skills, and talents other than the ability to play on men and look good. As their pimp, I was their life coach, so I had to observe everything about them. In due time, as they saw me and their sisters pursue our dreams, eventually, it would come to surface and they would follow suit. That's why my mind kept going back to owning a modelling agency, because all of them could pursue modeling. They all had the looks to do so. When I introduce them to people, instead of calling them hoes, I was gonna call them models. Bre, Heather, Sarah, and Jazz would be doing more prostituting than the others. Now with the modelling agency, my hoes' clientele would be legitimate tricks such as rappers, politicians, businessmen, and athletes. With customers as such, there wouldn't be any bullshit like there was on the track and escort sites. Everything would be on a professional level.

At that masonic meeting, they didn't do anything but push my hand towards the agency. To be honest with you and myself, I was not getting completely out the Game. I did plan on making the steps to get all the way on the legal side. It was going to be tough for me, but I would make it if I was breathing.

For three weeks, I took about four hours out of each day to do research on owning a modeling agency. The only problem that I had was not having a business license to start it. That meant I had to go to college for the license or find a good co-owner who had a degree in business administration. I was not going to school, so that was out the question.

Other than having a co-owner, everything was set. For my modeling agency, I set myself at a $100,000 budget. After doing the research, I made a list of things I would need to start this business. Five to eight thousand dollars would be for a used utility van, Apple I-Mac OSX-$1,000, photoshop-$500, video cameras and photo cameras-$400, backgrounds-$400, $2,000 worth of cosmetics for wholesale, insurance of all kinds that probably would cost $5,000 and up, $24,000 for travel and other expenses. Rose was the only one I could trust and depend on being my secretary. The only two I needed to hire was a co-owner, and a video crew.

The more I started thinking and spending time preparing the things that I needed to start my business, the more hype I got about it. Every day, for hours, I talked nonstop to my hoes about my plans and vision for us all involved. With this agency, my hoes would be getting paid $500-$1,000 an hour. To maintain those prices, I had to promote the fuck out of them and the company through multiple outlets such as TV commercials, photoshoots, runway models, magazines, and social media. I would have it as a service-oriented business with retail-style quality. I was going to strive to have the best and most successful modeling agency in Dallas. Once I accomplished that feat, I planned to have one of the hottest agencies in the U.S. I knew it wasn't going to be easy. It was going to take a lot of persistence, dedication, and hard work on the heads and everyone involved with this company.

During those three weeks, I rented and moved into a 1.2-million-dollar home to own in Health's Buffalo Creek. A suburban neighborhood eight miles from Bush Turnpike and 25 miles from Dallas. It had six bedrooms, four bathrooms (plus a pool bathroom), a two-story formal dining room with views of the backyard and negative-edge pool/spa, a study, a media room with a projector and screen, game/exercise room, wine room, and a small room I made into a studio. If I didn't rent everything in the studio, it would have cost me around $150,000. I figured since I was planning on building our dreams, we should all be under one roof, that way we could help each other out and be on one accord.

It was just me, my eight queens, Claire's son, and Rose's son. I figured since they were boys they could live with us. It was better for them to live with us than with their babysitter most of the time. Claire and Rose needed to spend time with their kids anyway.

Even though, Rose's son was white, I took care of him as one of my own, and the same went for Claire's son. My B.M., Tiffany, let my son live with me, so I gave my son two boys to be around, and so I could be in my son's life more. The three of them slept in my room. As far as my daughter, I didn't allow her to come to my house because of my hoes living here, even though she knew I always had a lot of women around me majority of the time. I'd just pick her up like two days out of a week and take her out to spend time with her.

Out of eight of my hoes, two of them needed minor fixes to enhance their physical. Sarah got a Brazilian butt lift. Rose got liposuction inside her lips from up under her arms, but she looked great afterwards. Although Bre needed to lose a little weight in her arms, waist, and small bulge in her stomach, I didn't let her get liposuction. The 25 pounds she needed to lose could be ran off and by watching what she ate. I got her a female trainer to help her out.

Jazz, on the other hand, had the same problem, but her fat was baby fat. I offered her liposuction for a solution, but she said she was scared of the procedure, even after I showed her a video of the process on YouTube. I offered her a trainer and to work out with me, but she declined all the help, so I left it at that. Even though they needed the fixes, I accepted their physical look as they were.

They all were still bad bitches in my eyes. The others were perfect the way they were.

In the meantime, without the modeling agency open and no record deal for Syn yet, my first project that I started working on pursuing was Syn's career, so I had her in the studio. I believed her career would help Rose and Claire's dancing career. It probably would help Erika in one way or another by having her act in Syn's and my videos. I categorized Syn as a pop artist because she had the look and style of voice to fit one. Not to mention that her favorite singers and most of her favorite songs were in the pop genre, so that pop sound would naturally come out of her.

Dealing with music was a long, difficult process if you wanted to become successful in music field. Love for creating music should be the main focus. Let me tell you, I worked hard with recording music and selling songs after I was released from the feds to get my record deal with Forever Records, an independent record label that's based out of Dallas, Texas. I took my feet off the gas a little once I signed because I had one foot in music and the other in the Pimp Game. I felt like I made it, so I didn't put in the work I needed to develop myself as a major artist, although I had the potential to be one. Still having a street mentality and being in the Game, it slowed me down from becoming a big artist. Doing so had been one of my biggest regrets, but I still had plenty of time to be what I wanted.

Before the deal, I promoted my music on Myspace and by performing at every small black club and bar I could get myself in. Thanks to my friend and masonic brother, Timothy, for the deal with Forever Records. It was a flexible deal I liked and one that I got paid 80% of my money from my records sales. The deal was for four albums, I already gave them two with 12 songs on each album. Between my album on the streets and the help from Forever Records, I'd sold over 100,000 units. I had 68k IG followers. I'd sold five records so far as a songwriter. Two of them were sold to a major artist that I still got paid 40% royalties for. Since I didn't get nominated for an award for any of those records, I didn't let that stop me from writing more songs.

Now that I had Syn on my team, I was pushing for the both of us to become major factors in the music game. I had Syn in the studio tough for over eight hours a day, off and on throughout the day, six days a week. About two days out of a week I'd hire a producer and engineer for her records. I had her do covers once a week, and drop them on YouTube and her Facebook page. I bought her pop songs from other songwriters and helped co-write with artists from my label for Syn to sing.

I put a lot of pressure on Syn for many reasons. For one, I believed she had the potential to become a superstar, on a level that Taylor Swift and Katy Perry were on. I talked to her for hours about how dedicated and persistent she had to be to reach those heights and beyond in the music game. She was a bit shy to perform in front of big crowds of people, so from time to time, I had her perform in front of me and her sisters at home to break down those barriers she had and build her confidence up. After a short period of time, she was comfortable with performing in bars in Deep Ellum and small clubs in the DFW area.

Syn recorded an eight-song mixtape. Seven of the songs were fire pop records, and one of the eight records was a slow-tempo ballad duet with me. I must have shelled out over $100,000 for the whole production of her mixtape to get the pop sound I wanted. I shot two famous pop DJs $2000 each to spin her music in the clubs and on mixes on the radio stations around the world. I prayed and hoped that money paid off in a major way, because if it didn't, she wouldn't be getting paid off any of those songs she recorded nor from the shows she was doing, until I got paid back. I owned all the rights to the songs she recorded except the ones that were bought and cowrote. I wasn't going to fuck her over, but I wasn't going to take a loss for this investment either.

Smoove Dolla

Chapter 4
Keeping Secrets
Christie

Keeping secrets from a man I'd shared everything with, even my darkest and most unpleasurable moments I'd ever experienced in my 46 years of living, was eating at me, consciously and unconsciously. I must say that it was nonstop. I wasn't good at keeping secrets neither, especially secrets that I was keeping from Herbert. For the first time since I'd known him, I'd had nightmares about Herbert discovering my hidden agenda and him killing me. It felt so real that I could feel him torturing me, scissoring off my fingers. Just as he would grab my tongue with grips to cut it off, I would wake up in cold sweats, screaming, "Don't do it, Herbert."

I didn't know if he was lyin' or not, but he told me I mumbled in my sleep that I was sorry and that I didn't mean to do it. One time, when I woke up screaming out loud and in sweats like someone just splashed me with a bucket of water, I looked over to Herbert's side of the bed to find him lying awake sideways with his hand on the side of his head. He turned his suspicious look into a concerned one and asked, "Baby, are you okay?"

"Yes, I'm good, just a bad dream," I replied back.

"Do you want to talk about it?" he had asked.

"No, Daddy. It's something that happened when I was a child. I don't want to talk about it, baby."

He probably thought it was bullshit because I always wanted to talk to him, no matter how I was feeling and what I was doing at the time. It was all about Herbert. At that moment, I was thinking, if he checked me about bullshitting him, I was going to lie on my father about doing something to me sexually when I was young, and that I was sorry for never telling him. I knew I would have to act my ass off, because he knew me better than any man knew me on earth.

"Whenever you feel comfortable about talking with me, I'm all ears," he said, and then passionately kissed me.

That shit surprised me. I wasn't expecting him to say and do that.

Without waiting for a response, he spoke again. "Get up, you're soaking wet. Go take another shower before you go back to bed. I'll change the sheets."

I looked at our digital clock on the nightstand—12:53 A.M. We'd only been sleep for almost three hours.

Holding things back from him was killing me to the point it was affecting my job as an attorney and my campaign to become a Dallas County mayor. My regrets made it difficult to concentrate. I was certain he will go crazy over the shit I did to Tunke. The way I was, if I knew he knew everything I did, our relationship would not be the same. I knew him enough to know I would feel like I would have to do a thousand cartwheels and jump through a million wholly hoops just to prove myself to him. And even then, there could be nothing I could say, everything I said would be questioned. Literally, I would have to speak through my actions. Our communication would surely die after a while, ending our healthy, long-term relationship. I didn't want that to happen.

I really was in love with Herbert Washington. Even though we were common law married, I still wanted an actually wedding. I didn't care if he couldn't have kids, we could adopt a baby. Herbert had always thought as a real pimp, knowing you can't fully trust women as far as you can see them. He truly lived up to his alias, Tight Game. Anyway, he was right, because of us women were fickle creatures, we changed up like the weather. Us women reacted according to how we felt. Some were stronger than others, more trustworthy than others, but we couldn't be fully trusted. I was down for Tight Game, but look, I was a living example of what I just explained.

No doubt, I needed Herbert. I needed him for almost every decision I made. You might say I was weak and stupid, but I don't care what you say about me. I had millions in my bank account because of Herbert. I owned two businesses and had my own firm because of Herbert. I was in the list of top 10 lawyers in the state of Texas, and I was currently running for mayor, so fuck you if you're saying I'm stupid. I was only stupid for what I did while Herbert was in the hospital. Herbert Washington had never misguided me, ever.

Everything that he had taught me and told me to do to better my life and upgrade my career had not just benefitted him but me, Christie S. Lewis. If it wasn't for him, I wouldn't be the lawyer I was today. If it wasn't for him, I wouldn't be running to be mayor. I owed him a lot. I owed him the truth, but I just couldn't tell him. What a shame.

Smoove Dolla

Chapter 5
Monopoly
The Thot House

My pimp partna, Luxury P, gave me a call while I was putting some pieces together for my business plan. "Wuz happening, P?"

"Just putting this shit together so I can take my pimpin' off to the next level, P. That's 'bout it. What's goin' on with you?"

"I called to give you some news you can use, pimp."

"What is it?" I asked.

"You ever heard of the Thot House?" he asked.

"Nall, is it some hoing goin' on in that mothafucker?"

"It is, that and a lot more, P. It's some underground shit, twice a month. Cash Flow put me on Game last night. You know I had to inform my partna about the good news."

"Good lookin' out, P. We some big pimps in the city, so I don't know why we wasn't informed 'bout these parties. How long have they been goin' on for?"

"For three years now, Cash Flow say. That's over wit', I'm 'bout to come up in this muthafucka in mo' ways than one. Get yo' shit together, pimp. I'll text you the info when we hang up."

He did just that when we hung up. The digital flyer said it was five days from now, on a Saturday. It also mentioned something about fight night. The contestants had to register before Friday. When I told Erika about it, she wanted to do it, so I had her call to register for the fight.

When Saturday night finally rode in, I had hoes load up on condoms, baby wipes, towels, toys, dildos, and different kinds of lingerie. I drove in my Rolls Royce with my hood niggas, Poppa, Kendrick, and Tyrell. My hoes were in Rose's Bentley, and in my Range Rover.

The Thot House was in Nawf Dallas off Northwest Hwy. After turning, I drove 30 seconds, 10 mph to get to the parking lot. It was ducked off pretty good.

If you didn't know this spot you would pass it right on up. I expected a regular size building, but it was a big three-story building. There were a lot of cars and trucks around the building-with people pulling up.

I saw a lot of bopped up bitches and hoish looking hoes walking up to the building like it was a billion dollars in The Thot House and they would do whatever for it. Everything they wore was tight fitted, no matter if it was dress, skirt, jeans, and tights. I didn't see too many niggas, but they were here from the few pimped-out slabs in the parking lot. Plus, there were a lot of freshly cleaned and waxed foreign whips outside. I saw Aston Martins, Audis, Bugatti S, a Ferrari, Jags, Lambos, and a Maserati, among other vehicles I didn't care to name. It looked like I was the only one riding in a double R. From seeing those cars, instantly, I knew there was big money inside.

When we walked in after paying and getting searched, I saw so many hoes getting at some paper it was like three of the biggest ho tracks put together that made one whole big one. This was too many hoes in one spot. I was definitely coming up with at least one ho tonight.

It seemed like every big drug dealer out the city was inside this bitch throwing money up in the air at these strippers. All the big money niggas in here were jeweled up and wearing designer gear like they were trying to outdo each other. This shit reminded me of the Player's Ball. As for sure, Player's Ball is for pimps. It seemed like the Thot House was for drug dealers, without the awards but with street cred on what nigga, hood, and clique was making the most money and doing the most in the city. I even saw my nigga, Damu, out of Hamilton Park in North Dallas in here with two other niggas I didn't know, and they all looked like money. One of the niggas had a fat blunt in one hand and a huge Henny bottle in the other hand, standing behind some stripper while she danced on him. Damu and the third nigga were throwing money on two other strippers. Damu was a getting money nigga, and he let it be known. They had about $100,000 in ones on the table wrapped up in bundles like a mountain.

It was crazy up in here. The DJ was spinning a track by Rick Ross featuring Wale & Pusha T, named "Fuck Wit' Me You Know I Got It." Every baller, every ho, every stripper was screamin' fuck with me you know I got it. The ballers were speaking through stunting and how much money they threw. The hoes and strippers were speaking through their sexiness, their bodies, their attitudes, and the good conversation they gave the patrons.

After I picked a spot to handle up, I gave my hoes instructions on what I wanted them to do. I sent Syn, Ross, Claire, and Erika to dance, and Heather, Bre, Jazz, and Sarah to go walk around to catch a trick until I said otherwise. Before we parted, I told them when they caught a trick to take them upstairs. I had Poppa, Kendrick, and Tyrell be their security because majority of the people here were black. But judging by the cars to jewelry to dress code to all the money inside The Thot House, it couldn't be too much drama, if any at all. Theses hoes would probably start fighting before these niggas would, unless it was some kind of outside beef between these niggas here.

After a minute of walking around peeping the scenery, two strippers that were dancing on the main stage caught my eye. They were introduced by the DJ as Magic and Spyda. Automatically, I started looking for Rose to check them out also, but found her about 10 seconds later close by, already looking at them. I couldn't help but smile. Rose never ceased to amaze me. She was a real student of the Game, always learning new things she could use to get paid.

They performed to "I Don't Mind" by Usher feat. Juicy J. Spyda had enough body strength to hold herself in the air in a shape of a C without her feet touching the pole for about five seconds. She then put the pole right between her legs up under her pussy and then crossed her legs. Her body stood in a straight line in mid-air while still holding on to the pole. Her long, pretty black hair hung down towards the stage floor. Magic, on the other hand, was already dancing on a higher end of the pole. She wrapped her left hand around the pole above her head and her right arm was extended out lower holding the pole. She squatted in mid-air from her legs being held up in a missionary position. She slid down, landing one of her heels on top of Spyda's lower thigh and one on her upper chest. She started popping her ass, making both genders go wild and rain money on the strippers. Don't let me forget these two strippers were bad bitches, so the people were amazed at what they saw.

The strippers didn't stop there. They were so talented, some-how, Magic had the strength to flip herself around and put herself upside down, holding herself up by tightening her thighs on the pole and crossing her ankles. Spyda landed on her heels on stage. She grabbed onto the lower end of the pole and then turned herself up backwards until she was upside down. Magic wrapped her arms around Spyda's waist and upper ass cheeks. When Spyda was spread eagle in the air, she let go of the pole, depending on Magic's strength. Magic had her face all in between Spyda's ass while they hung in the air. The ballers around the stage threw more stacks of ones up in the air at them. The whole stage was covered with one-dollar bills.

After their show, I looked at Rose who was looking at me. I nodded my head at her, signaling that I hoped she took notes on their performance. Afterwards, I made a tour of the building to see where my hoes were going to be around in this club. First, I took the elevator to the second floor. There was even a security guard for the elevator riding with me, three hoes, and three tricks. After the elevator doors opened, I waited until all six of them were off before I stepped inside the hallway. When I did, the smell of pussy and sex hit my nostrils. It was thick in the air.

There was another Big D-Bo looking bouncer that was in the hallway sitting down on a short stool, looking like he just woke up when he heard the elevator door beep. The three couples disap-peared one by one until they found an empty room.

The entrance of the rooms had no doors, so you could see what went on in every room. I counted 16 rooms by the time I got to the end of the hallway, 8 rooms on each side. Out of 16 rooms, there were about 10 rooms they were fucking in. I went up to the third floor and walked to the end of the hallway. It was the same thing going as it was on the second, except I saw a nigga hog tied to the bed, ass up, getting spanked with a big long paddle by a bitch, surprising me that somebody black was doing that weird shit. When I got burned up, I told myself, 'let me get my ass back downstairs.' While on the elevator going back down, it stopped on the second floor again. One of the chicks I saw get off with me got back on the elevator. Except this time, she wasn't hugged up with the trick like she was the first time. They were four feet away from each other. The trick looked satisfied from his experience since he had a smile on his face.

This fine ass ho was staring a pimp down with a curious look. I gave the ho a stone-cold look without smiling. I knew if I had smiled she would have taken that as a weakness. A sucker would have smiled at her. A real pimp would have done what I did or said something to the ho. I didn't say anything to the ho because I was cooking up a plan to knock this ho.

She was the first to look away when the elevator door beeped. When the door opened, I walked out to see if she would follow me. She didn't. I turned left, she went straight. I didn't pay it any mind, it was still early. I had all night to get at her.

I was surprised when I heard Sub O on the mic hosting this live event. His videos were some of the hottest videos on the web. He finally left the East Coast to come down south and get some of this good money. It really was good down south because the hoes and strippers didn't have to work extra hard to please a trick like they did on the East Coast. Down south, women didn't do things they did to make money. The women up east had to be more aggressive because of their more aggressive tricks. The tricks down here were easier to please than the ones up east.

"Listen up! Listen up! It's time, yo! I want all Phat Puff models to report to the floor. Get butt ass naked. Show these niggas how we do it in the East Coast!" Sub O said loudly on the mic.

Close to 10 women started stripping off what they had on and turning up for the onlookers and Sub O's camera men and photographer.

This underground shit was turned up to the max. In my seven years, I'd seen a lot of shit concerning the Pimp Game, but when it came to the low-level of the Game, a strip club and a bad ass hoe house, two in one building, The Thot House took the cake. Here, a pimp could catch a ho, a ho could catch a trick, and a ho could make some real money. This was the place to be.

The ho that was staring me down on the elevator was watching a double dildo show involving Rose and Heather. Poppa watched over them. I walked over to him. "Look out, Poppa," I said, tapping him on the arm. I ran down the play on what I wanted to be done.

Poppa went to her. After chopping it up for about two minutes, they both walked to the open elevator and got on. I waited until the elevator came back down to get on it, which took about four minutes. I went up to the third floor. When I got off, I called him to let him know I was walking down the hall. Supposedly, when he felt his phone vibrate, he knew to cause the commotion.

As I got closer to the end of the hallway, I heard the effects of a hard slap and then a light scream from her. When I finally found the room, Poppa had his hand up in the air about to strike her again, but I ran behind him and pushed him hard. He fell off the bed onto the floor. I went over to him and hopped on top of him. The only thing she could see was my arm being raised.

I swung at him like I really hit him hard but in actuality, I hit the wooden floor with the side of my fist. She came around the bed and tried to kick him with her stiletto but missed him.

"Get yo' ass up out of here! Hurry up! I got him. You got paid, right?"

"Yeah," she said, nodding her head.

"Alright, go downstairs."

She started walking backwards. Once I thought she couldn't see Poppa anymore, I swung four times that ended with my fist hitting the floor. I looked back to see her heading out the door and then turning the corner.

"Pappa, you good?" I asked him.

"Yeah, I'm straight. Can you get up off a nigga now?"

"Nall, not yet. I don't know what she's doing," I said, as I looked at the door and then back at him. "If she walks back in here, act like you're knocked out. Let me go see what's going on." I got up and walked towards the door. When I looked down the hall, I saw the bouncer was heading my way alone in a fast pace. I didn't see ol' girl anymore.

"Get up, Poppa, you good."

When the bouncer finally made it, looking like he wanted to rough someone up, he looked at me and then at Poppa, who was dusting himself off. I could tell he wanted to rough someone up.

"Waz goin' on in here! Alicia told me her trick started tripping and slapped her," big dumb ass said the girl's name.

"Everything's okay, big bro. I took care of it," I mentioned to him.

"You the one that helped her?"

"Yea, why, wuz up?"

"She told me to tell you to wait outside for her. She went cross the street to Taco Bell to use the restroom. Said she don't like using it here."

In my head, I was saying the shit worked. I was coming up with this ho, watch. All I needed to do now was play my cards right with finesse game and then she'd choose me.

Poppa and I went downstairs. After talking with him for two minutes, I broke him off five bills and then he went back to watch over my hoes.

I didn't go look for her. I wanted her to come look for me. By me not going after her, it would make her want me even more. I saw my pimp partna, Luxury P, chilling by himself at the bar, so I went to holler at him. "'You come up or what?" I asked him, knowing damn well he did.

He laughed, showing his diamond, iced-out grill. "Monopoly, wuz my name? You know a ho wants to be around Luxury, that expensive shit. I got two hoes getting my choosing fee together right now as we speak. You know dis shit don't stop. "Nigga, did you come up?"

I wasn't sure if I did, but I did know this Alicia chick wanted to see what I was about. I believed I had her attention, I just had to lay down proper game so she could choose. What I did, in a way, probably didn't mean shit to her. The effect all depended on what type of ho I was dealing with. If anything, maybe it affected her a little bit. I could see if she was at a hotel room with a trick by herself, with no security, and I saved her life when she was getting attacked. But we were here, she had all the protection she needed here. Eventually, that D-Bo looking motherfucker would have come to her rescue sooner or later.

Maybe I was wrong. One thing I knew, when a man really saved a woman's life, the woman felt she really owed him something. Some women did it by giving money. Some did it through cooking for that man. If the woman has nothing to offer, they know there's only one thing left on earth to give that would leave him satisfied. That one thing was sex. Even though she was a bad bitch, I wasn't after her sex. I was after the cash she made. Some weeks, maybe a month later, after she'd paid me, then I might dig in her fine ass. That's how the pimpin' goes.

"Yeah, I came up on one ho," I said, feeling like he wanted to compete with me. There was nothing wrong with that, it was all for sport. That's our thang to do, especially in a setting like this. I wasn't gon lie, luxury P's catch game was live. It wasn't liver than mine, but it was live.

We debated about whose game was liver a lot, to the point we would go out where a lot of women would be and make a bet on who came up the most. He'd win sometimes, I'd win sometimes. I won the most by a tad bit, so my catch game was liver. I didn't feel like betting on that tonight. I believed in my game to the fullest. With all these hoes in this spot, if I went out to pursue a ho, I'd have more than five hoes choose up by the morning. Here and now, I wanted a bitch to come to me, not the other way around.

About twenty minutes later, I got a tap on my shoulder along with, "Excuse me, can I talk to you?"

"Excuse me, P," I said to Luxury P and then I slowly spun my stool in a 180-degree angle to face her. "Yeah, wuz going on?"

"I been looking everywhere for you. Did Big C tell you what I said?"

"He told me you went across the street to Taco Bell. Something 'bout you don't like using the restroom here," I said, not telling her all that he told me. Really just setting her up in my trap.

"That's all he told you?" she asked.

"What else was he supposed to have told me, what, that you chose a pimp?"

That's when she saw me smile for the first time, showing my diamond platinum grill. She smiled and then said, "Oh, you got jokes, uhh?"

I stopped smiling. "Nall, I'm serious than a mutherfucker."

"We'll see. Anyway, can you take me to the Budget Suites down the street? I just wanna get to my room and chill."

I looked at my Rolex and thought, *this is a lazy bitch.* "What, you already done working? It's only 10:42."

"I been working all day. I done made close to $3500 today. I'm tired."

I wanted to look at Luxury P when she said $3500, but I didn't because I didn't want to make it seem like I was surprised. I wanted to know how she made that much.

When Big C mentioned that she went across the street to use the restroom, I thought it was a lie. I thought she went to go buy some drugs, but then again, I was sure there were a few people inside this club that had it. If she wasn't a dope fiend, then she was a getting money ho. And on top of that, she was a bad bitch. She was a tall, fine, young ho in her mid-twenties. She was slim, weighing about 135 pounds, with thick thighs and a real phat, juicy, square ass. Caramel candy complexioned. Brown eyes. White-blonde color sew-in weave in her hair; small, cute nose. Full lips that would make a man want her lips around his dick. I thought Pinky and Erika were bad, but this ho took the cake.

She wasn't a bad bitch just because of her looks, tho'. On top of her looks, it was her income. It took a bad bitch to make $3500 in a single day. Now I had to get her to choose me and break herself.

"How often do you go to The Thot House?" I asked her as I drove.

"I go every other Saturday. That's the only times it's open. This gotta be yo' first time coming to The Thot House, I ain't never seen you before."

"Yeah, it is." *I'm glad that me and my hoes did come. I'm coming up on over 30 bands and another ho tonight. That's blessings on top of blessings from the pimp God.*

"Where you from?" she asked.

"I'm from the sawf. Sawf Dallas. Where you from?"

"I'm from that Greedy Grove," she said proudly.

"Where at in the Grove?"

"Red Cloud."

"You gotta know Trill Black, Know Love, Pimpin' Buck, can't forget Buck's nephew."

"How I know you was gonna ask that? Yes, I know them. I've hoed for Know Love and Buck. Buck turned me out."

Even though I'd talked and hung out around all those pimps multiple times at hotel rooms and mostly in the club with other pimps, I still didn't know them personally. They'd even been to some of my parties and events before, but I'd never gone out pimping with them in Dallas nor cross country. I'ma put it this way, they were friends of my pimp friends, and that's how I knew them. Buck,

Know Love, and Trill Black had me by 10 years or better. From word of mouth and what I'd seen with my own two eyes, they were good pimps. I had nothing bad to say about them. I might hit Buck up to get some information on Alicia to see what's up with her.

"See, all three of them niggas could pimp they asses off. Buck held the title of being the biggest pimp in the Grove. I held the title of being the biggest richest young pimp in the whole DFW," I said, doing some bragging to her.

We made small talk until we made it to the Budget Suites. When I walked in, I saw that her room was spotless and it smelled of Passion Grape, which told me she kept herself and her spot clean.

"Let me get in the shower and then we can talk, okay."

That gave me confirmation that she really was a clean ho. "Yeah, okay, go wash those tricks off yo' fine ass."

She went into her room, taking off her clothes. I sat at the end of the couch, so where I was I could see her flawless, shapely body while she dug in her closet for something to put on. She wanted me to see her naked, bending over with her ass up in the air. She was testing me to see if I was going to be a sucker and attempt to fuck her. I wasn't, so I stopped looking at her before she turned around. Instead, I got on my iPhone to text my homeboys to see what was going on with my hoes at The Thot House.

When she walked out the room, she said, "Monopoly, give me 15 minutes, I'll be right back."

I looked up from my phone to look at her and said, "Do you, I'ma wait on you," then gave my attention back to my phone.

She left the bathroom door wide open while she was in the shower. About 20 minutes later, she stepped out the shower soaking wet. She dried off, wrapped the towel around her head, and then brushed her pearly whites. Afterwards, she walked out the bathroom butt ass naked while saying, "It's some lemonade in the ice box if you're thirsty."

"I'm good. Thanks tho'."

Five minutes later, she walked into the living room in her bra and panties, and then sat down on the couch two feet from me. I checked this ho with the quickness for playing with my pimpin'.

"Put some muthafuckin' clothes on. You ain't paid a pimp yet to be walking around me like this. You think you slick. You tryna get a pimp to fuck, that ain't gon' happen." I stood up before she did. "This here is real pimpin' that's standing in front of you, ho."

I wasn't mad at her. I just had to let the ho know don't try to play me like a sucker. Believe it or not, there were some pimps that would have ended up fucking this fine ass ho without getting paid first. I wouldn't ever come at a prostitute like that, no matter how fine she was. A ho was going to pay my pimpin' ass.

She stood up, taking baby steps away from the couch while looking at me as if she was shocked.

"And while you at it, go get my bread and pay a pimp. My choosing fee is five stacks for a ho like you." I got my business card out my pocket. "If you ain't got it, just give me a call when you do." Then I threw the card on the living room table and walked towards the door.

If that didn't work and it ended up blowing the bitch, so be it, lesson learned. There were plenty of hoes at The Thot House I could get at.

"No, don't go. I got the money in the room. I'll be right back," she said, rushing to her room. Seconds later, she came back with a big Gucci bag. She pulled out a big wad of folded cash. "It's 44 hundred. I can call one of my tricks to get the money within an hour."

"Aight, that's cool. Sit down." After we sat down, I started reading Alicia her rights. I ran down my rules for close to forty minutes, until I got a text from Erika telling me how long I had until the fight started. I excused myself and returned her text. "I'm down the street. I'll be there shortly."

She texted back three times. I didn't read them nor send her back a message, so she called me. I didn't want to answer it because

I was busy doing my best to give Alicia my undivided attention, and on top of that, some real live instructions to follow. I knew my ho, Erika. I knew she wanted me to see her fights. I excused myself for the second time.

"Hurry up, Daddy, I'm 'bout to fight in 15 minutes," she said as soon as I connected the call.

You know I had to check a ho for telling a pimp to hurry up. "Bitch, don't hurry me. Fuck's wrong with you. Bitch, if you don't see me that mean I'm out pimpin', ho," I said, really just causing a scene. Sometimes you had to start shit like that so your pimpin' could go smoother. I never really had an issue with nothing Erika did, but every once in a while, a pimp had to dry trip about shit. A pimp couldn't be easy going all the time.

"I didn't mean it like that, Daddy," she had told me.

"I don't give a fuck how you meant it. Don't never, ever say hurry up to me. I bet six Gs on your first fight. Plus, I wanna see you fight," I told her while looking at Alicia in the eye the whole time, talking with Erika. I had her on speaker phone.

"I know you do," she said, sounding a bit better.

I softened up because I was too hard on Erika in that moment. "Look, baby, I came up on another ho. I'm getting her straightened out. I'm wrapping it up now. I'm supposed to be your coach anyway, so I wouldn't miss that for the world. Are you suited up already?"

"No, not yet. I was waiting on you to help me."

"Aight, I'll be there within five minutes, eight at the most. I'm right down the street, okay baby?"

"Okay, Daddy," she said, sounding like a little girl.

I hung up. "Alicia, I'm 'bout to leave, I'll be back around 12. Have my choosing fee in hand too. Be dressed, because I'm taking you to my penthouse so we continue talking. When is your room up here?" Even though she didn't give me bad vibes, I still wasn't comfortable being at her room. I didn't know her; I didn't know what she had going on here at her room.

"In 12 days. I paid for a whole month."

"Aight. I'll see you in a little bit."

When I walked in The Thot House the Dj announced that the fight would be starting in a couple minutes. While I was gone, they had set up a nice-size ring. I looked around until I saw four of my hoes surrounding Erika. I rushed to them as they stood outside of the ring. Erika smiled when she saw me pull up.

"Thank y'all, I'll take it from here." Seconds later, I started putting on her left glove. Her right hand was already taped up, glove on, and tightened. "You know what you gotta do, go beat that bitch's ass."

A bell started ringing from the speakers for seven seconds, and then Sub O called the first two fighters to the ring, which were Erika and a good-looking light-brown-skinned chick.

I put her helmet on and her mouthpiece in her mouth. "Do yo' thang, baby."

While she was climbing up on the ring, I tapped Erika on her phat ass that made her ass jiggle in her boy shorts. All my hoes outside the ring on the floor cheered Erika on. Even Jazz was cheering her on, my ho' that got beat up by Erika five months ago. They forgave each other and got over their little beef.

"In the red boy shorts, we have Erika. Weighing 142 pounds, very well proportioned, 5'8, fine as a muthafucka. With all that phat ass, you need to come join Phat Puffs models. I got a job for ya. Erika's representing Stop 6 in Fort Worth, Texas. In the black boy shorts, we have Pretty J. Weighing 122 pounds, 5'7. Pretty J, you so pretty I have three pages just for you in my next issue. Holla at me later so we can talk about that. She's reppin' South Oak Cliff, yo. Let's see if they fight as good as they look."

After the referee made them touch gloves, the bell rang for them to fight. They squared off in the middle of the ring. They stepped side to side until they traded places with each other without swinging. I smiled. Erika had her game face on.

Pretty J threw a quick, wide two-piece, missing Erika's face and hitting her forearm. Erika responded by swinging a low hook to Pretty J's rib, and followed it with a hard punch to the stomach that stung Pretty J. She bent over in pain. When Erika ran up on her swinging a right hook to the side of her helmet, Pretty J wrapped her arms around Erika so she wouldn't swing anymore. I saw Erika's lips moving, so she had to be talking shit.

Seconds later, the black, fine-ass referee broke the hold. As soon as the referee backed out the way. Erika hit her with a right jab, and then hit her with a mean left hook, knocking her to the floor. The crowd went crazy, overpowering the Lil' Jon track that was playing. Niggas and females started throwing money up in the air into the ring. My hoes went crazier, jumping up and down, yelling.

Some dark-skin pimpish-looking nigga was screaming 'get up J' in her corner as the referee counted to 10. She got on her hands and knees from lying on her side when the referee made it to 10.

When the referee said it was over, I gave my winning ticket for $6,000 to Rose and told her to put $5,000 on her next fight. I climbed up on the ring to help Erika get in between the ropes, and then on to the ground. We were all proud of her for winning, representing us. I took her helmet up off her head and gave her a bottled water.

"You did a great job. All you gotta do is keep that same shit up, and you'll win again."

The next two women were about to touch gloves, so I told Erika to watch how both of them fought. This fight was weak to me. Even the crowd didn't get too hyped up about it. There were five rounds in all. One round went for three minutes. They both were throwing wild, bullshit-ass punches the whole fight until they ran out of gas in the fourth round. The prettiest one caught the other one with a good lucky punch to the chin and knocked her out, something that made the crowd uproar.

While they were waking her up, I told Erika she didn't have to worry about her at all. There was no doubt in my mind if they fought, Erika wouldn't lose. She had that fight all day.

The third fight, I wasn't too much worried about either. I guess if you like two fine-ass bitches fighting it was a sight to see. For me, I wasn't impressed and wouldn't have put any money on the fight because it was hard to tell who would win. The thickest girl from East Dallas 415 won. Like I said before, I wasn't worried, and neither was Erika. You know how I know these last two fights wasn't about shit, was because they didn't throw a lot of money in the ring. Between the last two fights, they threw money in the third fight on the strength because they looked the best.

Now this fourth fight was one to see, it was one of the most anticipated fights tonight, with two stud bitches fighting. The one with the red and black dreads was KK. She was a little skinny, light-brown-skinned bitch out of New Orleans. This was her first time fighting at The Thot House. Three dudes next to me were in conversation about KK being fast with her hands and on her feet. She was an undefeated champion at Onyx. On the other hand, the undefeated champion, Ivery, rocked a D-Town shag with big waves on the top and side of her head. She stood at 5'7, and weighed 138, weighing 18 pounds more than KK. She had broad shoulders that made her look stocky. Sub O announced that Ivery had been holding it down for six months, that's 12 times that she'd won the $10,000 pot at The Thot House.

Actually, they put on a good fight from round one to round five. KK could move her ass off. This stud knew how to weave, block, drop under an opponent's swing, and swing her punches. She had a small fist, so her punches didn't do too much damage to Ivery. She took the licks like a G. Because of KK's speed ability, Ivery only caught her with one out of every three to four swing attempts. Now every time Ivery got a hold of her ass, she caught her with a bad ass punch, shaking her up. She knocked KK down by hitting her in the nose with a mean jab. That punch made her nose bleed. She couldn't fight any more because it took too long to stop bleeding. Ivery won by disqualifying KK.

Erika won her second fight with ease. Erika made her tap out in the second round from beating her up so bad. That was nine bands I had won off of both fights that Erika fought. I had to give the house $100 off of every $1000 I won. I was so confident in Ivery winning the sixth fight that I put that $9,000 I won on a straight up bet that Ivery would win. And she did. Her fight went quick also. Ivery knocked that fine bitch out in the first round. That was the best knock out so far. Ivery vs. KK was the best fight yet.

Lethal Lipps would have a performance in between the sixth fight and championship fight. I'd seen some of Lethal Lipps videos, and she was a super freak for sure. I wondered what she was going to do for her live performance, because all her videos were throwed.

Two fine-ass bitches in lingerie spread out a big plastic wrapping across the top of the main stage. Sub O got on the mic once again. "Yo! Yo! Yo! I welcome one of the best porn stars in the industry to the stage. Lethal Lipps, bring yo' fine ass out here."

She walked butt naked up the stage in all her majesty, with some medium-built, dark-skinned nigga, wearing a muscle t-shirt and Versace blue jeans shorts. Lethal Lipps was fine, thick, and pretty from her body to her face.

"Yo, listen up. This my homegirl, Lethal Lipps. She calls this the Five Finger of Death," Sub O said.

Lethal Lipps got on all fours. The dude got down on both knees. Dude wrapped his left arm around her upper ass, straightened his fingers on his right hand, and then eased his hand in Lethal's asshole slowly, knuckles deep. He went in and out of her 10 times before he went in deeper.

She looked as if she was enjoying every second of it. He didn't have no small arm either, and he was digging all up in her ass as she moved back and forth, clapping her ass on his arm.

After five minutes had passed by Lethal grabbed dude's arm out of her asshole. While still holding his arm in her hand, she got on her knees right in front of him. I couldn't hear nothing of what was being said, but it looked like she told him to standup. He stood. Now she told him to put his hand in her mouth. He looked surprised and asked if he heard her right. She responded with nodding her head while saying, "Yea, yo, in my mouth."

I swear to God, seeing this nigga stick the same arm in her mouth that he put inside her ass was some nasty shit, but you know what, the crowd was making it storm with dollar bills. It was the most money I'd ever seen be thrown on a woman before. She did what most woman wouldn't and couldn't do. She did what paid the most money. Even though this was some disgusting shit, I couldn't do nothing but respect and love that. It was part of the Game.

After Lethal Lipps' performance, we prepared for the championship fight. As I tied Erika's glove, I let her know, "This fight is not gonna be easy like them other two fights. You gon' have to come with it. Fight dirty if you have to. You hear me?"

"Yes, I hear you."

The bell rang for them to walk to the middle of the ring. I put her helmet on and then her mouthpiece. "Go do yo' thang. Shine on that bull dyking bitch."

A minute later, they posted up in front of each other. Erika was the first to throw a punch, a left and right jab that Ivery blocked. Erika blocked one jab from Ivery, but she hit Erika with a right jab and left body shot to the ribs. The first round they did nothing but exchange punches and blocks the whole fight.

During their break, as I poured water in her mouth from a Thicky water bottle, I told Erika, "Keep doing what you're doing. Block more, punch less. Let her punch. All you got to do is tire her out. Whenever you do punch, add in some of them bad ass hooks."

That worked on the second round, but Ivery didn't get tired. Erika was the one who got tired. Erika got a few good punches in, but Ivery was getting the best of the fight in the third and fourth round. The only punch Erika got in the fifth round was a good hook and an elbow to her helmet. If she could have connected that elbow to the face, she would have done some damage and maybe won. That elbow made Ivery mad. That's all she needed to get on my ho's ass to the point I wanted to throw the towel in to save her from an ass whipping.

I wished I would have threw it, because about 15 seconds later, Ivery hit her with a five piece. A right jab dead in the face, a left hook to the side of her helmet, a right body shot, a hard left hook to the top of the head that dazed my ho and followed by a hard-cocked back jab to the chin that knocked her out cold. She woke up when she hit the floor.

The crowd went wild. Niggas was throwing money and shooting it out the money gun onto the ring. I wasn't expecting Erika to get beat up bad nor get knocked out, but I had to give it to Ivery, she was bad with those hands.

My hoes and I were in the ring before the female referee got to 10. Rose and I put each of Erika's arms on our shoulders. I thought about letting her sit down on the short stool, but I changed my mind. She was too outta there, so we just took her to my car.

"Rose, I'm 'bout to go out pimpin' on this new ho I caught earlier, then take Erika to the penthouse. Y'all keep doing the same shit, and keep making my paper. I'll be back later."

"Ok, I got you. I'll see y'all later."

I called Alicia to tell her I was on the way to come pick her up. She was already ready. She had texted me about 40 minutes ago telling me she had got the rest of my choosing fee.

I talked to Erika after she came to on the way over to the Budget Suites. "Even tho' you lost, you still did good. I'm proud of you. Plus, you won us $16,000 on top of the $9,000 I won from ol' girl's fight." I had put $5,000 on Erika winning the fight, plus $3,000 that she wouldn't get knocked out in the first round. They had a bunch of bets going on there, like betting on what round Ivery would win in to betting that she would win. Majority of the people at The Thot House had a lot of confidence in Ivery. I did give it to her, she was a beast with those hands.

She smiled and said, "Thanks. I wanna fight that bitch again next time. Can I, Monopoly?"

"I liked the scenery and we made a bunch of money but fuck that shit. I'm tryna go legal. I'll think about it, tho'. We'll see."

Alicia came out in three minutes after I pulled up. She had on a white, tight-fitted, short-sleeve t-shirt that showed her stomach and tight-fitted, light-blue jean pants that looked painted on her with blue-striped, white Adidas on her small feet. Her body was so curvy it shot fire and desire to my dick head. Too bad I couldn't go in her fine ass. I respected the rules of the Game. Fucking her would have messed up a good ho. I had to get some racks out of the ho before I put my dick inside her.

She went to the passenger side door and was about to open it until she saw Erika in the front seat. She got in the back seat behind Erika, filling my Rolls Royce up with perfume that made me desire her more.

"Hey, Monopoly," she said, sounding glad to see me again.

"Wuz up, Alicia?"

"Nuthin' much. Been up there watching *Power* until you came."

"Alicia, this is my ho, Erika. Erika, this is my new ho, Alicia," I said introducing them both.

After they spoke to each other, Alicia asked Erika, "You were the one that fought tonight, right?"

"Yeah, I'm the one." Erika replied back.

"How did it go?" Alicia asked.

Erika chuckled. "I won two fights, lost the championship. It's cool, tho'. I'ma fight again if Daddy lets me next time."

"Yeah, Ivery is a tough girl to beat. I've never seen her lose. She been holding it down for months. You gotta be tough yaself to make it to the championship," Alicia said.

I was liking the fact she was being friendly with my ho. That let me know that she was a people person. Also, she wasn't like most hoes who acted like they were too good to be friendly with a new ho they didn't know. Picking someone's brain was the whole point in having a conversation with someone you wanted to know about. Women who weren't friendly were either hurt by a woman they were close to or they had insecurities with themselves, making them jealous of the next chick.

"Yeah, I'm a good fighter. Shit, I made Monopoly 16 bands tonight, just from my fights."

I joined in the conversation. The three of us talked the whole way to my penthouse. Our conversation was flowing so good, instead of having Erika go inside my room so Alicia and I could talk, she stayed in the living room with us so they could get to know one another and kick game. Erika wasn't bruised bad, she only had a small knot on her forehead and a little cut on top of her lip, where she put ice that was wrapped up in a towel. That helmet and mouth piece helped her to not get seriously hurt. She was good for the most part.

Everything went damn near perfect tonight except one thing. My ho, Heather, was so distant that it bothered me. I talked to all my hoes except for her, which was a little weird because nothing had transpired between us to make her act this way towards me. When I thought about it, she didn't even stand by me during Erika's fights. Even when I tried to talk to her before the fight, she'd make up an excuse to get away, saying she was heading upstairs to meet a trick. I didn't check her ass right then and there. In my head, I was saying, 'Yeah, bitch, I got something for yo' ass.' Depending on my trap that I would get from her whenever I called it a night for us, it would decide on the punishment I would have for her.

I took Alicia to her room at 5 A.M. I left The Thot House at 12 and didn't go back until after 5. I picked my people up and then we headed to my spot in Health's Buffalo Creek. Everybody was tired than a bitch, including myself. All three of my homeboys were sleep on the way to my house.

When I got there, I checked my trap from Heather. She made $745, when she should have made over $1,500, like Sarah, Bre, and Rose did. They were my white hoes, and they made more money than all my hoes. Between today and tomorrow, she was going to pay for what she did.

I took a shower and went to sleep afterwards.

Chapter 6
Monopoly
Disciplining Heather

Heather was a fine lil' stallion, with bread embedded in her DNA. The type of ho any pimp would be blessed to manage. Things were okay between Heather and me, but our relationship wasn't progressing like I wanted it to. The shit she pulled on me two nights ago was out of line. She was the only ho out of all my hoes that wasn't responding like I wanted her to. I thought getting a mansion for us to live in would have them all acting accordingly to how I wanted them to. All players know you can't penetrate every woman's mind with the same Game. Understanding that I came up with something that might lock her into my game, I could have asked my mentor, Tight Game, what was the proper Game to use on Heather to make her respond like she should.

But due to what took place at the meeting, I passed on that idea. There were older players I could have went to also, but I just took a chance on my own Game. When I chopped it up with my pimp partna, B Magnifi¢ent 9000 aka *Mr. I Need A Bitch,* about the play, he didn't reject my offer to participate in it. So fuck it, I went ahead with it. Magnifi¢ent was from Houston, Texas with Galveston, Texas roots, and relocated to Dallas a year ago. He, like all boss players, took his show on the road and had developed several different styles like a truly seasoned pimp should.

He was a natural-born finesser by all accounts. I knew a couple of pimps in the DFW area that were certified macks and lethal when it came to conversation. I chose Magnifi¢ent because he fit the play perfectly. His intelligence and convo was just what I needed to make this play successful. He was living in a $350,000 home in Irving, Texas, and it was damn near a straight shot from my penthouse. I offered to pay him $1,000 for the play. He agreed. The play consisted of Magnifi¢ent calling my ho from an ad she posted on an escort site.

I gave him $500 extra to give to my ho just for conversation, nothing sexual.

Well, the first time I saw Heather on my white leather sofa with her legs folded up Indian style on the phone texting, she was beet red from blushing. I was heading outside, so before I went to the pool, I asked her, "Who the fuck you texting? You better be getting at some paper with all that blushing and shit." Saying that shot me back to that ho, Brittany, setting me up to be robbed months ago. In this case, I planned this whole thing. I still regret I didn't catch on to what Brittany pulled on me.

"A trick I met early this morning. He's paying me $500 just to text and talk to him on the phone."

"Alright, ho," I warned. "I bet not find out you playing games. You betta be gettin' at my scratch."

"I am, Daddy," she said dryly. "Do you want what I got right now instead of tonight?"

"Nall, ho, give it to me tonight," I said before I walked to the outside pool.

The second time, same day around 11:39 A.M., I was at the bar talking with Rose when I overheard Heather talking to Magnifi¢ent on the phone, passing through the living room going upstairs. She didn't pay us any mind. She was lost in conversation with him. She mentioned that she was glad that he had called to talk to her and that she had been enjoying their conversation. That wasn't a lie, she was really feeling it. She was all smiles. My partna was a true mutherfuckin' mack. He had knocked a lot of women off with just his conversation.

The third time I saw her in her and Sarah's room at home, I walked in like I was looking for Sarah when I saw her lying in bed, texting. She looked at me with a Kool-Aid smile. I walked up close to her and snatched the phone out of her hands. "Bitch, give this mutherfuckin' phone. You doin' too much smiling in this mutherfucker with this nigga."

"Daddy, I'm getting paid to do that."

"Bitch, shut the fuck up with that bullshit! Ho, you can't play me!" I ignored her and started texting Magnifi¢ent 9000 on her phone. "I'm so ready to meet you. Are you at home? I want to come over."

Before I came into their room, Magnifi¢ent 9000 and I talked on the phone for about 30 minutes about the whole play, while he was texting her. The message I shot to him through Heather's phone let him know the play was official.

"We sho'll 'bout to see. Get dressed. Put on something sexy. We going to his house," I demanded her.

"How am I just gonna go to his house without being invited?"

"From what y'all talking about, he gon' invite you over. He ain't married, is he?" I knew the answer to my own question, I just asked so she couldn't catch on to the play.

"No, he's not married."

"Here." I gave her back the phone. "When he text back, tell him to send his address and then you'll be on your way." I went back to my room downstairs, sat in my king throne, and called Magnifi¢ent 9000.

"Wuz up, P?" my pimp partna asked.

"I just told the ho to get dressed. Has she text back yet?"

Yeah, P, she told me to send my address. I'm 'bout to send it to her now, P."

"Alright. We'll be on our way after she finishes getting ready. Whenever we make it, just do you, pimp. You might just come up on another ho."

"You already know how I do, bring the ho thru so we can see where her head is at."

I had already taken a shower this morning, but I only had on a muscle t-shirt and Nike Jordan gym shorts. So, I changed into a dark Puma jumpsuit with the same color blue and white Puma tennis shoes. It was 95 degrees outside, but I wasn't going to be outside. I would be in the AC of my Rolls Royce.

Twenty minutes later, when I walked back inside, she was in her bathroom doing her makeup in the mirror.

"Sarah's gone in the car; she won't be back until later. You gonna let me take the Range Rover?" she said, looking at me through the glass.

"Nall, I'm taking you on this date."

"You know tricks don't like that. You don't think he—"

I cut her off with, "Ho, I know that. And I told you he not a trick. Just hurry up and get ready, everythin's gonna be good. Let me know when you finished."

I must add, she was really showing out the way she was dressed. She had on a tight, red, thigh-high dress. Her shoulders were exposed and she had a strap that was tied around her small waist. Within about an hour, we were going to see how much she was really feeling Magnifi¢ent. From the looks of it, she was feeling him.

I wanted to know what was really going on in her mind. I had an idea of what it was. She probably was wondering why I was letting her go to another pimp's house, if he really was a pimp. I could tell she was surprised when I mentioned he wasn't a trick. She wasn't going to agree with me nor question me about him being a pimp because she was curious about meeting him.

I pulled up in front of his $350,000 suburban home in Irving, a house I'd been to on numerous occasions. "Go handle that."

She looked at the house for a couple of seconds and then got out my Double R. Halfway up the sidewalk, heading towards the steps leading to the porch, Magnifi¢ent 9000 stepped out the house to the porch, standing at 6'4 and 220 lbs of southern fried pimpin' with a deep Texas drawl and a slow delivery, "Dripping" with IZM.

It was a little after two o'clock, but he still was dressed to impress in a burgundy cashmere Polo cardigan with the short-sleeve, black Polo shirt underneath with collar 'popped.' He also had on some black Balmain fitted jeans, with some burgundy Mauri gator loafers with no socks. His Cartier Aviator shades were cognac-tinted, his quarter-karat canary earrings, and the $50,000 white-gold and Cartier white-diamond grill were the true definition of the words bling bling!

I could tell she was smiling as she walked because I saw her dimples poke out as she walked towards him. Magnifi¢ent smiled at her. Once she stepped on the porch, she hugged him while saying, "It's great to finally meet you."

Before she got out my car, for her safety, I had her call my phone so I could listen to what was going on.

"It's great to meet you too. By the way, you look like a bottle of Bel-Air that's been on chill all evening just for me." Bel-Air was one of the finer champagnes that a pimp sipped on occasionally.

She giggled, "Wow, thank you."

"Look here, Heather, my name is B Magnifi¢ent 9000, and the B stands for Blessed, ya dig. And Blessed truly comes when a ho of your caliber, entertains a Boss such as myself. You been under some real 'ISM' so you're a sure shot. I made you grin, bitch, so come on in."

Heather was speechless, probably taken away by surprise by what he had said. Before I stepped out the car, I disconnected the call. I walked around the car to stand on the side of the hood, looking their way. She looked at me for two seconds, then back at Magnifi¢ent, and started shaking her head while slowly side stepping down the stairs.

When she turned and started walking towards me, he got loud to where I could hear him too. "This ya last chance, ho, to put it in a pimp's pants. So, come on, sock it to my pocket. And I'll make ya career take off like a rocket."

Heather acted like she never even knew his voice. At that point, Magno gave me a big smile, and said, "You got one, P. Text me later, Boss!"

"Daddy, let's get out of here," she told me when she reached me.

"Bitch, don't tell me what to do, ho. I'm the pimp, ho. We 'bout to stay here until we get some shit understood."

"Daddy, what are you talking about? Get what understood?"

Magnifi¢ent just stood on the porch looking at us while I checked my ho. "Ho, out of all my hoes you the only one that's been bullshitting a pimp."

"Daddy, I—"

I cut her off with saying, "Ho, shut up and let a pimp talk. Ever since I had you, you been holding back from a nigga, even after I showed and proved to you that I really am Player Personified. You know what, ho, fuck you, stay here. I'll pack your shit and bring it to you later."

After I said that, I turned towards my whip. She grabbed the sleeve of my Puma jumpsuit. "Don't leave me here. I want to go with you."

I looked at her, giving her an evil look. "You wrinkling my shirt. Get yo' palms off me."

She let go and then grabbed my left hand. "I'm sorry, Daddy. Please forgive me. Don't leave me."

"I'm good, baby. Choose Magno. Since I can't make you give me 100% of you, you don't need me. Maybe Magno can do the job. I'm gone." I looked at Magnifi¢ent as he was chopping it up with one of his fine ass white hoes. "Lookout P, you can have the ho." I was putting on an act that I hoped would work. Although I wanted her to stay, I didn't care if she chose him.

"I'm not choosing up with him, Monopoly. Daddy, can we please talk about it? I'm sorry. I'll do whatever I gotta do. I don't want to lose you."

"There's only one thing you can do for me to prove to me you really want me."

"What is it, Monopoly?" she asked, anxiously looking into my eyes.

"I want you to walk to my penthouse bare feet," I told her without smiling.

"Really, Monopoly?" she said, shocked.

I snatched my arm from out her grasp and started heading around to the driver's door. "I'm gone, pimp, you can have the bitch."

"No. Okay, I'll do it. Here," she said while taking her red-bottom six-inch heels off her feet.

I got into the car and rolled the window down. "Drop 'em down on the floor." As soon as she did, I raised the window back up and drove off.

I really didn't want to do it to her, but I felt that I had to. One of the reasons why I did it was to test how down she was for me. The main reason I was doing this was to get the best results I needed to lock her down. I figured while driving that I wasn't about to let her walk over two hours to my penthouse, so I stayed in the area. I went to one of my favorite fast food spots, Wing Stop. I ordered a big cup of lemonade to drink and a 20 piece of boneless garlic wings. After I ate, I did some research on the modeling agency to get my business plan together to present to a potential co-owner.

After being there for about 20 minutes, I called Heather. She didn't say nothing after answering. "Hey, My Queen, pick your head up. Shit gon' be just fine."

I could tell she was still walking because I heard wind hitting up against the phone as well as passing cars. I knew her head was down as she walked. A bunch of thoughts had to be running through her head right now. Her mind was jumping back and forth from thoughts like, 'I can't believe he's makin' me walk to his pent-house.' 'Should I keep walking and stay with Monopoly? Or should I call Magnifi¢ent to choose up with him? No, I can't leave my girls.' 'Should I call Rose to tell her what Monopoly is making me do and tell her I'm leaving Monopoly?' 'Maybe I should stay with Monopoly. He's really not that bad of a pimp. Plus, I like him.' Those kind of thoughts amongst others were going through her head.

"Daddy, where are you? Are you around?" She was probably looking around for my Rolls Royce. The reason why I called was to play with her mind and emotions. Without watching her, I knew she would have her head down in deep thought about her next move. So I called to encourage her to keep walking and to reassure her that I still wanted her to be my queen. "No, I'm not around."

"Can you please come pick me up? I'm sorry for holding back from you. Forgive me."

"No, I'm not picking you up. I'm surely not forgiving you. Now, if you don't believe you can make it, let me know, because I'll come and take you to a room." After I said that, I hung up.

For the last test I had for her, I needed Magnifi¢ent once again, so I text him.

"Look out, P. My ho walking bare feet. Text the ho and tell her that you heard she needs a ride. Or whatever you want to say with that same meaning, ya dig?"

"LOL. I dig, P. I see you up to your old tricks but yea, I got u. If I call you within 20 mins, that mean I'm callin' to serve u, P."

"I dig it."

She text me 16 minutes later.

"I can't make it, Daddy. My feet is blistered up. My legs and feet hurt. Please come get me."

I ignored her text. I waited five minutes to call her. I couldn't wait any longer nor play anymore. I wanted my ho. Let me tell you, Heather's a strong ho. Majority of hoes would have never passed that test. "Where are you?"

"I'm at a McDonald's off uhh, uhh, 35, and I'm in the parking lot."

"I'm on my way. I'll be there shortly."

On the way there, I called my old school pimp partna, Pretty Jay, out of 64 out the Greedy Grove massage parlor. He had white, Mexican, and Chinese masseuse working for him. I set up an out call for myself and mainly Heather to get a massage. I wanted to back door the pain I put her through with pleasure. I knew her lower body was sore as well as her being mentally and emotionally hurt.

When I pulled up in the parking lot, I saw Heather sitting on the thick curb that the foundation of McDonald's was on. I parked on the side of her. I got out and walked around to the front passenger side door to open it. Heather tried to stand up, but I stopped her with my right hand, palm facing her. "Sit yo' ass back down on that curb. You not 'bout to do no walking." I turned to slide the passenger seat back to the max so her legs could stretch her feet all the way in the front seat. I walked to her, putting my hands under the back of her knees and the middle of her back, and picked her up. Before putting her in the front seat, I asked her, "You gon' quit holding back on a pimp?"

"Yes, Monopoly."

"You'll give me all of you now?"

"Yes, I will. I'm sorry, Monopoly," she told me.

We gave each other two pecks on the lips, and then I put her into the Double R. Before I shut the door, I squatted, and then raised her feet to me. Heather's feet were fucked up. Her feet had two shades of redness. The bottom of her feet had three wide pus blisters with dirt on them.

I always keep a washcloth or big towel around at all times for hundreds of reasons, like in this situation. There would be a time where you would need to wipe something down, wipe something off your body, or cover your face or wound for survival. I got the towel from out the backseat. I had Heather pass me the half bottle of Ozarka water out the console. I poured a little bit of water on top of the towel, outside of my Rolls Royce so I wouldn't get any water in my whip. I started wiping down her right foot with the wet side and then dried it with the dry part of the towel. I did the same with her left foot. It didn't look as bad as it did with her feet dirty. Knowing that her feet would become sore in minutes to a couple of hours, she wouldn't be able to walk on her feet for at least a whole day or two. I'd have her off until she was 80% healed, and then she would be ready to make a pimp some money. I believed in the Game. I knew when she started working again she would be dropping off a bigger sack than she usually did. Plus, she would respond accordingly how I wanted her to.

On the way to CVS, I kicked Game to my Queen while I held her left hand. "I wanna let you know that I really care about you, Heather. I'm doin' my best to be the best man and pimp to you. I want a rider on my team, a muthafucker that's gon' ride with me and for the Game like I'm gon' ride for the Game and for mine. That can't happen if you holding back from a nigga and not comfortable with being with me. I set up everything that you went through today. I gave that pimp your number and gave him some info on you. That's how he knew what to say to get you all opened to drop your guards. You can't play me. I'm not gonna let no ho play with my pimpin'. If a bitch not happy with me or don't want to be with me, the bitch can tear her ass. Why stay around? I thought you didn't want to be with me. That's why I gave you chances to be with another pimp, with a pimp you actually liked. Anyway, next time I see you holding back from me, you gone, my Queen. And I mean that shit."

"Monopoly, I told y—" she said as I let go of her hand.

"I don't give a fuck 'bout that shit. I don't want to hear your sad story. I'm not your ex-pimp. What that nigga did, wasn't pimpin'. What I been doing since you been mine, is really pimpin'. You better understand that, ho. I'm Monopoly."

Hearing a ho's sad story was a waste, most of the time. I say that because what that nigga did to her was a gorilla move. I wasn't a gorilla, I pimped for real. I used good Game without putting my hands on a ho to get the proper results out of a ho. That was really pimpin'. So, fuck her sad story. The ho should have left him sooner. In these days, if a ho wanted to leave her pimp, she would find a way to. That was if she really wanted to. I wasn't feeling sorry for her.

At CVS, I bought a bottle of peroxide, two wrappings, and a small blade, all for her feet. I had a small bottle of Percocet at my penthouse that she could take for the pain. About ten minutes out from my penthouse, I called the massage parlor to tell the Asian to come over. I toted Heather all the way to my apartment on my back. I sat her on the counter of the sink to help her disrobe, taking of her dress and lingerie. I took off my jumpsuit, leaving my muscle t-shirt and Gucci boxers on, and then went to run her some hot, soapy bath water in the big tub.

Heather was staring me down and smiling like she was all in love with a nigga. It's weird, but she liked the way I played her. A real ho respected real pimping. It was crazy how proper Game gets the results you want out of someone. How could a person deny Game? Oh man, I was really in love with this shit.

After going to get the bottle of Percocet out of my room, I gave her one. I emptied the rest of the contents on the sink's counter. I grabbed a big white towed out the cabinet, and then went to kneel down in front of Heather. I started cutting an inch of skin on her biggest blister. A mixture of blood and pus instantly shot out onto the towel. I did that until all blisters were cut and all the dead skin was removed from her feet.

The Asian masseuse, named Sue, showed up to the penthouse while Heather was still bathing. I stopped to let her in. I had her set up right by the window overlooking Downtown Dallas and went back into the bathroom to get Heather out the tub. She rode my back to the living room, and I sat her on the long, portable massage table. I had her lie on her stomach and put her face into the cushion where her head went.

Sue went high and began to massage Heather's temples. I went low and massaged her feet because I was the cause of them being in pain. I didn't know a lot about massaging. What I knew came from experience through massaging some women's bodies I used to fuck with in the past. All I had to do with Heather was do what I knew while listening to how she responded from the moves that I made.

I poured baby oil on my right hand, enough for both hands to get oily for one of her feet. I started rubbing my fingers in a circular motion into the bottom of her feet without applying too much pressure. Before I moved up to her legs, I massaged both feet for about eight minutes apiece.

It was quiet as a mouse inside the penthouse, no one said anything. Even Heather didn't make a sound. I started to think that Sue and I weren't doing a good job, but soon after going up to her upper thighs, she sighed. I was quiet for a reason. I didn't want to say anything. I wanted her to enjoy this moment in peace by getting pleased by Sue and me.

After massaging her ass cheeks for a little bit, I had her turnover. She had a big gap between her fine, toned legs. I spread them apart by inches and started massaging her right thigh. She was in heat. Everywhere I touched was hot. After grinding my hands in her thighs for about four minutes, I went to rub her pearl tongue with my point and middle fingers. Slow turned into fast. Her moaning got louder every time I sped up.

I went to mack on my ho while I pleased her sexually and Sue massaged her shoulders.

"Who yo' muthafuckin' pimp, ho?"

"You, Daddy!" she said, moaning.

"Who, ho? Say my name, ho. What's my name?" I said as I rubbed her pearl in a circular motion.

"Uhh, uhh, Monopoly."

"What, ho? Say my name five times." I went faster.

"Oh, Monopoly!" she said as she was told. She attempted to put her legs up and spread them wider.

"Put yo' muthafuckin' legs back down," I said as I laid her legs down on the massage table. "You do what I tell you to do. Now spread yo' legs wider."

She did it so fast that her left leg fell and hung off the table.

"Hang yo' other leg off too."

After she did, I put two fingers inside her love box, and started working my fingers in and out of her. I worked them fast. Her pussy was slippery and made wet noises. The reason I was doing this was because I wanted my ho to feel good as possible. At the same time, I was trying to teach her a lesson, not to pull that shit she had pulled by holding back from me. By doing this to her, I was penetrating her mentally and sexually without putting my dick in her. I was really pimpin' at this ho.

"It's what pimp say, ho. Not what ho say and ho do. You hear me, ho?" I said as I started playing with her pearl with my other hand while fingering her with the other.

She couldn't control herself. Her body was going all over the place. "Yes! Yes! Yes, Daddy!"

"Be still, ho, and listen. That shit you tried to pull, it bet not happen again. If you do, the consequence is gonna be worse, or I might just fire yo' ass."

"Daddy, please don't. I'm sor—" she said as she moaned.

"Bitch, shut the fuck up, a pimp's talking," I said, then started going faster. I must have done that for another twenty minutes. She was loving every minute of it. She busted four nuts on my fingers as I played with her pussy.

I stopped and let Sue massage Heather's whole body. I washed my hands and just chilled on the sofa, returning some of the messages on my Facebook and IG as well as got on Twitter. Sue finished up in an hour. After I paid for the extra time, Heather and I talked on the sofa.

"I knew you was gonna be some trouble when I first saw you, but you know what?"

"What, Daddy?"

"You're a strong woman. I'm glad that you had enough courage to choose me. I'm also glad you went through the fire for me today. It meant a lot to me. It takes shit like this to make relationships better. As long as you don't bullshit me, I won't bullshit you. You hear me?"

"Yes, I hear you. I'm really sorry, Monopoly."

"I forgive you. You proved yourself, and I know you want to be with me. I understand what you went through."

"We talked for a little over three hours about the life in general, the Game, and the plans I had for the family. After what she experienced today, it made her receptive to everything that I kicked to her. Majority of the time, that's what it took to make a pimp and ho's relationship better. Until the next time they decided to trip out again. Then more game would be called upon to use. I believed what I did today broke her from the pain she experienced with her last pimp. That's how you pimp. She knew now I was the right nigga for her.

Smoove Dolla

Chapter 7
Advance Models

From Monday through Friday, I got help drawing a business agreement for a potential business partner, contracts for my models, and a mission statement ready by a business lawyer that I hired who knew many things about modeling agencies. I was really glad that I went through a lawyer instead of trying to do it on my own. All I did was let him know my vision for the agency. He tweaked it up, drawing it up how it should be with things that would make it a good and original modeling agency. He even showed me how to find potential co-owners online. All that costed me $75 an hour, and it came out to be $225 at the end of each day, $1125 at the end of the week. It was well worth all of it.

After surfing the website, I found two people who had the qualifications that I needed for the job. My first interview was with a 32-year-old white guy named Josh, and it was scheduled for 10:00 A.M. at my house. Once he got buzzed in at the front gate, I waited on the porch for him to pull up. He parked his XKR-S JAGUAR right behind Rose's Bentley Mulsanne.

As he walked to the front door, I peeped his style right away. He was for sure a ladies man and pretty boy. That was kind of a good thing, that meant he had charisma, which was cool. The company needed it to pull in new models. The bad thing about that was he could use that for sex from the models instead of using it to inspire them. He was tall, standing at about two inches taller than me, around 6'4. I couldn't tell what kind of suit he wore, but it was grey and tight, complementing his slim-built frame. He had on a blue tie with blue Adieu shoes on his feet. I didn't know if he knew this or not, but blue represented trust, stability, integrity, and confidence. That gave him points in my book.

Before coming into my home, we greeted each other with smiles and a firm handshake.

"Hey, Damion, how are you doing?"

"I'm doing great. Doing my best to get closer to the 'good life,' man," I told him and smiled again.

"It looks like you're already living the 'good life' to me," Josh said as he was walking inside the house.

"Naw, not yet, Josh. Honestly, I just know how to make it look good."

"You can't fool me. I see a Rolls Royce and a Bentley out front in your driveway. That looks like the 'good life' to me."

"Ok, you caught me, Josh. This is it, but I'm not content with all this. I'm trying to achieve more. Hopefully, you can see my vision and add to it so we can make it a 20/20 vision."

I wanted him to see the luxury lifestyle I lived. That's why I interviewed him in my home. He was probably used to the lifestyle already, driving a late-model JAG. Still, I wanted him to see how I lived.

"I hope I can. I have the experience, you know."

"I hope it can be some value to what I have for Advance Models."

We headed to the living room. To the right of us, Rose sat in a tall stool at the bar sipping on her favorite, a strawberry margarita. I called her over and introduced Rose to him as the manager, and Josh to Rose as our potential partner.

"Hello, how are you, Rosemary?" he asked with a pretty white smile.

"Hey, Josh, I'm great. How are you?"

"I'm good. I'll be doing a lot better if I can be of some help to you both."

"Well, let's get to it and see if you qualify for the partnership of this company."

He clapped both hands together excitedly. "Let's get to it, I'm ready."

I ushered him to my office. Before we made it there, Rose asked, "Excuse me, do you two want any refreshments?"

"Sure, do you have any bottled water?" he said before I could say anything.

"Yes, we have Ozarka water. Is that okay with you?"

"Yes, that's perfect," he told her.

She looked at me. "Bring me one also," I told her without her asking me.

After she walked away, heading for the kitchen, we went into my office. We sat across from each other with a big desk between us. I looked at my notes on him, and got straight into interview mode. "So, you tell me that you actually owned a modeling agency last year, correct?"

"Correct. I did."

"What happened? How did it fail?" I asked out of curiosity.

"That agency is still running. What happened was my business partner and I didn't see eye to eye anymore. The main reason is because he let one of the models come in between our friendship and most importantly, our business. I can't be around jealousy and someone that's a snake and against me, so I sold my shares to him, hoping that I could start over with another capital venture."

Rose showed up with four bottled waters on a silver tray. She handed us both one and sat the tray on the file cabinet that was 90% empty. After she left out the office, I asked Josh, "Did you start another business?"

"Yes, a marketing company," he said.

I nodded my head, because that could come in handy. "And how is that going? Is it taking off?"

"Business is a little slow, but eventually it will pick up. I've only been owning it for three months now. It's cool though, I'm not hurting for anything."

"That's good. So how is the company you owned with your ex-friend doing?"

"It's doing its best. Actually, it's one of the hottest agencies right now."

"What's the name of it?"

"Perfect Models."

"So, what races of women were you working with over at Perfect Models?"

"Mostly white. There were a couple black and a few Hispanics."

"Josh, if you had the chance to do something different while owning Perfect Models, what would you do to make it a better outcome?"

"Nothing. I don't regret any of it. It was best for us. Everything that occurred was a lesson learned to not make the same mistakes twice. People are who they are. Nothing would have helped the hatred he had for me."

I liked this guy. He was intelligent and wise. And he was a woman magnet, something I needed for Advance Models. "My plans and duty to this company will be to promote it, invest in the start-up, and insurance cost for Advance Models. As my partner, what can I and the models guarantee from yourself?"

"At Perfect Models, my job was to promote as well, like everyone should do. Also, I was the head scout. Since I've sold my share, I've come up with better ways to scout for foreign women, getting them a work visa so they can come out of their foreign land, bringing them to the U.S. At Perfect Models, we were only dealing with women from the U.S. To add to that, I still have my resources."

Automatically, I smiled. Those were good-sounding words to a pimp's ears. "How long has it been since you sold your shares?"

"Five months ago."

I handed him the business plan, the two contracts for the models, and the mission statement papers. "Take a look at those. Let me know if you can add to it to make it better. Take your time."

While he read, I checked to see if the phone call with Rose was still connected. I had her listening because I wanted her judgment on what candidate fit the job. Next, I surfed the web, looking at Perfect Models' website. You know I had to checkout one of my competitions. They had some bad white girls. There were some fine, slim Blacks and Mexicans also, but the white girls stuck out the most. He even had the sexy Marilyn Sunshine, a super model, an up-and-coming actress who played in one box office picture and in a couple other big films. Marilyn Sunshine was a fine white blonde. She copied Marilyn Monroe's hairstyle, but Marilyn Sunshine was much prettier than her, with a Lady Gaga nose on a flawless face. She was slim and tall with thick thighs, with a nice round ass.

Looking at her, I could tell why most men went crazy over her. She had that kind of power.

Majority of the photos on their website were of Marilyn Sunshine, like she was the face of the company. I didn't know what made me, but I went to her Instagram. A lot of her photos were at a bunch of events and in spreads in magazines. There was this guy who appeared in a lot of her pictures. I guessed it was Josh's ex-partner. He looked like somebody, probably because he had money. But he looked a bit dinky to me.

After scrolling through her gallery, I saw Josh and Marilyn hugged up together at The Oscar Awards. Josh and his partner were probably both fucking her, and then got into a bad fight over her. His partner ended up winning the girl and the company. More than likely, I would be choosing Josh to be my business partner, that was if he wanted to be mine. When that happened, I would definitely ask him about what went down between the three, because he didn't break it down in depth.

After fifteen minutes of reading the papers, he placed them back on the desk. He was smiling, and I knew he liked what I came up with.

"I see you've really put big thought into this. This is funny. I don't mean to be rude or anything. I don't have anything against your past. I looked you up, and I saw that you went to federal prison for human trafficking."

All I did was nod my head. I was glad that he did so I didn't have to tell him myself that I was a pimp. If he didn't like the fact that I went to prison for pimping, he wouldn't be interested in this interview to have the opportunity to own another modeling agency and do it better than he did before.

"I can really be some help to you, Mr. Johnson."

We talked for about 45 minutes. That conversation took me by surprise. He was really fascinated about me pimpin'. He thought it was cool to be in a pimp's presence. Anyway, he pointed out small errors I had in my contract and added two statutes to where my models would only be paid for their time on assignment, that she was not to accept money in exchange for any sexual advances. The other one was to where if a model got arrested for prostitution, that it couldn't fall back on the company, and then we would breach their contract. I told him I would give him a call when I was ready to have him sign the business deal.

The second interview was for 2 P.M, and she showed up at 1:47 P.M. My first impression of Helena Moore when we met was that she had a sense of style. She wore a pretty yellow, button-down casual shirt and black clam diggers, a white, plastic, stylish belt through the loops. To complement her pretty feet and white-painted toenails, she had on yellow, open-toe, three-inch heels, standing at about 5'10. Her blonde hair hung down to the middle of her back. From 1 to 10, I gave her face a 7. She had no lipstick on but she had just a dab of makeup on her face. Although, I could see she dressed fashionably and for the occasion, so I gave the 23-year-old some points for that.

After introducing ourselves, we repeated the cycle we did with Josh. She got a Coca Cola and I got another water.

"What made you want to accept my business offer as a partner in Advance Models?"

"Well, Mr. Johnson, the deal you offered isn't bad. Especially, when everything will be paid for. Plus, I love fashion, so I can see myself running a modeling agency."

I had emailed her, telling her I was about to start a modeling agency, but I needed help starting it because I didn't have a license nor a degree in business. And if they helped start it, I promised them 40% of the company and $20,000 for themselves. I was paying for everything to start the agency, so they didn't need to put in any money. All they had to do was use their business skills and their degree to start the business. Who wouldn't want to hop on that opportunity? I knew I would have if the shoe was on my foot.

"You just graduated college for business management last year. Congratulations on that achievement."

"Oh, thank you, Mr. Johnson," she said, smiling.

"You're welcome. I know that wasn't easy."

"Oh no, it wasn't. It was very difficult, but I had to pull through. It was worth it."

"Something worth having isn't supposed to be easy. That's good you graduated. So, tell me, what brought you into the desire to want to own a business?" I asked, crossing my legs, and then leaned back in my white leather recliner chair. Interviewing people for employment was a little different from interviewing prostitutes. It was natural for a pimp. If you didn't know, pimps were businessmen and entrepreneurs, so I was already business savvy. I was starting to like this.

"Well, I'm a child of seven. My family grew up poor. My father was a hard-working man. He worked for an oil field in Odesa. He made good money but taking care of his household and paying the IRS for old debts, we didn't have much money to live off of. It was hard on us when my mother divorced my dad for cheating and getting another woman pregnant. My mother, who had little job experience, had to start working. That taught me a valuable lesson. Taught me to learn as much as I can and to own my own business. I'm the only one out of my siblings to graduate from college. I have to make a way for my family."

The interview with Helena Moore lasted to 2:27 P.M. It went okay. I liked her, but she didn't fit the criterion to be my partner in owning a modeling agency. She seemed like she would be too bossy. I told myself that I would keep all her information for future reference.

After she left, Rose sat the back of her head on my lap on the sofa. "What you think about her?" I asked.

"I don't like her. She's too conceited for me. I know the girls won't like her either," Rose told me.

"I said the same thing to myself. Ya know, I'm not putting up with that bossy shit unless I'm doing it. I know she probably will say the wrong shit to them, and they gon' end up fighting."

She laughed and said, "I know, right."

"Hell yeah. I want the best for y'all, so I gotta find the right partner that's gon' see the 20/20 vision I see. Looks like it's gon' be Josh. I really like his views."

"Yeah, I do too. I think he will be a loyal partner and bring some good to the company."

"Me too. I got a good feelin' about him. Do you still want to open that pole dancing class?"

"Yes, I've been thinking about it for the past month. I'm gonna go to a couple classes in Dallas so I can see how they're ran. I should be ready within two weeks."

That same day, I scheduled a day with the business lawyer for Friday, which was two days from now, to add the two statutes to the contracts. The next day, I sent Josh the contract in digital form. After he signed it, I wired him the 20 bands. He seemed excited to get back into the modeling business. He wanted to get together as soon as I got time to go over the day we should launch our company and start buying the things we needed to run it. From being amped about it too, I told Josh tomorrow we could take care of the things that needed to be done first.

The next day, after ordering some things online for the agency, I gathered up all eight of my hoes in the media room. First, I introduced Josh and my hoes to each other.

"This here is Josh, he will be joining me on running this modeling agency. Introduce yourself, Josh." I gave him the floor by signaling both hands towards him to my hoes. All eight of them looked at him in curiosity.

"Hello, you all, I'm Josh. I used to own Perfect Models five months ago. Things didn't go right with my business partner and I, so I left that company. Now I'm here with you all. I have a year of experience of operating a modeling agency. I look forward to helping you all achieve whatever you are pursuing," he said, and then stepped back to where he was five feet away from me, side by side.

Damn near every ho in the room, except for Erika and Rose, looked at him like they wanted to suck and fuck Josh.

"Aight, you hoes, that's enough," I said, smiling while stepping up towards them. "Listen up, I want to thank you all for being loyal to me and the Game I love. I've discovered a bunch of things on my quest in this Game. I've discovered the real meaning of standing as a high-class pimp. Those are not the ones that's a time bomb, heading for destruction. High-class pimps succeed to their fullest extent in this Game. I believe in giving back to the ones that have stood down and have given to me and been obedient. With that being said, last week I dropped $80,000 on a modeling agency company for you all. It's for us to strive to be the best we can be in this Game as well as in life. Whatever you're striving for in life, this is the opportunity to do it. Advance Models agency will back you. I'm on a quest to success and you should be too. As a man, I'm a firm believer in being my woman's provider and protector. This is what a king is entitled to do for his queens."

I went to a small wooden table that was in the room and picked up the 24 sheets of paper I had for them. I had eight stacks crisscross every three sheets, which was two agreement contracts and the mission statement. I gave it to Rosemary first and then each one of them passed it on to who was on the side of them till the last three sheets went to Sarah. "Y'all take y'all time to read over them. Don't sign them yet."

While they read, Josh and I stood up and talked amongst ourselves. "Damion, you really are a pimp," Josh said excitedly.

"What? You thought what you read about me was a joke?

"No, I believe it. I thought pimps beat their whores for money, but it don't seem like that is going on with you."

"Bro, I'll rather whoop a bitch's brain with game than put my hands on a ho. There's better ways to break a ho than putting your hands on them. Josh, I represent B-I-G Game. That's what you gon' get out of me. I got taught by the best."

"I can tell, bro."

"I'ma show you how BIG my game is. You mentioned you wish you could have Marilyn Sunshine sign with us. Well, I can get her to choose Advance Models over that other company," I said with confidence.

"No, I don't believe that. You'll have to show me that. I don't think you can do it," he said, testing my game.

"If you don't think so, bet me 10 grand I can't."

His eyes got wider. "That's a bet. I want to see this."

"Excuse me, Daddy. We're done reading it," Rose told me after we stopped talking.

I walked up closer towards them. "As you can see, this agency is dedicated to excellence and to upgrade y'all's hoing to being up-scale models where y'all making $500 to $1000 hourly on your dates. This is it, my queens, but this isn't going to be easy to attain. Succeeding in that on a regular will require a bunch of hard work and dedication on everyone who's involved. I will help in all my power to promote you the proper way so you can get to the top and remain at the top." I searched in all their eyes as they stared at me. I could tell all kinds of thoughts and images were going through their minds. I sold them a dream that I knew I could make tangible for us all. Nothing they read or I said was bullshit that I didn't intend on doing for them. My Word was my Bond. "Now, if you want the best for your pimp, for the family, and more importantly, the best for yourself, initial and sign those contracts that I've given you."

The contracts mainly consisted of their conduct under our company, outlining their duties as well as the company's expectations that we planned on performing for our models, and its liabilities to the models employed. One of the contracts consisted of guidelines to protect and ensure a positive work environment for its employee's, where it would protect the integrity of the agency. If the models did anything that offset the order or conflicted the presence of management in those contracts, it would be deemed as a breach of contract and a reason to terminate employment immediately. The models agreed to do everything in their power to perform to the statement of this agency and instructed by management under contract for the full term of one year from the date of their signature. I knew they would all sign after reading the mission statement about how clients call upon my models to host events, to be in fashion and hair shows, dance entertainment, and other private engagements, getting paid $500-$1,000 an hour. What I was presenting to them was something new and one of the highest levels in the ho game. They had no choice but to hop on the bandwagon and ride with me.

After the contracts were signed, they were given to Josh. "This is one of the best decisions you will ever make in your life. Wet got y'all. You're with the winning team now. It's set in stone," I told them.

Later on, that very day, I chopped it up with Josh about Marilyn Sunshine. "How good do you know her?" I asked.

"What I don't know? I know damn near everything about her. We've known each other for years. We met at New York's Performing Arts School, uhhh, six years ago. Waaay before David and started Perfect Models."

"So, you wanted to be an actor too?"

"Yeah, man. I didn't get to get in nothing but three films we did in class. Opening up a business seemed more important to me, so that's what I did when I graduated. That's how Perfect Models came about."

"So, what were Sunshine's goals and dreams back then?" I asked, wanting to know so I could use it as a form of game.

"To be a big-time actress. She's a big fan of Paul Turner films. Her dreams is to be in one of his films one day. The reason she's a model is because of me. I knew it would heighten her acting career."

"David, the dude you owned the business with, were y'all both fuckin' Marilyn?"

"No." His jaws tightened up at the thought of David having sex with her. "I don't know about now, but back then, no. Marilyn and I were a couple, man."

"So, you don't mind her getting down with Advance Models after what happened?"

"No, I don't mind. I want her back, man. I'm not gonna lie. She'll be a very good asset to this company."

The only advantage I saw I had with Marilyn was to play on her dream of being in a Paul Turner film. After doing some research, I found out Paul Turner was a 57-year-old man who had produced 21 box office movies. He'd been nominated 17 times and was a nine-time Oscar Award Winner. His movies had grossed millions. He was one of the best in the movie industry. I definitely had to find a way to put Marilyn in a Paul Turner film.

It seemed like I had infinite benefits when it came to being a Mason. What it was though, Masons, we had our hands in everything. Like I said before, there's a Mason in every field and career. In different cities around the world, there were a few fields and careers that had their own lodge that they attended just for network-ing, building as a whole, and having something in common. In Hol-lywood, California, there was a 13-story Film Lodge that producers, directors, actors, and others in the Hollywood film industry at-tended. It took me three phone calls to my Masonic brothers that I didn't know in that lodge and five days to wait for a call back from one of them to get Paul Turner's cell number. I didn't know if every word got to Paul or not, but I had told them that I wanted him to produce my model's music video.

He told my Masonic brother for me to call Tuesday morning at 9.

"Hello, am I speaking with Paul Turner?"

"This is he. Is this Damion Johnson?"

"Yes sir, it is."

"Hello, Damion, how may I help you?"

"Mr. Turner, I own a modeling agency that's here in Dallas, Texas. I have a model that is about to drop a mixtape. I want you to produce her first music video," I told him.

"What is the song about?"

"Basically, it's about women pursuing their dreams in life. It's an inspirational and motivational song."

"Okay, I got it. Do you have a pen or pencil in reach?" he asked me.

"Yes, I do."

"For me to tell you a price, I want you to send me a link to the song to my email address so I can listen to it. Are you ready for the email address?"

"Yes," I said with pen in hand.

After he had given it to me, I prepared to send him the song while still on the phone.

"Mr. Johnson, do you have any suggestions that you've con-sider to be in the video?"

"Yes, I have a model that's an actress who appeared in the ma-jor motion picture *Fear Me*. I don't know what, but I want her to be in it."

We talked for about five more minutes and then we hung up.

That call strengthened the foundation of what I was building for Marilyn Sunshine, without her realizing it. I would put down some of my best game so she would drop Perfect Models and sign with Advance Models.

***

The Set Up
Rose

Syn hit Marilyn Sunshine up three days ago via email to discuss her being in Syn's music video. Syn gave her the choice of the meeting location. Marilyn Sunshine chose the Cheesecake Factory at the Town East Mall in Mesquite.

We met her because Monopoly and Josh didn't want to expose themselves to Sunshine yet. I agreed because it was better for us to meet her than them. When we arrived, she was already there sitting in a booth in the front, scrolling her fingers down her smart phone screen, waiting on us. I could tell she was a boogie bitch, having it her way. She had this boss bitch attitude about herself. Convincing her to leave Perfect Models might be difficult. We were gon' see.

A big, tall, bald, handsome, muscle-bound white guy sat across from her. Once we walked up on her booth, Syn said, "Marilyn Sunshine."

Sunshine and the muscle guy looked up at us. She smiled, he didn't.

"Hey, I'm Syn." She extended her arm for a handshake. "Thanks for agreeing to meet with us. This is my friend, Rosemary. She will be in the video as well."

"Nice to meet you two," she said, and then I mentioned the same thing she said.

The muscle guy asked Sunshine, "Will you be okay?"

"Yes, I'm good," she replied, nodding her head.

The muscle guy got up and went over to the bar facing us. Syn and I sat across from her in the same booth. Sunshine took the huge pink sunshades off her face.

"So, last night I listened to some of your songs, they're good. I like the song you have named 'Strength In My Corner.' It's very inspirational."

Syn blushed uncontrollably. "Thanks, Marilyn Sunshine, that means a lot."

"Us women need that, ya know. Let me tell you what my favorite song of yours is. It's a duet you have with some singer named Monopoly. That song shot back memories of my old lover. You two really sang that song."

Sunshine would be in a world of awakening when she found out who was behind this whole set up. Her IG was on fire. Eight days ago, she and five other models were at a club in Cancun going crazy. Sunshine got paid six stacks to be there, and she got over 20 thousand more followers just from taking a bunch of pics and making twerk videos.

Daddy was mentioning going to Dubai in a few weeks and said he would offer her 10 stacks to go with us. We were going to have to make it livelier than they did in Cancun. She was going to love this whole experience of being around the family. Syn and I had to make it seem like this video and being around us would take her career on a higher level so she could choose Advance Models to be her agency over Perfect Models. For this plan to be effected as Monopoly and Josh wanted it to be, we had to make all this seem as natural as possible.

After Syn thanked her again, they got down to business about the video. "My manager and the producer of the video decided on Rosemary, her being a gymnast, and you, pursue being an actress. My manager wrote it for different reasons. At first he wanted a song like "Strength in My Corner," so I could sing it at his fashion for breast cancer. And then, he thought about doing a video for that same song for inspiring and uplifting women. That's where you and Rosemary came into the picture. Rose, tell her your story."

"Well, when I was in high school I was a gymnast, the best in school. I ended up dropping out during the pregnancy of my son. I would have went to college for it, but you know. Our manager really believes in us and thought it would be a great idea to have me do gymnastics in Syn's video. Really, he wants me to do the video for my parents. We're not on speaking terms because of me dropping out and not going to college. Anyway, I've been training close to a month now. I don't know how Paul Turner is going to do your and my part together, but he's—"

"Wait a minute, I don't mean to cut you off, but did you just say Paul Turner?" she asked after she cut me off.

"Yes, why, is something wrong?" I asked, playing it off.

"No, nothing's wrong. Is that the film producer Paul Turner?"

"Yeah, that's him," Syn responded.

"Well, why didn't you say so earlier? I would have agreed in the email."

Since that was set in stone now, minutes later, I told her about Monopoly's birthday party on Saturday, which was in four days. I didn't tell her what kind of party. If she said no, I would tell her what kind of party it was. If she said maybe, I would tell her tomorrow, a day before the party. All she knew was that it would be an outdoor event, so she knew to show some skin since it would be outside. I wanted to surprise her. Monopoly told me to tell her, but I did otherwise. The reason was because I believed she would be suspicious of being hired to do a video with Paul Turner and being invited to a dirt ride, both of which she loved. I knew I'd be suspicious of that myself. That was why I played it like that. Since we told her that Syn would be performing at his birthday, she agreed to come to support Syn. All that needed to be done now was, Monopoly and Josh work their magic, then they would have her.

Smoove Dolla

Chapter 8
Monopoly
Rosemary's Birthday Night

Rose was really my queen on my chess board. She had the potential to be every piece position on the board besides one, if caused for. I believed with her by my side, I could accomplish anything I set out to be in life. I hadn't felt that way about any ho, ever. Rose was the first. Let me tell you why.

Rosemary's drive was beyond all others, not just in the lifestyle, but in life in general. She just needed a nigga like me to come along and bring it out of her. She was amusing, I loved playing the Game alongside of her as I did with Fancy and Shae. I was drawn to her responsibility and intelligence, and her seriousness to the Game we were in. The chances of me taking a loss with her were slim. With her, I would accomplish a lot. Although, it took her a while to fully open up to me. That was because she was careful not to get herself involved in something she would regret. I constantly strived hard to please her, win her, and fulfill her. And she did the same for me. Our relationship was smoother than any ho I ever pimped. We brought out the best in each other. I believed our bond would grow even stronger than it already was.

Tonight, was Tuesday, August 24, 2012, Rosemary's birthday, three days before my own. I could have flown us out of the country, but since we were prepping for my birthday party on Friday night, I decided to do something with her in Dallas City Limits. It really didn't matter to her, we were alone anyway, and she was happy as long as we were spending time alone together. To her, going out somewhere with me was just like going on a vacation. The Reunion Tower, known as the building with the ball on top of it in Downtown Dallas, was a five-star restaurant and hotel.

"What brought you into the Game?" I asked Rose as she ate her strip salad.

After swallowing her food, she said, "About six years ago when I was 17, I had gotten pregnant by my ex-boyfriend in high school. He died in a motorcycle accident three months into my pregnancy.

He left nothing, and his parents didn't want to deal with me either because they say I was the cause of him dying."

"How was you the cause of him dying?"

"We had gotten into a big argument about him not spending time with me while I was pregnant."

"He must have told his parents 'bout the argument before the accident."

"Yep, he did. Anyway, my parents were tripping super hard that I just left their house. My friend, Destiny, had her own apartment, so I went to stay with her. She danced at a club called Rick's in Euless. She took care of me for the remainder of my pregnancy until I could dance and ho on my own. Basically, that's how it all started."

"Did you graduate high school?" I asked.

Her mouth moved to the left of her face while she looked down for a second. I took that to be shame. The thought that came to mind was that she disappointed her parents. She shook her head and said, "Nope, I didn't finish school."

"When was the last time you talked to your parents?" I asked before I bit a piece of my well-done steak that had about five more bites left until I finished it.

"I don't talk to my dad at all. I spoke with my mom about my son a week ago. If it's not about Lil' Mike, we don't talk that much. Due to me dropping out and not going to college and dancing in the club, they don't want anything to do with me."

She mentioned without her telling me that, her parents were probably deep into the church and without a doubt, they had high expectations for Rosemary. They wanted her to do something better with her life.

"What were your dreams when you were in high school?" I asked her.

"I was a gymnast my whole entire time in high school. I was really good at it too. That's because I really loved dancing. Dancing makes me feel at ease. It releases all negative thoughts and feelings."

From being around her at the club and the house while she danced, I could see that to be true. Like Claire, Rose was a very gifted dancer with a lot of rhythm, not just in the club but a woman that could be a professional dancer. I was definitely going to have her pursue dancing. How she felt about dancing was how I feel about music and singing. Music was my calling for sure. I connected to it more than anything.

"Anyway, my parents were planning on sending me to college for gymnastics, but I got pregnant."

An hour later, before paying the bill and then leaving, I texted the receptionist at my penthouse building to put flame to all the candles in my penthouse, something I had set up for Rose. My receptionist at the front desk gave me a thumbs up once he saw us walk through the lobby, letting me know he did what I paid him to do.

I unlocked the door and let her go in first. Once she saw the romantic setting I did for her, she put both hands over her mouth. Earlier, around 3 P.M., I went to buy a lot of rose petals. I also took 200 one-hundred-dollar bills out of my safe. I put the rose petals and the hundred-dollar bills all over the floor from the entrance of the front door trailing to the bedroom, as well as on the sofa, on my king-size bed, and in the jacuzzi. The rose petals represented her and the money represented me. By me romancing her this way, I believed every time she saw and smelled a rose she would think of this experience with me.

A couple of seconds later, she said, "Wow, baby, you did this for me?"

I shut the door behind us. "You know I did, baby. All for you," I said, then took her hand, guiding her to the sofa, and we both sat down. I grabbed the $949 bottle of Moet Chardon Imperial Brut champagne out the silver bowl of ice. While I opened the bottle with the corkscrew, I told her, "I'm not a drinker, but tonight is your birthday celebration, which is a very special night, so I might as well get loose with you. It's nothing wrong with drinking a couple glasses of some of the best champagne in the world every once in a while, especially when we're living a luxury lifestyle, right?"

"No, it's nothing wrong with it, Daddy. Thank you, Monopoly. Thanks for everything."

"You're welcome, baby," I said as I poured us both a glass. I gave her a glass and got the other one for myself. "I want to make a toast." We raised our glasses up. "This toast is for our birthdays, our drive, our accomplishments, to the Game that's been good to us. I am proud of your performance and productivity over these last past three months. We have really accomplished a bunch since we've been together. You and I are a great team. Let's not stop making history in this life. It's us against the world, My Queen."

Then we toasted and drank the champagne in our glasses. I made up my mind that I wouldn't be drinking more than three glasses of champagne, just enough to where I would be feeling a bit tipsy. We talked for a little over an hour, and then I led her from the sofa to the front of a wall that had a long mirror on it. The red lights were dimmed perfectly, where I could still look in her eyes through the mirror while I had my arms around her from the back.

"Rosemary, you are really an amazing, gorgeous woman, you know that?"

"You think so?" she asked and smiled.

"I know so. You're perfect for me, Rose. And I'm not just saying physically, but also mentally, emotionally. I appreciate every piece of you, Rose."

"Thanks, Daddy," she said while moving her long red hair to the other side of her shoulder from the side my head was on.

I took that as a sign that she wanted to be pleased physically. I kissed the side of her neck three times, and then went to the nape of her neck until I ended up on the other side of her neck. I started licking and sucking all over her right ear while caressing her waist and tight, flat stomach. Her breathing became heavy, so I continued on doing what I was doing.

A couple of minutes later, I whispered in her ear, "I must admit, I'm glad I met you on May 14 on that Saturday. We came into each other's lives at the perfect time." I started tonguing her ear down again for about thirty seconds. "You made one of the best decisions of your life, choosing up with an outstanding pimp. We've accomplished a lot together in these three months we've known each other. With a pimp like me and a ho like you, we can accomplish a lot more."

I stopped talking to kiss and suck on her earlobe. I caressed her arms. After a minute had passed by, I caressed her face and then her red hair. I had to take my time with Rose before I went inside her. I couldn't just stick my dick in her. This was a special occasion and a very rare opportunity for her to get my dick.

In between kisses, she worked my Balenciaga shirt up off my body and head. I followed her lead with sliding her tight-fitted Dolce & Gabbana dress off her fine ass. Once we were naked, we went back to kissing. Seconds later, I picked her up and turned her body around, upside down into 69 position while standing. We held on tight to each other's waist while we gave each other head. I started out licking her pearl tongue. I went from licking the pearl for about 20 seconds to sucking on it for the same length of time. She had a half-inch pearl, so I was able to grab it with my lips, sucking it in and out of my mouth. While still in between my lips, I licked the tip of it as best as I could.

That treatment made her cum. Her cumming made me go crazy eating her pussy. I went back and forth licking around to in between her pussy lips. We both went hard. It was like we were competing against one another on who could make each other nut first. I won that giving head contest. A minute later, I came in her mouth. She sucked me dry, swallowing every drop.

I stopped eating her. A lot of pimps would disagree and wouldn't approve of kissing a hoe in the mouth and eating a ho's pussy, but it was what it was. I didn't do this with any other ho but my bottom. Her being my bottom didn't justify me that I could or should eat her pussy. It was the fact that I wanted to do it, to please myself and then my bottom ho. So, I didn't give a fuck what the critics would say, it was what it was.

She started slapping her left jaw with my semi-hard dick. She did it twice and said, "Get that dick hard for your ho again, Daddy! Come on, Daddy!" She then started sucking my balls and jacking me off at the same damn time, trying to get me back hard as a rock again. Don't forget she was still upside down while I stood.

After succeeding, she told me to put my body up against the wall. Once I did, she slid down my body into a headstand position. I put my arms up under her thighs so she wouldn't fall backwards.

"You don't have to hold my legs. I got it. I have good balance, Daddy. All you have to do is stand up, baby."

I let go of her legs and said, "Do what you do then."

Rose was 5'7, so in the headstand position, she was the perfect height to work her body while I was inside of her. She did just that. She popped her ass back and forth repeatedly. "That pussy good uhh, Daddy? You like the way your ho fuckin' this black dick? Uhh?"

"Keep fucking this black pimp dick, ho. Keep on, you dirty bitch."

Talking dirty to her that way made her go crazy. She moaned and talked dirty for the whole three minutes she fucked me. Next, she moved her hips side to side, making my dick touch the walls inside of her love box. It looked and felt so great. I slapped each of her ass cheeks hard once because she was going so hard.

After a while, she pushed off me, and she landed on her butt and feet. She got up to jump on me, putting her arms around my neck. She grabbed my jewel tightly with her right hand, went up and down on it, and then rubbed it on the surface of her pussy. She put me back in.

I had my arms up under Rose's legs, grabbing two handfuls of her little ass so I was in control of the way we fucked. I moved her body up and down on my shaft roughly while I pumped at the same time.

"Fuck the shit out that pussy. Dig in this white pussy with that big black dick. Fuck me hard."

I began pulling out, leaving the head of my dick in her and then slamming her down on me over and over. Every time I did that, she said, "Fuck it! Fuck it! Fuck it!" She moaned insanely while scratching my back with her short press-on nails.

A few minutes later, while walking her to the sofa, I moved Rose's body in a circular motion on me. When we made it there, I placed her on her back with me still inside her and then pinned her legs behind her head. I slowly moved her hair out the way from the left side of her face. "Oh, baby, you're so gorgeous, Rose. You know that?"

"Yes, yes Daddy," she said loudly while throwing her hips up at me.

I put one hand on the back of the couch and the other on the arm. My body stood over her like I was a bad storm with her body diagonal in the corner of the couch. I must have tried to slam all my weight into her about fifty times fucking her, making her run up the couch. It felt so good that I had to switch positions to keep from nutting.

I had her get up and bend over on the sofa. I placed my right foot on the sitting part of the sofa and then put myself inside her. Rose moved her body back and forth while I hit it from the back. A couple minutes later, I put my thumb inside her pink asshole and started fingering her. She went wild. She swung her head around hard in a circle, making her hair follow her like a star. Some of the rose petals that were in her hair flew out. She jerked her head around towards me, hair swung to the back of her neck. "Fuck the shit out of me, baby! Yea, just like that!" she said in a deep voice while looking me deep in the eyes.

After a few minutes of fucking her hard, I got the idea of wanting to fuck Rose in the ass. So, I slid out her pussy, leaving my thumb in her ass. "Scoot yo' ass down some more and toot your ass up," I instructed, while pushing her with the hand I had on her ass. I climbed up on the sofa right behind her.

Since her asshole was wet enough for me to go in without Petroleum Jelly or baby oil, I replaced my thumb with my dick. I slid in her tight asshole two inches and pumped slowly about fifteen times, getting her hole loose and comfortable before I went deeper and faster,

"Fuck that white asshole with that big dick. Fuck yeah! Go deep in that ass. Dig in that shit!" she said while moaning.

I gave her what she wanted, putting the whole length inside of her. She went crazy, throwing her body back and forth, matching me with every pump while holding her cheeks open for me to go deeper. I put my hands on the back of the sofa and started thrusting my hips into her body.

She began crying out in pain and running, then I busted in her ass after what seemed like fifty or more strokes. I pumped until I couldn't no more and then collapsed on her.

We went to go take a shower and went at it again the whole night until the morning.

Chapter 9
My 25th Birthday Party
Monopoly

My birthday party was tailored to the liking of Marilyn Sunshine, without her even knowing it. This party was going to be used as bait to sign Marilyn to Advance Models. It was a two-day dirt ride party in Mesquite. Josh was confident that this would work. He went in half with me, so I wasn't tripping if it didn't get her to sign. As long as she didn't renege on the agreement to be in Syn's video, it was good. I was working extra hard to get the attention I knew she deserved. I wanted her to blow up. I was confident in my Game. I knew one thing, I would make it my business that we had her. It wasn't about the bet money. Having her down with our team would do nothing but add status to the company and models.

I rented 10 acres, a field that was used for dirt and trail rides. I rented 20 each of dirt bikes, three-wheelers, four-wheelers, and five big trailers for the people with me. I hired Ced and another known DJ from Dallas to work, one for the day and one for the night. I even paid a few artists to perform at my birthday party. Also, I hired a big catering service based in Dallas for two days. They started today at noon to 3 P.M. for lunch, and then for dinner it would start at 5P.M. to 8 P.M. There were about 10 chefs for the catering service, and all 10 would be cooking at one time. Whatever meal you wanted would be custom made. We had the best of champagne, all kind of liquor, and beer to drink. All for free.

It was my birthday, so I had to go all out for it.

I invited damn near my whole immediately family, a bunch of my Masonic family, some of my fans, which were all women, a couple of celebrities I knew, a few pimps, their hoes, and people out the Bonton projects where I was from to my party. There were over 200 people that showed up within the 30 minutes of the party starting at noon, and the people were steady rolling in.

About forty-five minutes later, Marilyn Sunshine showed up in a new white Maybach. A big white dude I was guessing was her bodyguard got out the driver's seat and got out to open the door for

Marilyn as well as another skinny, tall, pretty chick. Rose and Syn met them at the entrance. Josh and I posted up at the DJ booth with my boy, Cedric. I got Josh's attention off Ced's laptop by tapping him on the arm, telling him that Marilyn had shown up.

As they talked while they walked, I saw that Marilyn looked better in person. She put Bebe Rexha shame. She was finer than all my white hoes. She had on a blue tank top that showed a lot of cleavage. She had the perfect tan, like she went to the spa yesterday just for this party. Her pretty ass friend had the perfect tan too. The blue denim daisy duke jeans Marilyn had on were skintight. The shape of her pussy was showing. I could see why a white boy like Josh could go crazy over something that beautiful.

I looked at him while he stared at her like he hadn't seen her in years. He had love all in his eyes and smile. They were still a good distance away. Plus, they hadn't seen Josh nor me yet. "Look out, Josh, introduce her to the party. Get on the mic," I told him, grabbing the microphone, and then handing it to him.

"Man, I'm not about to do that, bro."

"You can't be my partner if you gon' be scared to shoot at a broad. Plus, you ain't gon' never have her being that way. That's why you don't have her now, being scared," I said, challenging him to see if it would motivate him.

"I don't know what to say, bro."

I gave him a quick summary of what to say. He smiled the whole time I was telling him. He definitely liked that shit.

"Excuse me, ladies and gentlemen, I want to introduce this special lady that's been missing out of my life far too long. You all might know this A-list actress from the movies *Swampland* and *The Devil's Daughter*. Or seen her grace the pages of *Swimsuit Magazine*. I welcome you, the lovely Marilyn Sunshine," he said as he pointed his finger at her.

He did good, better than I thought he would. If I had said it to a woman, I would have juiced it up more and dedicated a song, but I liked what I heard from him. He got the response I knew he would get. She smiled the whole way to the DJ booth. We stepped down the ten-step, wooden stairway and met them at the bottom.

"Hey, Josh, it's good to see you," she said as they hugged each other tightly. I could tell they were both crazy about each other, but their pride was in the way to call one another.

"I'm a little taken aback. It's good to see you, too. How have you been?"

"It's been wonderful. I just been doing my best to climb up the ladder in the film industry. And by the way, I know this party is not a coincidence. You set everything up, didn't you?"

"Yeah, I'm the cause of it. But it's all real though. I did it for you, Mary," he said, calling her by her real name.

"Paul Turner producing the music video, is that real?"

I butted in, because that was too long to be quiet without being introduced and invited in their conversation. "Yes, it's real, Marilyn. You'll be working with your favorite producer."

"And you are?" Marilyn Sunshine asked me while looking me up down.

She knew I was somebody from my confidence, my swagger, and I was Balenciaga down, from my shirt to my shoes. Plus, I had on $100,000 worth of jewelry. "I'm Monopoly." We shook hands.

"This is his birthday party. He's the one who really put everything together," Josh told her.

"Oh. Happy Birthday, Monopoly."

"Thanks, Marilyn."

"And by the way, I listened to some of Syn's songs. I really like the 'Commitment' song y'all did with each other."

"Thanks. We will be performing that song today."

"I posted the song on my Facebook and Instagram."

Syn's IG and Soundcloud were blazing. I didn't know it was because of Marilyn Sunshine's post. That was all right. I knew I was doing the right thing by putting her in Syn's video. I knew by being associated with Marilyn, some of her fans would be Syn's too.

"I really do appreciate that. Who's your friend?" I asked Marilyn Sunshine, because ever since we all met up, she had a frown on her face.

"This is super model Elizabeth Simmons. You don't know her?"

She did look familiar, but I couldn't place where I had seen her. I thought hard and fast, and it came to me. I saw her when I was looking at Marilyn Sunshine's photos on Perfect Models' website. She looked damn good in person.

"I remember her now. I saw her on you all's website," I said, smiling as we shook hands.

"Nice to meet you. Happy Birthday."

After thanking her, I told my two queens, Elizabeth, and her bodyguard, "Let's enjoy what I have to offer at this party and let them talk."

As we were walking to the bar, I stopped. They stopped a couple of steps ahead of me when they noticed that I did. I was in the middle of the three women, and the bodyguard stopped about ten feet behind me.

"You all tell me, who's the best dresser out of you, you, and you?" I said, pointing at Syn, Rose, and Elizabeth, in that order. "Or me," I said and then spun around.

My queens grinned. Rose said, "You know you are, Daddy."

I looked at Elizabeth. "I'm not too sure about that. I know I can be on the cover of the *GQ* magazine and all, but I gotta give Liz that crown. The way she's dressed, she can do a spread on every page in a *Sports Illustrated* magazine swimsuit issue, and they'll sell millions of them for it. Am I right, my queens?"

They nodded their heads. "You're definitely right. I'll probably get off on that magazine," Rose said and then smirked.

Elizabeth looked Rose over and then chuckled. I wanted a laugh in some kind of degree to lighten up her mood. A chuckle was a good enough response.

I took back what I said about giving her the crown as best dresser out the four of us. She probably had more money than me, but I outdressed her today. She looked really great with what she had on. She had on a white MIU MIU blouse and pink pencil skirt with matching wooden sandals, and the thin, sleek, metal-trimmed Chanel purse that I knew cost damn near five Gs. She had her brown hair in a ponytail and her bangs hung at the front of her head that looked pretty on her. We were both overdressed for this dirt-ride party. I wasn't tripping, tho', because I had changing clothes in my trailer if I got dirty.

We went to the bar to have some drinks. Julie, the white chick that worked at Speed's where Tiffany and I used to play pool, was my bartender at my party. I made a decision not to turn her into a prostitute. The first time I had a conversation with her, I imagined her as a cheerleader. That's what we were working on for her. Josh and I had her apply for a job to be a Cowboys, Saints, Texans, Dolphins, Giants, and Bears cheerleader. If that didn't work, we would have her try her hand in their basketball teams. All we were waiting on were the tryout days.

Julie had lost my business card at that bar. Weeks later, she had hit me up through a comment on one of my videos on YouTube. I barely checked those comments. When I didn't respond, she found me on Facebook and IG. I got so many messages and was so busy that I didn't see her messages until almost a month later. She ended up signing with us a couple weeks later after launching our agency. I was glad she found me. She had a great personality. I knew one day she was going to be an asset to Advance Model.

After kicking it at the bar for about 20 minutes, Rose, Syn, and I bounced, Elizabeth and the bodyguard there. Even though I made Elizabeth laugh, I still had to watch her, and maybe the bodyguard. If he wasn't their bodyguard on a daily basis, he was Josh's old partner David's eyes. One of them was watching Marilyn and going back to David to report what they saw at this party. That was the whole reason why I pulled them away from Josh and Marilyn. I was glad no one told Marilyn about us owning a modeling agency. She didn't need to know about that yet, until the right time.

That would definitely create a big threat. By Josh being in her presence again, it was already enough of a threat in itself. Them going to tell David we had a modeling agency would have done nothing but started some shit between the two agencies, all over Marilyn. Maybe we could use the beef after we'd signed her, but now wouldn't be a good time.

On the way to my trailer, I texted Josh and Julie to tell them to not tell anyone that we launched a modeling agency. Until Marilyn was comfortable and she was coming around us by herself, she didn't need to know neither. Until then, the only way they would discover we had an agency was by them doing their research. Since some of my family members, a few children, and my models were under five huge umbrellas in a big area beside our trailers, I group texted all my models to tell them the same thing.

I pulled Rose to the side. We sat side by side on the trailer's steps to talk. "This shit gon' come together like glue, Rose."

"I believe it will."

"It's not gon' happen today, but it's gon' happen one day. All Josh got to do is take his time."

"Why was that bitch, Elizabeth, mugging like that?"

I broke down what I thought just seconds ago, but added, "She doing what she's supposed to do. She's loyal to David. You're loyal to me. I expect you to do the same for me but in a finesse type of way. In better words, with your poker face. You and I have history in the streets where we conceal certain type of shit to accomplish the plan. David doesn't. Majority of everything he tries to pull is in a direct way. That's how I saw it. Josh didn't even see it, and he was around him. She fucked up when she let me see that frown. I know how to deal with a boogie bitch like that. That bullshit ass joke I told wasn't about how she looks nor her dress code. I did it to make her feel comfortable. That's why I told y'all not to tell them about our modeling agency. She's only going to go tell David about it, if they don't already know. If he knew, he wouldn't have let her come here. We become a threat to him once he finds out. That's why Josh, you, and I have to establish business and apply proper game so she can choose with us. You see what I'm talking about now?"

"Yes, I see now."

At 3 P.M., we had a 14-man bracket tournament. Believe it or not, Marilyn Sunshine won first place by inches. Minutes before the race began, by seeing her warming up for the race, I could tell she really loved riding bikes. She gave me the $300 she won for my birthday. It told me she gave it to me because she was enjoying herself, thanking me for this event, and it was a birthday present. Even though I came in ninth place, I still had a lot of fun. This was my first time ever riding a dirt bike and attending a dirt-ride event. We had two more races involving the three and four-wheelers that I didn't race in. I watched and cheered on the sidelines for the people I knew who raced. The director of the races paid first place $300, $200 to second place, and third got $100. Everybody that rode had a blast.

Out of 365 people, I only received about 50 gifts along with $8,593 that came from about 100 people. I had Sarah and Heather put all my gifts up in my trailer. I even had a ho choose me tonight. It was a ho Solo knew out of Garland. She asked him about me, and he sent her my way. Since I still had Alicia working out of hotels, I had the new chick work with her until I said otherwise.

Tight Game pulled up in a new Bugatti to the party a little after 6 P.M. Some young dude got out the car with him. I guess he was the youngster he wanted me to meet. When I got closer to him, I saw that he favored Big Country.

"Wuz up, Unk?" I said, greeting him with a Masonic hand-shake.

"I had to make my way to see you on your birthday. Happy Birthday, nephew."

"Thanks, big bro."

"I got you a birthday present, but I ain't gon' show you till later on tonight."

"I wonder what it is. Is it a whip or something?"

"Nall, youngin', I'ma just say, justice gon' be served."

"Okay, okay. I can't wait to see what you got for me." I really didn't know what he was talking about. Justice gon' be served meant some payback shit to me. We'd see.

"Ok, by the way, this is Big Country's son, Elijah. Elijah, this is Tunke, one of my three nephews I told you about.

"Elijah and I shook hands and spoke to one another. "Let's go sit down over there." I pointed to my trailers.

Halfway to my rented trailers, Solo pulled up on the side of us, popping a wheely on the four-wheeler. "Wuz good, Unk? I see you finally made it."

"Yeah, you know I had to come thru for his birthday. You better watch yoself on that thang before you hurt yoself."

"I know what I'm doin', Unk. Us pimps catch on fast. I'm about to ride, I'll catch up wit' y'all later," he said, and then sped off.

An hour later, my brother, Juice Leeroy, opened up for me doing two of his songs. He set the mood just right with his mellow style. Next, Mos performed some of his most known songs with Rose, Claire, and Erika as his dancers. he hyped the crowd up with his fire songs. Most of the people here rapped his hits with him. I thought that was throwed.

After Mos's performance, I performed "Certain Passion," which went like this:

Chorus
I got this certain passion for flashing (girl)
like lights, camera, action
talkin' 'bout girl you mean the world
I'm braggin', not laughing or askin'
Wanna know what you mean to me
it's passion, complete with pure satisfaction
tryna put you on a house and hill so here's the deal
I'm smashing, I must admit I'm smashing
Verse 1
Now I'm dwelling on our history
'Cause it gets to me
Just the thoughts of you kissin'
me thinkin' 'bout the love we shared
'cause it meant something and I missed
Something's in between
Baby girl, you the one for me
the girl of my dreams
like sexin' you in limousines
And never once I had this thought you on top of me
And we makin' love properly
the windows sealed up airtight
Where no one can see
just you me (because)

Next, I sung my song called "Voicemail."
Verse 1
I need you, to pick up the phone
just give me a few minutes to explain what's goin' on
didn't mean what I said or what I did
I was acting like a kid,
I say I was acting like a kid (yeah)
Now my actions got your heart bleedin',
got me pleadin',
fightin' just to talk to you
Chorus
1 ring, 2 rings, 3 rings; 4 rings
straight to the voice, straight to the voicemail
It said I'm sorry you can't reach me,
leave a message at the beeps
I'll get back to, I'll get back to you (beep)
pick the phone so I can tell you that
I'm sorry, I didn't mean to do it

The last song I performed was a duet with Syn titled "Commitment," the song Marilyn Sunshine liked. I had her and Josh on stage for that one. I called my daughter to the stage before we began. We danced as Syn sang with the live band playing the slow-tempo instrumental.
Syn, Verse 1
Blind you my sight at times I felt like dying
You made me live for life, you got me flyin'
I've lived in the darkest corners for so long
to where now I stand in the light
For past times I fantasize
how I can be a better lover
your love is what I prefer
from past hurts, caused trust issues
so many times, I ran away from the truth
back then I didn't understand

till my last breath left is to succeed is the plan
broken pieces of my life I shared and you understand
this opportunity to love you
And getting loved by you
I'll keep in my hand
Chorus
This is my Commitment
to love you (forever)
This is my Commitment
to always be your boo
This is my Commitment
to stand true
My commitment

Me, Verse 2
Had a depression
Wasn't good at expression
My thoughts or love
I was seekin' some affection
You a goddess girl
The angel of my blessin'
My future wife, the woman I can grow old with
And there were times we cried
And often times we hurt
We had problems in our lives,
life was far from perfect
but we had love
so we made it
pain, is love, is time
and that's what we dedicated
to never break your heart was the promise
that I made it
Chorus

The crowd enjoyed all the performances. We had fun on stage.
My daughter looked like she enjoyed it the most. She had a huge

smile on her face. She thought it was pretty cool to be on stage with her daddy.

After Syn and I performed our song, she started singing Happy Birthday to me. She even invited the crowd to sing along with her. I ain't gon' lie, that made me feel better than I already did.

I walked over in front of my trailers where Tight Game, my momma, my pops, and a few more of my family members were. It'd been a while since my pops and I hung out like this together. We were never close my whole life, and still were not, but I was glad he attended my B-Day. We all talked for about two hours straight until Tight Game was ready to show me my present.

He sent me to get a bucket of ice water. Tight Game and Elijah were at the trunk of his Bugatti. When I looked inside, I saw that Tricks' wrists and ankles were tied up, laying on top of a long sheet of plastic. He was knocked out cold. Tight Game must have beaten him up pretty bad with more than just his fist, because he was bruised up and two golf ball-sized knots were on his forehead.

"You got him out of jail?" I asked as I looked at Tight Game.

"This muthafucka had a million-dollar bond, I had to post it," he said, then splashed him with the ice water. "Get yo' bitch ass up, you punk bitch."

Tricks almost jumped out of his skin when he felt that coldness. He looked around at the three of our faces one by one. His eyes got bigger with fear in them when he saw Tight Game.

He closed the trunk and told me to follow behind him. "When did you get that Lambo?" he asked after he saw me deactivate the alarm.

I smiled. "This my new toy, a present to myself. I copped it this morning."

I followed him to Big Country's house. As soon as we got out our cars, we headed to Tight Game's trunk. He had a short, wide, sharp-edged knife in hand. He cut the thick plastic from around Tricks' ankles, and he snatched Tricks up by his black tee.

"Get yo' bitch ass out. Now, I'ma give you a chance to save yourself. If I see you back around this way, I'm killing you. Now run that way," Tight Game said as he pointed towards the woods where a lot of tall ass trees stood, right beside the small pond.

I looked at Elijah. I was thinking, *He gon' bond him out, just to give him a chance to save himself?* Elijah shrugged his shoulders at me like he didn't know what was going on.

Tricks ran fast alongside the small pond into the woodland that met at the middle of the pond. I looked back at Tight Game to see what he was up to.

"I've thought about a hundred and one ways to kill that mutha-fucka. Only a few brought justice to what he has caused me, my family, and operation. He's the cause of me having to kill my main Queen on my chess board. He's the root to why one of my best friends is dead. If I could kill him for every effect he's caused and wake him back up again, I would, but I can't. Only one came out to be perfect."

He ushered us to a plastic unfolded table about 20 feet away, a table I didn't see until now. There were night vision goggles, a small flashlight, a hunting rifle, a Glock, and a sharp knife next to cam-ouflage army fatigues, three of everything, except there were two knives.

Tight Game looked at Elijah. "This is a game your father loved playing and created, called Find 'Em, Kill 'Em. There are no rules. All you have to do is get it done. The winner gets $10,000. Get dressed if you want to play," he said as he was taking off his clothes.

We dressed out in the army fatigue uniform. "Elijah, your father knew these woods better than he knew the back of his hand. He won every single time except for once. Us three will be splitting up, go-ing in different directions. The one that kills him, will call the other two to notify them. Let's see what we can do. Y'all be careful."

Tight Game went in the woods one way. Elijah followed the trail Tricks went. I went in along the other side of the pond.

Once I made it to the end of the pond, I started jogging. Tricks took off running, had gotten a three-minute head start. I kept in mind that he was a short little chubby muthafucka, so he couldn't have ran for a long time. I stopped jogging after two minutes. I cut on the flashlight and put it beside my rifle. It helped out a lot because it was pitch black out here.

I heard something to my left. I looked with my rifle pointed in that direction. It was a big, long snake going about his business while moving some of the leaves on the ground. I didn't bother it, it was going in another direction, not the way I was heading.

Not hearing any gunshots in the distance meant no one had found Tricks yet. I was glad, because I wanted to find the mutha-fucka first. I wanted to be the one to kill him.

After walking for two minutes, I started jogging again for one minute. When I stopped, I heard some branches and stiff leaves off a tree cracking under someone's feet rapidly behind me. On my way to look, someone pushed me hard to the ground. My rifle flew out my hand about eight feet away.

After taking the night vision goggles off my head, I attempted to roll over but felt a hard kick to my ribs in mid-turn. I rolled on my stomach in pain. Seconds later, I slowly reached for my Glock, but when my right hand got two inches from it, he put his right knee on the back of my right hand and followed it up with putting his hands over my neck to choke me with his left arm.

"You gon' die this time, you bitch nigga! Go to sleep!" Tricks told me.

I thought fast. I remembered the cutter in my knife holder. Four seconds into the choking, I wiggled my head from the brace of his arm. I used that for a distraction so I could get my knife. Once I retrieved it with my left hand, I bit down hard on his arm. He screamed in pain while taking his arm up over my head. I rolled quickly on my side and stabbed him in the chest, over and over, four times.

He laid on top of me until I pushed him off. I laid there for ten seconds, and then stood up. "It's you the one that's gonna die." I pulled the Glock 40 out, and gave him two shots to the dome.

I sat down Indian style on the ground. I called Elijah first and then Tight Game second. "It's a done deal, Unk. I'm somewhere out here."

"Alright. I'm about to go get the golf cart. Put the flashlight upside down in the ground. I'll find you."

Twenty-five minutes later, I was getting out the shower in Big Country's house.

I got paid, said my goodbyes, and went back to my party. I made it back to Mesquite at 1:52 A.M. Majority of the people that were there were gone. The people that were still here were either sleep or up chilling, outside smoking, talking, and drinking. Ced was gone, but I could hear music still from one of the cars.

After I talked to some of the niggas from my projects for about 10 minutes, I went inside my trailer. I was tired as hell from all the activity I participated in earlier today. I walked to the room and saw that it was full with Sarah's daughter, Rose, and my son in the bed asleep. I collapsed on the pallet next to Rose, Heather, Pinky, Syn, and Sarah.

Even though I went to sleep late, I still woke up early at 7:24 A.M. Most days I was like that, other than when I was really exhausted, then I'd stay asleep. I loved the morning more than any time of day. I guess it was the opportunity for me. To wake up was a blessing. It was even more a blessing to wake up to make money and do something you love doing. Sometimes, when I was alone at my penthouse, I'd look out my big window. I was on the 27th floor in my penthouse, so where I was at, I could see I-35 and lots of people going about their business in the streets downtown. Looking at that for about 15 to 20 minutes gave me the motivation to accomplish something that day.

I put on a muscle t-shirt, Nike gym shorts, and some Jordan house shoes. After getting myself together, I woke up everybody in my trailer so they could get something to eat. Breakfast was served from 6 A.M. to 8 A.M. Since it was almost 8, I paid the catering service extra to wait until 9 to shut down the breakfast. I wanted Josh, Marilyn, Rose, and whoever else to get a chance to get breakfast. The only things that were precooked were grits, oatmeal, biscuits, cinnamon rolls, and bagels. Everything else was custom. I ordered fish, grits, and turkey bacon as well as a liter of orange juice.

In between bites, I called Josh. He and Marilyn Sunshine were up already, getting themselves together. I let him know when he was finished to come to the food area.

Marilyn Sunshine ate with my queens and the children while Josh and I ate together. "I see you had a good time last night."

"Yeah, bro, I had a great night. Yeah, man," he said. putting emphasis on it.

"Y'all had sex?"

"Yeah, we did."

"So, what she talking about?"

"Just a lot of catching up on her goals and how David is handling his business since I've been gone."

"Did you mention to her that you wanted her to be under Advance Models?" I asked, making sure he didn't tell her.

"No. I thought you didn't want me to tell her?"

"I don't, not yet."

"Even though she had a good time, I don't think it was a good time."

"I'm thinkin' the day of the video. Oh, yeah, check this out. I'm going to Dubai in three weeks. Tell her to clear her schedule. You two can join me if you like. Tight Game, Elijah, the dudes you met yesterday along with some of the girls. We should bring one of our scouts too."

"Hell yeah, I'd love too, man," he expressed excitedly after swallowing his food.

"Don't ask her, tell her. Don't forget to tell her everything will be paid for. We're flying in a private plane."

"Okay. I got it. Let me go over there. Her bodyguard just pulled up."

"Aight, bro. I'll holla at you when you get back."

The whole weekend turned out to be one of the best birthday parties for me. We had a lot of fun until late Sunday night. I couldn't wait for the next one. It would be even bigger and better.

Smoove Dolla

Chapter 10
I'm Fiending for A Dose
Christie

A loud noise that sounded like a scream woke me. I was a heavy sleeper, so it had to be loud to wake me. I took a look at the clock on my nightstand, and it read 11:38 pm. I heard loud, distant screams again, this time for a long period of time. I got out of bed in my flannel nightgown and walked towards my room door.

I slept with my door half-closed. Herbert wasn't here, since he was out of town on business again. The only person that was here was Elijah The sounds were coming from upstairs where he was. It couldn't be anyone here. The alarm was still activated.

Before I walked upstairs, I switched the light on. Immediately, I saw a gagging ball on the third wooden step. When I got to the 11th step, I picked up a long, black rubber whip, that was on the 12th step.

The screams were getting louder as I eagerly got closer to Elijah's room. I didn't want to just walk in front of his wide-open door, I wanted to give him privacy, but I was curious to know what was going on in my home. I snuck through the hallway into the bathroom that was diagonal to his room. I could see right into his room.

I couldn't believe my eyes. There was a naked, black-haired, attractive white girl on a big wheel. Both arms as well as legs were tied, all spread apart on the wheel. She was upside down. She had a big, black, long dildo in her ass. Elijah held the dildo at its half mark, pushing and pulling the dildo out of her while striking her with a whip. Instantly, that made my pussy wet.

I had to enjoy this show. I hurried to climb up on the sink's counter and the one with the door on it. From there, I had a straight-shot look into Elijah's room.

I tied the thick end of the rubber whip around the metal towel holder on the wall in front of me, and then I put the thinner end around my neck, leaving a three-foot space in between me and the gap. I rubbed my bare pussy. I went back up to my pearl and rubbed away. "Oh, shit!" I said to myself. Dominatrix excited the hell out of me. I loved being dominated. I loved pain.

I leaned back so it could tighten more while I rubbed my pearl and watched Elijah perform. Elijah turned the wheel upright, then took the dildo out of her. He grabbed a handful of her hair. He grabbed his eight inches and then rammed it up her asshole. It was like he was a porn star because he stood to the side like it was a camera nearby.

I could see his meat enter and exit her rectum roughly. She screamed louder and louder than she did the first time.

I got so lost in playing with myself, and leaned further back than I should, because the left nail on the towel holder snapped out of the wall. It caused me to fall back and make a loud sound.

After I caught myself, I looked outside into Elijah's room. The commotion made him look towards my way. I hurried to close the door. I loosened the knot on the whip around my neck and sat there for a few seconds, thinking about what I was going to do next. I hoped he didn't see me, but if he did, fuck it. It was like I was being punished by Herbert for some reason. I didn't know because I hadn't been getting my dose of torture by him. Herbert had been going out of town a lot on the regular now.

It hadn't been a full two months yet since he awakened from his coma, and already he had gone out of town eight times, three out of the country, the others in the states. He'd only taken me once, the trip to China, but that was because of how busy I'd been. I had a busy day ahead of me tomorrow, so I should've been asleep right now.

Anyway, sometimes he would take Elijah, but if not, he was here with me. Most times Tight Game came back to Dallas, he barely would come home and spend time with me. He would leave again a couple days later. I never said anything because I didn't deserve an explanation on why he was doing what he did. For my actions of what I caused, I just took it as a form of torture from him.

I didn't think he knew what I'd done. He would have killed me already. He was far from dumb, tho'. I knew he knew I was holding back something from him. He had to know something. If he didn't know, whenever he did find out, I was ready for my punishment. Whatever the consequences were. I still didn't have enough courage to tell him, just to see that look on his face when he did find out. I sure didn't want to see it.

After sitting for a while, I asked myself, *What the fuck am I ashamed of? Surely, not this shit. It is what it is, this is my house!*

I jumped down from the sink's counter and opened the door. Elijah stood outside of his doorway in nothing. His dick was hard as a rock. I bit down on my bottom lip until he said something.

"Are you okay?"

"Yes, I heard some noise like somebody was dying, but I see what's going on now," I said as I looked at his body. Elijah was a big, dark, bulky young dude, with the body of a heavyweight UFC fighter. "Get back to what you were doing, she's waiting on you."

I went back downstairs to take another shower in my bathroom and finished the job. The whole time I washed myself, I was thinking about how I was going to bring the opportunity to Elijah that I wanted the same treatment the girl on the big wheel got. Since Tight Game was neglecting me, I was going to Elijah's corner. Only if he accepted me.

Smoove Dolla

Chapter 11
Dealing With This Court Shit
Monopoly

There were two women and six men inside the 297th Judicial District Courtroom in Tarrant County when I walked in. Even though I was dressed down in a plain, dark-blue Steve Madden, two-piece suit, dark-blue tie, white long-sleeve shirt with dark-blue Steve Madden dress shoes, people still stared at me when I walked inside the courtroom and walked down the aisle.

I had on no jewelry other than a 50k Rolex. The female D.A., a female C.O., both in front of the courtroom, a black older lady, and black man in his mid-30s sitting on the benches all looked at me when I sat on the forth row, left side at the end of the bench by the aisle. I didn't want that attention, but I guess it was the natural-born charisma my presence held that caught their attention.

A white lawyer came out the side door from talking with his client. The attorney and the D.A. went back and forth in conversation for about four minutes before the D.A. went and started talking to the judge. It was probably some fuckery going on in this muthafucker. The lawyer came back to where we were to talk to an older lady in her late 50s. I was in earshot of what was being said between the two.

"Good morning, Ms. Collins. Sorry I missed your call. I've been pretty busy lately."

"Hey, Mr. Phillips. It's okay. Tell me something good," she said to him.

"Ms. Collins, I did my best to get him the lowest sentence possible. They're not going down on the 15 years."

She started shaking her head. "I told you on the phone my baby's not signing for no 15 years. That's too long. He told me y'all court-appointed lawyers not 'bout shit. He's not signing for that," she said, speaking her mind.

He looked insulted. "Let me see if I can get them to lower that sentence again. Excuse me, Ms. Collins."

As he walked past her to get to the middle aisle, Ms. Collins grabbed his left hand and looked up at him. "Mr. Phillips, I'm sorry for what I just said. I'm emotional right now. I want my grandson home. Just do the best you can, please."

"I understand. Let me go see what I can do. I'm gonna tell you now, she really wants to give him the 15 years. If not, she's willing to take him to trial. I wouldn't prefer that."

"Like I just said, please do your best," she said, then let his hand go.

My intuition told me that lawyer wasn't looking out for their best interest. I didn't know what the charge was, but 15 years was stiff. I knew for a fact if that attorney was getting paid or another paid lawyer represented him, they would get that sentence lowered. In these situations, money talked.

So, when he walked off, I got up and went over to where she was. Being the man I was, I had to see if I could help in any way possible. I didn't want to ask how she was doing, because I already knew from what I heard in her conversation with that attorney. "Hello, Ms. Collins, my name's Damion. I want to tell you if you want help getting a paid attorney, I'll help. I know some attorneys personally. You don't have to pay for nothing, I got the bill," I said, giving her a solution to her problem.

"'Don't be telling me a lie, boy, are you serious?" she asked seriously.

"Yes ma'am, I'm serious. I wouldn't have wasted my time coming over here to tell you a lie. I really want to help. I know it's some crooked stuff going on with this judicial system. All I want to do is get your grandson out as soon as possible."

"Oh, baby, I can't believe this is happening." She put both of her small hands over her face, covering up her eyes, and then looked at me with a white smile. Her fangs had gold on them. After seconds passed by, she made prayer hands. "Thank you so much, Jesus. Thank you Jesus for this blessing," she said a little too loud.

"My lawyer will be here in a few. I'll talk to him about your grandson. After he's done with my case, I'll have him come talk to you. Okay, Ms. Collins?"

"Okay, young man."

Let me tell you, I made this woman's day this morning. It made me feel great doing it for them. I had to post this on the Book, the Gram, and Twitter with a picture of her and me. I posted, "This woman has a grandson who's locked up. They're trying to give him 15 years. If he doesn't sign for it, they're taking him to trial. When I saw that his court-appointed lawyer was no help at all, I had to give a helping hand and pay the whole bill for them a new lawyer who's willing to do his best. This judicial system is crooked."

We exchanged numbers and talked for about 10 minutes before my attorney showed up. He walked in front of us holding a thin brown briefcase in his right hand. He switched hands, putting the briefcase in his other hand. I stood up so we could shake hands. "Mr. Johnson, how are you?" he asked before he sat down next to me.

"I'm good, man. Just ready to get this over with. How are you doing?"

"I'm great, busy as usual, you know. Anyway, they're still at 20 years. I know you're not signing for it. I wouldn't even have you sign for that, knowing your case is extremely weak. Also, I've called the supposed victim multiple times, and she hasn't answered not one call."

"That's a good thing. I told you that I wanted you to keep setting my court dates back. But after thinking about it, file a motion for speedy trial."

"Are you sure?"

"Yes, I'm very sure. I'm ready to get this over with."

"That's fine with me. The chances of us winning are great, the balls are in our court on this one. If we go, it will be 90 days from now, so we'll be well prepared. The investigator I hired will do his job. I will do whatever extra I have to do and I will get back with you in a month. Will that do for you?"

"Yeah, it'll do. Mr. Lowes, how good are you with aggravated robbery cases?"

"I'm okay. I specialize in human trafficking and human trafficking cases. There's good attorneys at my firm that will do a better job than me."

"Okay, that'll do too. I'll be paying for everything." I pointed to Ms. Collins on the side of me. "This is Ms. Collins, her grandson is locked up here for aggravated robbery with a deadly weapon."

They introduced themselves and shook hands right in front of me. "Here is my card." He handed it to me to give to her. "Give me a call around 3 P.M. I'll direct you to a good attorney."

After my lawyer left, seconds later, her grandson's lawyer showed back up with a deal for 12 years, which was kind of good for that kind of charge in Tarrant County, and plus, this was his first felony charge. We still took our chances with a paid attorney that probably could get it down between 6 to 10 years. She apologized to him for the second time and thanked him for his time. Ms. Collins and I talked about five minutes before she left the courtroom while I waited on my lawyer.

Being here in this courtroom dealing with a pimp charge brought me back to the reason I got locked up the first time in the feds. I was on Sunset Blvd. at the strip club when I got a call from my black ho, Tamika. As soon as I answered the call, she told me, "Monopoly, I'm at the Greyhound station. I'm leaving you."

"Bitch, why are you calling me for? Ain't no chains on you, bitch, go. Thanks for telling me," I said, nonchalant, using trick psychology on her. I didn't want her to go, but at the same time, I didn't care about it if she did.

"Okay, but I have the key to the room and your laptop is in there. My bus is leaving in two hours to Dallas."

I had four hoes at that time. Three of them were dancing at the club. I didn't want them to have to leave the club to pick up my shit. I had to do it because I didn't want to lose my laptop and have to buy another, so I told her, "I'll be there in like 30 minutes." Without saying anything else, I hung up. I wasn't going to beg any woman to stay with me, ever.

At the time, I thought the ho respected me enough to call me to give me the news and not run off with my shit, but boy was I wrong.

I knew now she only wanted attention. I should have told her to tear her ass with my laptop and hung up instead of telling her I was coming to get it. I regretted that. Sometimes a person has to know when to take a loss. That should have been the time for me.

When I arrived, Tamika was sitting down at a netted mental bench out front of the Greyhound station on 1760 E 7th Street. She stood when she saw my white 745 pull up, leaving her bags by the bench with the key and laptop in hand. After she had given it to me, I attempted to put the car in drive, but she placed her hand on my wood-grain steering wheel.

"Monopoly, you just gon' leave without saying nothing?"

"Bitch, you got three seconds to get yo' funky ass hands off my steering wheel, or I'ma drive this car with your hands on it," I said, not meaning it.

She let go. "I don't want to leave you. Please, can we talk?"

I regretted not burning rubber on Tamika. See, I'd had problems with her insecurities a couple of times. She always wanted me around her. It was built-up insecurities from her childhood with her father not being around. I didn't know that until after going to the feds over the bitch. "I didn't bring you here. You found your way here, so find your way back to the room. I could have came up on a ho at the club by now, but I'm here. Bring me $500 back for wasting my time," I said, putting my feet in my mouth.

"Daddy, I got the money right here," she said while digging in her bra. I didn't know if any laws were watching. This ho could be setting me up for all I knew so, I told the ho, "Find yourself back. Bring it to the room. When you get there, call me. I'll make some time tonight so we can talk." Then I burnt off, going back to the strip club.

Four days later, Tamika and an Asian ho I had named Kim got arrested in a sting operation and brought the feds into my life. I spent 50k to get 17 months in the feds. I did a whole year, all because I failed to hang the phone up on that ho when she called.

While in prison, I came to the realization that I couldn't blame her. As a man and pimp, it was all my fault. Being who I was today, I was a fool to be mad at that ho, Tamika, for snitching on me.

There's not a lot of men that truly understand the woman they were with. A man would have to put in a lot of energy to truly satisfy a woman into staying down with him through thick and thin. There's no half stepping when it comes to dealing with women, if you do, you're going to be the one taking a loss. The men who don't understand get in their feelings when a woman does something that the man does not agree with, and what women do in a crisis that leaves a man in bad situations, it's a man's fault. A man should always take full responsibility to know when a woman was worth fucking with and when she was not.

Twenty-three minutes later, I got my court date set and then walked out the courtroom. It was 10:49 A.M., and Pinky's doctor appointment was for 12. I'd been taking her once a month, for four months now, and today would be the fifth.

Shae was four months pregnant with a girl, Pinky was five months pregnant with a girl. I didn't need any kids, but I was happy to have them on the way. I knew every move I made I had to have them in mind, for their future, if I wanted them to be raised the correct way. That's why I did my best to be in my BM's lives during their pregnancy.

Sometimes I was disappointed at myself because I didn't meet my expectations on giving them the proper time. I needed to at least be around them four days out of the week instead of two to three days a week. Even though I leased a house in Mansfield, Texas for Pinky, her mother, and sister for them to live in, it wasn't enough. I had my ex-ho, Selena, and her two kids move in with Shae so she wouldn't be lonely at home, but that wasn't enough. A woman appreciated a man that took care of her materialistically but being present in their daily lives meant more than being a good provider. Especially when you're a good man and they loved your ass. Not being there physically put strain and stress on the woman, and eventually on the unborn child.

Since I was here in Tarrant County Jail, I put $300 on D-Mack's books. I'd only been to court twice since I bonded out. Every time I went to court, I would visit him, except for today because of Pinky's doctor appointment.

After leaving the county, I went straight to Pinky's spot. I had my own key to the house, so when I went in, I didn't see anybody, but I heard laughter inside of Pamela's room, Pinky's mother. I walked close by the entrance of the door, enough were I could hear and not be seen at the same time. Pinky, Pamela, and Amanda, Pinky's mixed sister, stood at the edge of each side of the bed folding clothes in conversation.

"Change a man. A man like Tunke is going to do what he wants and have it his way. I saw that the first time I saw him. He really cares about you, tho'," Pamela said to Pinky.

"I know, Mama."

"I know he really loves you. When he's ready, believe me, he'll come around."

Amanda must have felt my presence, because she leaned to the right a bit and saw me. "Tunke, what are you doing?"

"Chilling, just walked in the house," I said as I walked in the room at the same time. Pinky started blushing uncontrollably when she looked back and saw me. "Lexi, what you blushing for?" I asked, knowing the answer.

She walked her fine, pregnant ass over to me with a smile on her gorgeous face. "I'm just glad to see you, that's all," she said as she wrapped her arms around my waist and then hugged me.

"I'm glad to see you too. I almost got a ticket the way I sped over here to see you after getting out of court," I said, making her feel good.

She slapped me playfully on my chest as she said, "Quit lying, Tunke."

It was a little over an hour until her appointment, so she knew I was just charming her. I gave her a kiss on the lips. "You know I missed you, tho'. How's our baby doin'?"

"She's good, but she's tiring me out a lot. All I been doing is eating and sleeping."

Pinky had gained about 26 pounds since her pregnancy, but she was still fine as hell.

It made her hips and ass poke out more, even her thighs were thicker. All that looked good to me. I liked that shit.

I looked at her moms, who was smiling. "I'm sorry, Pamela. How are you?"

"I'm good, Tunke," she said, sounding black a little bit. "How 'bout you?"

"I'm great. Just got through taking care of some business. "How you doin', Amanda?"

"Good. Can I go with y'all to the doctor?'"

I looked back at Pinky, who was facing me. She looked at me like I bet not say yeah. "You know Lexi want to spend some alone time."

Amanda's lips turned into a pout.

"I tell you what, after we go to the doctor, we'll come back to pick you and yo' momma up. We'll all go out as a family. That sound like a plan to you?"

"Yep, it sounds like a plan," Amanda said as she smiled at Lexi.

I looked at Lexi and asked, "Why you not ready yet, Lexi? You know you gotta be at the doctor at 1."

"I know, I was helping them with laundry. I already took a shower. Give me 10 minutes," she said and hurried to her room.

"So, Pamela, how has Lexi been lately? She been aight?"

"No, not really. She be depressed a lot. Always worried about you. Always talking about you."

Her 12-year-old sister butted in the conversation. "She ain't lying either. She be like Tunke this, Tunke that, Monopoly this, Monopoly that. All the time."

"Girl, shut up. Two grown people are talking. Anyway, Tunke, I know you're a busy man, but all I ask you to do is be there for her as much as you can. She really needs you. I thank you for everything you have done for her, for us. We're getting along quite good now as a family. Thanks for getting her off drugs. I'm so scared she's gonna get back on drugs. She sleeps a lot, not just because she's pregnant but because she's depressed. I don't like seeing my daughter like that."

"I know you don't. I don't like seeing her like that neither. I can promise you that I will do my best to make things better for her. I just can't promise you that I will be with her. I'm not saying that

I'm in a relationship with someone else. I just have too much going on for a committed relationship. I just opened a new business and I'm pretty busy, but I will make more time," I said, not saying too much about my lifestyle or the women that I loved in my life.

Even though I didn't want it, now I understood how some men only wanted to deal with one woman. While some could deal with more than one. Speaking from experiences, it took a lot of energy dealing with mutiple women at one time. At this current moment, I was dealing with nine prostitutes and three square women. Damn near half of them I wasn't spending a lot of time with. It was never on purpose; I just never had enough time in the day to spend time with them like I wanted to. It felt like every one of them was pulling on something on my body and clothes for my attention. Still, though, that didn't make me want only one woman in my life. Whenever I was done with pimping, if Shae couldn't accept Pinky being my woman, and same vice versa, I wasn't going to be with one who chose not to accept it. I knew Pinky was going to accept me being with Shae. I was 80 percent confident Shae would too.

"You proved you love and care about her. You wouldn't have bought this house if you didn't. Lexi really loves you. She wants you to spend more time with her. I'm gonna need you to spend more time with her. I don't want her getting back on boy," she said, using street terminology. I forgot, even though she was white, she still was from the hood.

In my head I was like, she bet not get back on heroin, especially while she's pregnant. I was a pimp, who majority of the time I always knew what I was gonna do. But if that ever happened, I just knew it was going to be fucked for her. I quit thinking about it before I got mad.

On the drive to her monthly check up, I told her, "I know I don't be spending time with you like that. If you wasn't pregnant you'd be by my side hoing, but since you is and out the ho Game, that's how it's gonna be for a while. I'm making big moves for us and it's taking a lot of my time. You can't touch me, but we do Facetime each other every day. Is that not enough for you?"

"No, that's not enough, Tunke. I'm pregnant with yo' baby, and I need to see you in person every day."

"I'm not gonna make a promise I can't keep. I'm not promising you every day, Lexi. The most I can give you is four days."

I thought about Lexi not having a car. Since I'd been knowing Lexi up until now, I didn't want her having one because of controlling reasons and her drug habit. But now, I was thinking differently for her, our baby, and her mom's sake. "You want me to buy you a car?"

"Really, Tunke?"

"Yeah, really. That way, when I can't come to you, you can come to me with a friend or your sister if I'm in town." I was doing this because I knew she needed me around, and I didn't want her getting back on heroin.

So, after the doctor's appointment, we went to the car dealership. She picked out a new late-model Benz that I helped lease in her name. I co-signed it for her. Next, we went to my penthouse. I knocked her down because I wanted to make love to her and make her feel better. Two weeks ago was the last time I fucked her. Fucking her and spending time with her would keep her at ease for about a week.

After a hot shower, we changed clothes here, putting on new ones, and then headed to her mom's to pick them up. I drove, but we rode in Pinky's car to the Dallas World Aquarium for two hours, and then a five-star restaurant named Eddie V's Prime Seafood.

I was glad I took the time to spend with them. We all enjoyed ourselves together. I left Pinky's place at 9 P.M. and went home to my hoes.

Chapter 12
The Video Shoot

All 32 of Advance Models, Pinky, Shae, Marilyn Sunshine, Poppa, Lil' Kenny, Elijah, and I flew out to Los Angeles, California on American Airlines a day before her scheduled date to film Syn's video.

Josh couldn't make it. He had gone with Julie to Florida for a tryout to be a Miami Heat's cheerleader. We got eight rooms at the Beverly Hilton near UCLA.

Two weeks back, I made a call to the president of the university to explain my plans for Syn's video, who's producing it, and that I was an R&B singer. He agreed to let us use their university's gymnasium and students as extras in the video, under two conditions. Syn and I had to do a mini concert for his students, which I agreed to do. We needed the exposure anyway.

That same day, I typed up a notice for students who wanted to participant in the video as an extra for pay; sitting in the stands cheering. I tagged the extra job as well as our mini concert on UCLA's Facebook page. I paid a female student there to post the notices all around the campus. I tagged it up on their Facebook page every day for two weeks until the day we flew to LA.

I met up with Paul Turner at the campus 30 minutes before we were to meet with President Shawn Penning. Paul Turner was a tall, humble man who weighed about 250. He wore black specs. The hair on his head, beard, and mustache was all white. He had 'a great vision,' and I couldn't wait to see what he had to offer us. Everybody with us was excited to be here, except for Mr. Turner, who was very calm and ready to work.

After we met up with the college president, the 42 of us got so many stares it was crazy. The homies and I got a bunch of lustful looks that I knew I was going to come up on a few females after this was over.

An hour later we sat in unfolded plastic chairs and talked while Rose was practicing with her trainer, Tessa Esterling, who showed up 20 minutes after we did.

"So, Mr. Turner, are you working on any films at the moment?" I asked the seventh question within the thirty-two minutes that we'd been conversing.

"I'm producing an action picture. It's a Transporter meet Equalizer type of film. I feel good about it. I believe it will get me another Oscar. We have some big names in the picture."

"When you do I'll be right there in the auditorium as well as at the premiere of the movie. I like your work. What else are you intending on working on afterwards?" I asked, wanting to know his plans for the future.

"Well, Monopoly, I've been thinking about winning another Academy award for a while now, but I haven't had the time because of the past three films I've produced."

"What kind of film were you thinking about producing to win an Academy award?" I asked, not knowing at all what it took to win an Academy award. I didn't ask either. I'll have to do some research on it if he didn't tell me.

"I'm thinking a rich thriller, maybe two to three series. I don't know what kind of thriller, but it's got to be rich."

"Mr. Turner, I have a proposition for you."

"What is it?" he asked after taking his attention off my models.

"I've been brainstorming on a movie to put Marilyn Sunshine in to boost her acting career but nothing has come to mind until you mentioned the thriller. If I can find you a great rich thriller as you say and buy the rights to it, can you put Marilyn Sunshine as one of the head actresses."

"If you can bring me a rich script I can make that deal with you. From seeing what you have come up with yourself and models, you seem like a creative young man. I would love to see what you find."

"Thanks Mr. Turner. That means a lot coming from you. I'ma pick out a great thriller."

"Monopoly, I have to ask you." He leaned in closer towards me like whatever he had to tell me was top secret. The closest female to us was my ho, Sarah, who was 10 feet away. I don't think she was close enough to hear us talking anyway unless she was ear hustling. "With all these women around, do you ever have sex with anyone of them?"

My plan was working. The night before I told my hoes to wear nothing but spandex, booty shirts, and daisy dukes to this video shoot. They weren't wearing it for the video but to flaunt their good looks around Paul Turner. An old white man like him couldn't resist a variety of fine ass women of different races. That was the whole reason why Sarah was in front of us dancing in daisy dukes and every now and then look back to look Paul Turner in the eyes. Whenever we were done with Rosemary's solo video, they will all put on UCLA's one piece garment that the gymnast use.

Instead of answering him, I said, "If you want to you can have any of them except for her, and her." I pointed at Shae, Pinky, Marilyn Sunshine, and seven of my new latest models that I just signed with Advance Models. "And they would be willing to do anything. They can do some amazing things behind closed doors. I mean, what are you into?"

He had already moved back into his chair so I leaned closer towards him. He did the same towards me, and whispered, "I have a fetish."

I was glad he kept it to himself and didn't say what he was into. I didn't want to know, I didn't care. That was my hoes job. I called Sarah over to us. "After this is all over today, I want you to get with Mr. Turner here to see what he wants and supply it for him."

After she walked off, I told Paul Turner, "I got you. I really appreciate doing business with you. This is a big move for me and my models. You don't have to worry about any bullshit going on a long as you use protection, everything will run smoothly. I promise you will be satisfied." I meant every word. Before I said that, I had thought about filming him while my hoes performed and blackmail him but decided not to. I asked myself what would be the purpose for it. It wouldn't have been a good choice. I know my hoes will show him a good time on the strength of me, to make him come back to do more business with us.

I hired one of the top three gymnast coaches in the USA training Rosemary. Tessa Esterling has been training the female gymnasts on the USA Olympic team for 12 years now. Tessa has been Rosemary's trainer for a month now. The first ten days of that month I had Rose visit Wisconsin where Tessa lives with her family to start her training. The last 20 days I sent Tessa$5000 before I had both of them back to Dallas where she would finish Rose training. I paid all of Tessa's expenses on her stay in Dallas and here in LA. I had to go all out for my Queen Rose. She had been a great ho, she deserved it and more. I wanted Rosemary's parents to see Syn's video that she was in, not her solo video that we were doing now. I wanted her and her parents to be in each other's lives.

We only had one life to live and got one set of biological parents. I knew if she didn't get to have a good relationship with her parents before they died, that would cause Rosemary and her parents to become bitter. With that feeling, they still wouldn't pick up the phone to call one another to heal their relationship. I didn't want any of that to happen. I was gonna create that connection myself. I wanted all my queens to be happy in all aspects in life and strive for the greater good.

Before Rose began her performance I gave her a little motivation. "It's time. This is what you been working towards for a month, 5 days a week. You perfected this shit. This is what is gonna jump start your business and career in modeling. I want you to give it your all. Lose yourself out there. You got this. Let me hear you say you got this."

"I got this," she said loudly, and then smiled.

"Now go get it girl."

As Rose walked to the balance beam, Shae, Pinky, all models, the other gymnast, and the students sitting in the stands all cheered for Rose. A song by Ciara named "Body Works" came on the big speakers.

Rose jumped high and landed on the beam in a split. She placed her hands on the side of the beam, and then started popping her ass.

There was a cameraman fifteen feet away from her off the floor of the balance beam. Paul Turner was on the side of him telling him to zoom in on that footage, getting a good shot of her jiggly ass.

Another cameraman was 20 feet away on the other side of the beam, recording her from a different angle.

Somehow, she arched her back even more than it already was. She started moving the middle part of her back and forth like she had a dick behind her.

After she did that for about 20 seconds, she stood up, balanced herself by kicking her leg out three times. She jumped up in the air doing a split in mid-air, and landed on both feet on the beam. She did that twice before she jumped high off the beam, doing one forward flip in mid-air, landing perfect on the floor.

Everyone in the building applauded her except the two white cameramen who were filming what was taking place. She did a great job on the beam, like she never lost her touch.

Next was her performance on the uneven bars. A song by Kelly Rowland, called "Motivation," came on before she started. Rose walked up the lowest pole and then jumped to grab a hold of it. She started shaking her ass and thighs as she held on tight to the bar. Even though she was petite, she had a tear-drop booty that clapped and jiggled.

She raised her legs up in the air in front of her to where her whole body was a L. she started rocking her body back and forth five times until she had enough speed and power to spin all 'round the pole. She did that slowly three times before she went flying to the second bar that was a couple feet higher. She swung around twice and then flew back to the smaller bar.

She made it around to the top, stood on top of the bar, and leaned off the bar with her arms stretched out to get a good hold on the higher bar. She swung around fast twice, let go, and did two back flips. She landed on both feet but lost a little of her balance. She caught her balance by putting her left foot in front of her.

If I was a judge, I would have given both her performance and landing a 99. All models and most of the UCLA gymnasts ran to Rose excitedly, telling her how great she did.

Thirteen minutes later, she was ready to perform on the floor to Beyonce's "Dance For You." Rose ran full speed vertically until she made it to the middle of the floor. She jumped up doing two cartwheels, and then did a summersault in the air. She landed in a split. She started popping her ass. Eight seconds later, she put both hands on her ankles and leaned sideways while she popped her ass.

After doing that for ten seconds, she leaned forward using her forearms, then both hands in a headstand position. She balanced herself and then started p-popping for about 30 seconds. Rose let her body fall to where she was in a female push-up position. While she pushed up, she clapped her ass at the same time. She leaned her body forward while clapping her ass on her hands and knees. She repeated that going back and forth four times. She got up and started twerking and then moving her hips until she reached the one of the corners.

She ran diagonal until she got to the middle of the floor. She did one front flip, a cartwheel, and then two front flips, all in that order. The flips and landing were perfect.

Her whole performance was amazing. She performed on every platform like she hadn't quit doing gymnastics five years ago. She was very flexible and a very talented gymnast. Seeing her doing something she loved to do made me feel some kind of regret for her that she didn't go to college for this. I was definitely going to ask Tessa Esterling was Rosemary good enough for the Olympics. If so, I was going to pay Tessa to use some of her connects to get Rosemary into the tryouts whenever they did it. I sure did want to see my queen succeed in that.

Anyway, if she had gone to college, she and I would have never crossed paths at that hotel when we first met. The Game brought us together. At this moment, her past didn't matter now. The present was the best phase of her life. One of the best phases of my life. I planned to make it the best phase of all my models as well. We were on the road to the top. I believed this gymnastic performance would have the effect we needed to entertain her fans, supporters, and new viewers. It was going to get her a lot of exposure.

We did Syn's video all in the same day. Rose had to perform a clean version on every platform again. In the video she finds that she has breast cancer but through all the struggle she survives the cancer. She doesn't give up on her dreams which is being a gymnast. We filmed Marilyn's part at a Hollywood studio, where she had played like she auditioned for a movie. A couple scenes later she gets a call back from Paul Turner telling her that she got the part. Everything was muted except the music but you could understand what's going on in the video.

The next day, we got together and did all the editing for both videos recorded.

Paul Turner and I looked at the video over 10 times before I posted them both on YouTube as well as each of my models Instagram. The video turned out pretty good, exactly what I wanted it to be but with Paul Turner's flavor in it. Now I needed as many views as we could get..

When the next morning came our business was done to the next time I needed his skills for the movie I'm going to present to him. My queens showed Paul Turner a great time that he wanted my girls three nights in a row. He even told some of his film industry buddies about how good of a time he had with them that they wanted to date them also. He really likes Rose for some reason that he told me that he wanted her to escort him at the upcoming Oscar Awards in March.

I was proud of them all for doing their best. I even talked Bre into doing porn. I got in contact with a big porn company out here in LA and set it up. Bre did a 46-minute video with Mr. Marcus and Wesley Pipes with a condom at a mansion in Beverly Hills. It turned out pretty good. Plus, she liked it, and said she would do it again. She got paid $4,500. I was glad that I thought about that. It made me think of future possibilities with my other hoes.

We set the mini concert seven days after we did the video. That turned out great. My name had been ringing at UCLA since we did the videos. I copped two hoes and recruited five models just off of who I was as an artist, and the model company. Coming to Cali turned out to be very profitable, and our future could only get better and brighter. We all had to make our way back out this way.

I wish that I could have this moment for life
for life, for life
'Cuz at this moment I just feel so alive, alive, alive

Smoove Dolla

This is my moment, I waited all my life
I can tell it's time
Drifting away
I'm one with the sunsets, I have become alive
I wish that I could have this moment for life,
for life, for life
'Cuz at this moment I just feel so alive, alive

Chapter 13
Pimpin' in Dubai
Monopoly

We flew into the atmosphere of Dubai, United Arab Emirates at 3:13 A.M. That's what my iPhone read. Actually, my Patek Philippe read 6:13 PM.

That was the time it was in Dallas. So time out here was nine hours ahead. So it was September 17, Thursday, in Dallas, and September 18, Friday, here in Dubai. I was glad we made it safely. It took a little over 16 hours to get here from Dallas. While the pilot of Tight Game's private jet was preparing to land on Dubai International Airport airstrip, I looked out the plane's small window. The first sight of the lights on the high rises as well as the structures of the skyscrapers was breathtaking, a bit staggering. I would rather look at the lights on the buildings than Christmas lights on houses in a high-income neighborhood. It was that beautiful. It was something I'd never seen before in any city. I couldn't wait to explore Dubai.

There was a limo waiting on us. Tight Game, Elijah, Solo, Josh, and myself rode in the limo. My hoes, Solo's hoes, and Marilyn Sunshine hadn't made it yet. Their tricks bought them first class tickets, and Marilyn flew with them. I thought of that idea. I didn't want it to seem like we were human trafficking across the country on a private plane.

Tight Game taught me years ago to never drive a ho to a date, let her drive herself or let her board a plane by herself.

While pulling my Louis Vuitton luggage towards the entrance, I looked up at the one-story building. I stopped in my tracks to enjoy the beautiful sight. The hotel building was a masterpiece. From being a Free Mason and a man of study, I could tell the building had traces of Arabian architecture. There were a few tall palm trees outside as well as a landscaped garden. Once we passed security, we entered a lobby that was styled like a wealthy woman's tasteful living room. There was a range of well-crafted Italian furnishings. Sofas and chairs, upholstered in Versace fabric. It had classy, ornate trimmings in the lobby with Versace vases sitting on top of them. Hanging high from the ceiling was a Bohemian chandelier. The floor was checkered with the Versace signs around each square.

We went to one of the three marble desks and gave the Arabian man our booking info. Days ago, I had booked my hoes four deluxe Versace creek view twin rooms and the signature suite for myself, that's built only for a Boss Pimp.

As we walked past the desk through the east wing to our rooms, the smell of a Versace fragrance entered my nostrils and it became stronger with every passing step. My room was really pimped out. It had parquet flooring, a canvas of elaborate white and cream boiserie's, and a postel pallet of silk furnishing, furnished with the Versace Home Collection.

I pulled my luggage to the foot of the bed and sat on the edge of the bed. The bed was comfortable, large, and dressed in powder blue and golden linen with Versace patterns. I looked around the room. There were two Versace chairs of the same blue and gold color cushions with Versace symbolic print, by a small coffee table. There was a 55-inch LED TV hung up on the wall in front of me. I could get used to living like this.

I opened up my Louis Vuitton suitcase to get my silk Louis Vuitton boxers, a Givenchy outfit I bought two days ago, some of my jewelry, and hygiene, to lay it all out on the bed.

The marble bathroom had mosaic wall ornamental over the hot tub. There were Versace toiletries. This whole hotel was symbolic of the Versace lifestyle. For about forty minutes, I took a bath. I called to talk to my hoes I had in California to check on them and my trap, until my hoes had called me telling me they were here at Dubai's airport.

***

We had the driver take us to the airport. Tight Game was the only one that stayed in his room. We picked up Marilyn Sunshine, ten of my hoes, and six of Solo's hoes.

We headed back to the Palace Palazzo Versace Hotel in downtown, which took us fourteen minutes to get back to. When we arrived, our hoes and Marilyn Sunshine rushed out the limo before Solo, Josh, and I got out of the limo we were in. They went to the mosaic of the Medusa Head that was outside of the entrance of the huge building. Marilyn Sunshine took pictures of my and Solo's stable posing together. Afterwards, they ran back to the limo to grab their luggage. They were very excited to be here. That probably would only motivate them to get more money out their tricks they had set up. I gave Solo a pimp handshake for making the move to bring our hoes to Dubai. It was some good pimpin' on both of our part. Everybody went to their rooms except for me and my women. After I gave them the keys to their rooms, I told them, "I want y'all to take a shower. Be ready in a hour. Before y'all start y'all day in Dubai, I want to show y'all something. And remember to dress appropriate."

Two weeks ago, Tight Game mentioned to Solo and me that we had to make sure our hoes were covered while here in Dubai and to look it up for ourselves to get the knowledge on it. When I did, I found out they couldn't be dress inappropriate like they did in the USA. They had to dress modestly, covering their shoulders and legs.

I told my women to not wear any sleeveless shirts, sleeveless dresses, mini-skirts, and short shorts out in public. They didn't need to wear that type of shit with these rich tricks anyway. I had them shop for something sophisticated when they went shopping at the North Park Mall in North Dallas.

***

An Hour Later

Before coming to Dubai, I did some research on must-visit places to go to. I found the hot air balloon ride at Balloon Adventure Dubai. I love watching the sunrise, so I decided that would be the first thing we did here. Solo and his hoes came along with us. The sunrise would be a good time to give them the motivation they needed in their individual dealings with their tricks today. For two weeks, I had my women network on all social media and some dating sites associated with men in Dubai, to find potential tricks to date. The ten of them each had two to five tricks apiece lined up for ten days that we would be here for $15,000 to $20,000 for each date. It surprised me how Rose, Sarah, Syn, Heather and Bre, all of them white women, got four to five tricks when my black hoes got two to three tricks. I thought it would be the other way around. Solo brought it to my attention that majority of the women in Dubai were slim, that there weren't too many thick women in Dubai. Looking around seeing for myself, it was true. My black hoes were thick and super fine. My white hoes were fine as fuck too, but they weren't as thick as my black hoes. I guess they were used to that. They got paid $5,000 before boarding a plane to come here and the rest when they met up with their tricks. It was 5 A.M. when our hot air balloon went above the thick of the clouds, floating 3,500 feet above, behind the Hajar Mountains and desert dunes. There were 20 people on this hot air balloon ride, that was including the pilot of it. Solo was on one end of the balloon with his hoes, and me and mine were on the other end as we all sailed through the clouds.

I started talking to my women. "Y'all know what's so great about the morning and seeing the rising sun?" I asked my hoes.

"What, Daddy?" most of them said at the same time, and the others said it a second or two later.

"Each time you greet the morning, it opens opportunity. Another opportunity to devote yourself to a particular cause. Another chance to go fulfill your dreams and take on another challenge that will benefit you and make your life better at the end. Downtown there in Dubai," I said, pointing at the distant view of the downtown skyline, "or any city and down in the streets and on the highways are the most traffic in the morning. In about 25 minutes, the traffic in Dubai will be a super car traffic jam. People are on their way somewhere, majority is going to work, and while others for other reasons. No matter where they're going, all of them have some kind of goal they're hoping and doing their best to accomplish. Some of them are living their life's purpose. Some of them will have more money than they had yesterday. Some will be better fathers and mothers than they have been all year. For some people, this day will be the best day of their lives. As y'all know, 98% of the time I love waking up early mornings, even if I been up most of the night. For me, it means a lot to wake up and take another breath. It gives me another chance to pimp another day. It gives me another chance to be a better man than I was yesterday. Another chance to see you gorgeous queens and appreciate you even more. Waking up gives me another day to push you towards you all's dreams so we don't have to live a life of crime anymore. The Game is, no, not the Game, but the laws are getting fucked up every passing day. It's in our best interest to strive for our dreams in life instead of just living the life. I want y'all to know I love each and every one of you. I wish the best for y'all. With me, there's no limits, you will reach heights unknown," I said meaning every word. And they knew it too. My actions added up with my word.

I talked with them for about 10 more minutes, until I saw the head of the sun coming from above the fluffy clouds. Minutes later, we saw a lot of full-grown and baby falcons fast approaching the side of the hot air balloon about 15 yards away from us. They made noises as they flew past us. The rising sun was in the far distance, looking amazing.

For almost 20 minutes, we watched the sunrise in silence, enjoying this experience. It was really beautiful. We must have taken over 10 photos by then.

We landed in the desert 38 minutes later. My crew got into three 1950 vintage Rovers and drove us to a camp site in Royal Deserts retreat. That's where we took a photo with our pilot and driver, and then we ate a delicious, customized breakfast amidst the tranquility of the desert.

Afterwards, they drove us back to the rented limo Tight Game had for us, and then we headed back to our hotel. We made it there at 8:37 A.M. I went to my hotel room by myself and called Shae.

"Why you just now calling me, Tunke?"

"I did say I was going to call you when I got here, but I had to take care of some business as soon as I got here. Duty calls, you know how I am. How y'all doing?" I asked, referring to her and my unborn baby.

"We're good, just missing you."

"I miss y'all too."

"So, how is it out there?" she asked curiously.

"It's beautiful. It's clean. It's built for kings and queens like us. It's long money. You know I wish I could have taken you out here back in the day. You would've been a superstar out here," I said before laughing.

She laughed a little. "Yeah, I bet. You know it ain't never too late," she said, letting me know I still had her in that way. What it really was, was she missed the hell out of me and would do almost anything to be by my side.

"Na'll, you good where you're at. One day we'll fly out here for a vacation."

We talked for 43 minutes until Tight Game called, telling me to come to his room. He opened the door in a live Versace robe and Versace house shoes on his pedicured feet. Hair hanging down to damn near the middle of his back. When I walked in, I heard "Atlantic" by The Isley Brothers playing in the background. "What you got going?"

"Getting ready to go to the Jumeirah Mosque for Jumiah Friday. You ready to become Muslim, Tunke?" he asked seriously.

"Nall, Unk. I'm good. I got too much going on to be dedicated to being Muslim."

"I understand. I'm not going to force you to change. I know when you're ready you're gonna cross over. I'ma just say quit while you're ahead, youngin', you're already a multi-millionaire. Anyway, I want you come to Jumiah with me since you know how to pray. I want you to meet some wealthy friends of mine after service."

Tight Game had asked me to become a Muslim multiple times while I was in prison. Even though we were Masons, we still could be Muslim. Being a Mason was just being a part of a huge fraternity.

From my research, Islam was a religion. In better words, a way of living a righteous life. I knew eventually I would make that move, I just didn't know when I'd do so.

Although I wasn't ready, I did know how to pray as a Muslim. During my bid in the feds, I had a couple of Muslim homeboys from South Dallas that I was tight with. They gave me insight on Islam and taught me how to pray. I did it because Tight Game used to kick Islam and Masonic knowledge on our visits and phone calls. I had a strong addiction to the Pimp Game, something I didn't want to fight against. When I was in the feds, I was planning on getting released to pimp hard and not be a stomp-down Muslim. I wasn't about to play with no religion, most of all God. Throughout the years, I barely prayed. When I did, it was to pray for a desire, family, and thanking the creator for an accomplishment. With that being said, I didn't mind going to Jumiah with Tight Game.

After talking for a while, I went back to my room to take another shower and put on a Steve Madden three-piece suit with no jewelry but my platinum Rolex. This was my first time going into a mosque. I had no clue to what was going on inside, other than worshipping Allah and other small things. The building was huge, it favored a beautifully built castle, the color of a light-brownish sand. It resembled the mosque in Irving, TX. Although I only drove by it on the interstate, I believed Jumeirah Mosque was bigger.

We walked through a concrete passageway with a metal shed over it and small bushes on each side of the pavement until we got to the big ablution area. We performed Wudu, which consisted of washing our face, hands to the elbows, wiping over our heads, and then washing our feet up to the ankles. That was something done to be clean before performing the Muslim prayer. There were about 10 men and women doing the same thing at this big ablution area.

After walking into the lobby, immediately, I saw all the women in hijabs walking up two flights of stairs while at the same time the men were heading in under them in a different room. Also, I noticed there were two stands side by side, with Islamic pamphlets on one stand, and the same cover Qurans in multiple languages on the other stand.

Before going into the prayer room, we took our shoes off by a large area where there were hundreds of pairs of shoes of many kinds.

There were hundreds of men praying in racks. I peeped up at the balcony where some women sat, and some prayed on the carpet. The women were separated due to their beauty and the attention it demanded. It was preferred there were not loud perfumes either. Man was created weak. The last thing you need is for a gorgeous sister to be within sight during the Khutbah nor in bowing in the rank before you whom God has blessed with a curvaceous nature and swell figure. Also, the Muslim leader was in front for he was responsible for his family, beginning with his wife, or women. It was his job as the man to protect his garden by erecting barriers and boundaries. This protection was foremost #1 as his duties, and this could only be fulfilled by being in front. Take the lead! It was required of a real man.

Tight Game and I got in the fourth row, made prayer, and then waited on the Imam to give his sermon.

***

Three Hours Later

After the services, we went to a private lounge owned by Muslims at the Madinat Jumeirah with two of Tight Game's business partners, their wives, and children. One of them had two wives and three children. The other Muslim man had three wives and five children. I ain't go lie, I really liked seeing that. Islam had a little pimpin' in it.

A feast of lamb and mutton, which were halal foods, was brought out to us after ten minutes of being there. Dates, carrots, green beans, and tea were served with our meals. The males sat at one end of the long table, and females sat at the other half of it. Three Arabian male bodyguards stood on three sides of the table, about fifteen feet away from the back of their kids and wives.

Between bites, Baaqir, Klaaliq, and Tight Game all caught up with each other about what had taken place in their lives since Tight Game was last in Dubai six months ago. They talked for a little over an hour before I was brought into the conversation about what I did for a living. I told him everything, except I left the pimpin' out of it. They weren't impressed at all, but it wasn't like I was trying to impress them. To express myself in a better light, they were nonchalant about what I told them. I was guessing because they were Muslims, and everything I did wasn't 100% agreeable with Islam. Only the business side of it was, if I was being exact. Even with all that, it seemed like they accepted me and at the same time, respected me. That's what mattered to me the most, was the respect.

"Tell me about yourself, Khaaliq. How did you become so successful?" Tight Game had told me on the way that this was just one out of the five restaurants he had, and he was the most successful out of the two men.

"I'm the owner of the biggest construction company in the country. I own Khaaliq Properties and the Islamic Bank here in Dubai. We have built eight skyscrapers to date, two that I personally own. We have built multiple buildings in the city. With one of my wives, we own five restaurants Downtown."

I nodded my head and asked Baaqir a similar question. He began with, "Back in the early 90s, my father and two of my uncles opened a manufacture and distribution plant for fuels and petroleum jelly. Petro dollars were and still are pouring into Dubai. The petroleum industry that I took over after my father and uncle's deaths, helped develop the city's economy. Dubai is now a financial and shipping center with a multinational population. It took prayer, hard work, and dedication to make this all possible. I can continue to make history."

Now I was the motherfucker who was beyond impressed. These Arabs were wealthy. They had over half a billion dollars in their bank accounts. The three men in front of me, that's including Tight Game, were talking about coming together to spend over 100 million dollars to build a skyscraper, and once it was built, they'd be making millions each year from businesses they were going to put in there. I was surprised and thankful when they asked me did I want to contribute a business once the skyscraper was built, which would take three to five years from now. I believe that's why Tight Game invited me out here, really to show me what kind of level he was on and to invite me into an opportunity. That showed me that he really cared about my well-being and success in life, like a true masonic brother should. He wanted me to change my life. I took all that to heart.

After we shook hands and said our see you laters, we got into the limo. "You heard how big those two brothers are doing it?" Tight Game asked me.

"Yeah, they're fuckin' with some major money."

"Major is not the word. They've surpassed major. They're on the level I'm doing my best to reach before I die. Right now, my network is close to 30 million dollars, I'm not even close. I know I have what it takes to reach it. Tunke, I brought you here to see how big money is being made in this world and how a real man is supposed to do it in life. See, there's nothing wrong with praying and believing in something other than the pimpin'. What you've accomplished with the modeling agency is a wonderful thing. What you're doing for your women is even better. That is what a real pimp, no, I'm not going to say pimp, I'ma say a man. It's what a real man should do for his woman, no matter how long a woman stays in your life. You have to make a woman better while she's under your instructions, at the same time making yourself better. Like the Imam said at Jumiah, it's about getting from level to level. I love what you're doing, but you have to do something bigger and better with yourself. You have to get your hands in more things that's gonna really generate you millions every year. Year after year, you're supposed to have made more money because you have your hands in multiple things, or you just fucking with some huge shit that's really booming. Either way, you supposed to be getting at some real muthafuckin' paper. You have what it takes. You're a unique individual. I just want you to succeed in all aspects of life up under my wing."

"And I will."

"I surely muthafuckin' hope so, nigga. Don't let me down."

"I won't, big bro."

***

The next day at 7 A.M., Heather, Rose, Erika, and I went to the big gym in the Versace Hotel to workout. It'd been a couple weeks since we worked out together. We all had been tied up in some kind of business one way or another. My adrenaline was still pumping from our workout, so I went out to jog around the city, and plus, I needed to look for places for a photographer here in Dubai to take photos of my models.

I jogged from the hotel to the Kite Beach that took 18 minutes to get to, and then headed towards the Al Warsan Lake.

As I ran through the trail, I saw a woman that favored Baaqir's daughter's frame, even though she was in a hijab. I did a double take because I wasn't sure that it was her. I stopped running and started walking. When I got within ten feet of her, I could tell it was her. I couldn't forget that gorgeous face she had. She was feeding the exotic birds in the Al Warsan Lake.

When I got within six feet of her, I said, "Assalamu Alaikum."

She looked up at me with her right hand in a white Mrs. Bread bag. "Alaikum Assalamu."

When we were at Khaaliq's restaurant, I didn't look at her more than twice nor did I talk to her. I wanted to but out of respect for Tight Game, Khaliq, and Baaqir, I didn't continue to look at her. Now that we were alone, I was good to have a friendly conversation with her. Plus, I wanted to get to know her. "You're Baaqir's daughter, right?"

A big, muscled Arab man walked up on the side of me, and touched me on my shoulder. I looked at him like he was crazy and brushed his hand off of me.

"It's okay, Haadee. He's Muslim. He's a business partner of my father's."

Haadee went back to where he stood 20 feet away across the wide sidewalk without saying a word and watched our every move.

I wanted to ask her name, but I thought about the fact that I wasn't Muslim. If I asked her what her name was, she was going to ask me what my Muslim name was and probably what it meant if she didn't know already. Knowing that I wasn't Muslim, I knew she couldn't talk to me as far as dating went. I wasn't going to lie to her to make myself seem bigger than I really was in her eyes. I absorbed my surroundings because I was about to take control of the conversation and small talk with her about something of her interest, other than Islam. "How often do you come here to feed the birds?"

"Every day since I was eight. I'm 21 now," she said, looking up at me.

"Wow, that's a long time."

"Yes, it is," she said in a strong accent.

"Pretty girl like you, your favorite gotta be the doves. Am I right?"

While blushing, she said, "How did you know that?"

"It was just a wild guess. Although, it does seem like you have taste."

"You guessed right, but I have two favorites. The doves and the moorhens."

"Which ones are the moorhens?"

She pointed to a black medium-sized water bird with a red and yellow beak. "Those are Indian moorhens. Six years ago, there were hardly any moorhens here. There are about 50 of them here in Dubai."

"Give me a couple slices so I can help you feed them," I said, as I held my hand out.

She gave me three slices of bread. "So, this is your first time in Dubai?"

"Yes, it is. How did you know?" I asked as I tore one fourth of a slice of bread, and then tossed it six feet away from me in the lake so one of the doves could eat it.

"I can tell from the way you absorb everything around you."

"I'm a man that pays attention to details and likes to know what's going on around me."

"How old are you?

"Twenty-five."

"You seem older than you are. I don't see a prostration mark on your forehead, and you're not wearing a Kufi. How long have you been Muslim?"

After I threw more bread for the birds, I answered her. "I'm not Muslim, as far as I haven't taken the shahadah yet."

"Why haven't you taken your shahadah yet?"

"To be totally honest with you, I haven't done so because of my present lifestyle, that I'm not going to mention to you yet. I don't want to become Muslim while I'm still indulging in things going against Islam. To me, it would be like I'm playing with the Almighty Allah."

"Is it the modeling agency you mentioned when talking to my father?"

I didn't know she was listening to us. So, she was checking me out then.

"No, not really, it's a part of it but it's far darker."

"Don't you know that once you take your shahadah that your sins will be washed away, that you will have a clean record? Let me tell you my father's secret. My father is a religious man, but even he lets go of Islam every other weekend to indulge in wild parties in the high rises doing what Allah forbids of. My father and Khaaliq don't think I know, but I do. Even though he does that, I still love him and Allah does too. Allah still shows my father favor, grace, and abundance. What about the Khutbah, did you not listen to it?"

"Of course, I listened to it." Before she asked me what the Imam talked about in the Khutbah, I told her. "The sermon was about levels, steps from Muslim to being Mumin as well as the five greatest prophets. Jesus, Noah, Muhammed, Moses, and uhh, uhh, it starts with an A. Oh yeah, Abraham, about their steps and attributes."

"It was nice to meet you, Damion, but my interest in you is gone. Since you're not Muslim, I can't talk to you. Don't speak of this to my father," she said, and then turned towards Haadee. She waved for her bodyguard to follow her.

"It was nice meeting you also. I'll see you around," I said, loud enough for her to hear.

I ain't go lie, I really liked and wanted a Muslim woman. It was because they were more loyal and abided by the laws of Islam. Majority of the Muslim women were righteous believers. I could tell it took a lot within her to deny me. She wanted to talk to me, but she was a believer in her faith. I was glad she did, that told me she was loyal and a strong woman. That's the type of woman I wanted by my side. You're probably asking yourself what part I wanted her to play in my life since I was pimpin'. It's not a ho, that's for sure. If things go right between us, the next time we encountered each other's time, I'd consider becoming Muslim and dating her. Why not? She was Muslim and the daughter of a wealthy man, from a wealthy family. He'd be a billionaire one day. I was like, fuck it.

The next morning, I jogged to the Al Warson Lake at 9 A.M. She was sitting on a blue-painted, metal, mesh bench, wrapped in her blue hijab, feeding the doves, her favorite birds. She saw me approaching her, and then looked at Haadee, who was heading towards us. She held up a hand to him, letting him know she's good.

"Can I join you?" I was about eight feet within her reach.

She ushered her hand for me to come closer. I walked up and sat down next to her. I took the bag of bread out of her hands. I took out two slices and sat it between us on the bench. I started feeding the doves with her. I broke the silence a minute later. "It's crazy how you can meet a person one day, and that night, that same person has an effect on your mind. You constantly crossed my mind last night."

"Be serious, Damion."

"I am serious, as I always am."

"That might be true, but whatever you're into, got you playing yourself. You said it yourself, you're not ready."

"Let me take you out on a date tomorrow."

"No, that is something I can't do."

"You're grown, who says you can't?"

"The Quran that I faithfully follow. I'm a believer, Damion. Plus, my father would never approve because you're not a believer."

I pulled out my business card and tried to give it to her, but she didn't accept it. "Call me so we can talk on the phone until I become a Muslim."

"I can't accept that. We can't talk outside of this lake."

I put the card back in my pocket, and then tore the other slice of bread in tiny pieces. I dropped them right in front of the doves to make them come a little closer to us. When I turned towards her, she looked at me with curiosity in her eyes.

"I gotta go handle some business. It was nice seeing you again. You have a great day." I said, and then got up to leave. I started back jogging without waiting on a response from her. There was nothing else to be said.

I gave her a chance. She couldn't get another until I gave her another chance. I wasn't about to deal with her on her terms. That was my last time showing up here and her seeing me until I became Muslim. I didn't know when that would be, though. If she married a Muslim man before I could become one, then so be it. I could find about twenty stomp-down, pretty Muslim women who were from a wealthy family. She couldn't find another nigga like me, I was the only one. She probably would expect me to show up tomorrow, but she wasn't going to see me. It might be months until she saw me again.

I went back to my room to take a quick shower. Afterwards, I grabbed my laptop to read a couple more TV scripts for Paul Turner and Marilyn Sunshine. Since Erika wanted to be an actress, I looked for something for her to play in as well. If Paul agreed to it, I was sending her to acting school.

After five hours of reading two scripts, I felt the last script I read was the perfect series script for Marilyn Sunshine to star in and Paul Turner to produce. The first fifteen pages of the drama, mystery thriller had me hooked.

It was 7:36 P.M. here in Dubai, and 11:36 A.M. yesterday in New York where the young guy lived who wrote the script. He answered on the fourth ring. I let him know that I was interested in buying the script he wrote, but before I did, I had to run it by the Paul Turner. That information excited him. I told him to hold off on selling it, and that we would notify him after Paul Turner did what he does.

Next, I called Paul Turner, but he didn't answer the two times I hit him up, so I left him a message and sent him the script via email.

Earlier, Solo had asked me did I want to go to a club or a bar tonight, but I declined, telling him I was handling some business. Solo and Elijah had been tearing down the city since the day we touched down. Business was first and foremost with me, and then the fun next. Lately, for me, most of my business had been fun. I could go out with them now since I was just waiting for Paul Turner to return my call.

Solo answered on the third ring. "You at the room or y'all already gone to the club?"

"Nall, we still here."

"Y'all still going or what?"

"Hell yeah, we still goin'. We leaving in 'bout 20 minutes. You rollin'?"

"Yeah, I'll meet you down in the lobby in 20."

***

Thirty-Five Minutes Later

When we walked in, I was surprised to see a mixed crowd of Americans. I only saw two Indians, and they were a couple. That's what I wanted. An Indian and an Arab woman, something foreign, not a visitor. It was a nice size club that played a variety of Gogo and pop music. I was about to tell him let's go to a pub or another club, until I saw three young American women at the bar, two white girls and a mixed-breed black chick. I tapped Solo on the arm to let him know we were heading there first, because we had talked about going to the VIP section.

The whole time we were headed that way, I sized them up. They looked like they had money, so I decided to use a debate to invite them in a conversation to get their attention.

Solo, Elijah, and I started with a normal conversation about football. A few minutes later, we began debating about whether women should directly compete with men in sports for about three minutes. I knew they heard our whole conversation because we spoke loud enough to where all three of them heard us. Plus, we were four stools away from them. We started out talking intelligently but then started having fun with the subject because of the environment we were in.

"Man, I understand all that equal stuff, but a woman don't want to go head-to-head with all this pressure coming at her," I said, making the women beside me giggle. I looked their way with a mean mug on my face. I eyed the tall Amazon closest to me.

"That's what I'm talking 'bout. Too much pressure," Elijah had said while flexing his muscles in a men's tank top. I had on a tight-fitted Givenchy shirt. Solo had on a loose Gucci fit. Solo and I looked like basketball players because of our height, and Elijah looked like a linebacker from his muscular body and weight size.

"Look, let's get these gorgeous women's view. Their opinion counts in this conversation too. Excuse me, ladies," Solo said after getting off the stool he was sitting in. He walked towards them. After they turned around in their seats, Solo asked, "How are you ladies doing tonight?" He smiled at the three of them, showing off his diamond platinum grill that cost him over 80k.

Two of the white girls said they were great and the black chick said fine. The white girl on the end asked how was he doing.

"We're here in Dubai living the good life. I can't do nothing but be happy. Is it possible you three can bring peace to our debate about whether or not women should directly compete with men in sports?"

"Yes, it's possible," said the white woman I wanted.

"Alright, why do you?" he asked while he pointed at the white girl he wanted.

"Because there's women who play professional sports in every single sport that a man plays. You have women who are built and would love to play against a man in sports. Anyway, that's what I believe."

Solo looked at the other two women. "Do you two have your own opinion, or do you two agree with your friend?"

"Yes, for the most part. Yeah, she's correct," the Amazon next to me had said.

"Yeah, I agree with her. She summed up the question," the pretty black chick said.

"Okay, that's four to two. Point made. Anyway, I'm Solo," he said as he extended his arm for a handshake from the white girl he asked first for her opinion.

"I'm Suann. Nice to meet you," she said, smiling.

"Nice to meet you also. Introduce your two friends here."

"This is Amber," she said as she pointed her hand at the mixed chick. "And this Rebecca. My two besties."

"Suann. Amber. Rebecca. This is my brother, Monopoly, the entertainer. Here's Elijah, the future in football."

After we spoke to one another, Solo told everyone, "Since we're coupled up, let's go to the VIP section to get more acquainted with one another."

They accepted the offer. We ordered high-dollar wine and clear and brown liquor. Once we were seated in our booth, Elijah talked with Amber. Solo talked with Suann. Rebecca and I entertained each other.

"So, tell me about Rebecca," I told her.

"Where should I start?" she sighed and then continued. "Okay, I grew up in San Francisco. I currently reside in Beverly Glen, California with my husband and three children."

I cut her off. "Hold up, wait a minute. As gorgeous as you are, you look 21 years old, you really have three children?"

That made her smile. "Thanks. Yes, I have three handsome boys, ages 11, 9, and 7. I had my oldest when I was 18 with my high school sweetheart, which is my husband now."

"You look amazing to be in your late twenties."

"Thanks, Monopoly."

"What do you do for a living?

"I'm a major real estate agent."

"How major are you?"

"I find mansions, condos, and penthouses for the rich and famous."

"Is it your dream? Do you love what you do?"

"Oh, yes. I talk to and meet so many famous people that it's the norm now, and I make a lot of money doing what I love doing, selling houses."

"That's wonderful. Rebecca, you deserve a toast." I poured us a shot of Armand de Brignac.

"For what?"

"A lot of people aren't able to do it. You deserve a toast for living your dream and your great health. You're doing an awesome job," I said as we toasted.

We talked for about forty minutes before we even talked about myself. We all entertained one another for about two hours before we all agreed to go back to our hotel rooms.

When we got to my hotel room, Rebecca and I sat on the sofa on the balcony. We had been there talking for about 25 minutes before she got on top of me in a sitting position, facing me. She started giving kisses to my neck. Then she went to my earlobe, sucking my ear.

"You know we ain't got to do this?" I asked her that because I was a firm believer in not having sex with a woman that I wanted to develop a friendship with, especially if there were benefits involved. Sex really did fuck up certain friendships. It wasn't because she was married. I didn't give a fuck about having sex with a married woman. She had her reasons on why she was here with me. Her eyes and facial expression let me know she was telling the truth when she told me she wasn't happy with her husband. She was stuck in a marriage that she was bored with and was in because of her kids and her parents. She didn't have to tell me that nor tell me the truth, but she did.

"I know we don't, but I want to," she whispered in my ear. She raised herself up and got down on her knees. She pulled up my shirt, and then unbuckled my Givenchy belt to pull my dick out through my zipper.

That was how it started. I must have fucked her all over my hotel room like we were professional porn stars.

Even though I wasn't planning on moving to California, it was good that I met a woman like Rebecca. In the future, I might plug a partner, some of my models, or someone I knew in with her for a loft or mansion. Although our sexual escapade was great, it wasn't about the sex with me. I enjoyed more than just experiencing a sexual trip with a woman. That's why I wasn't quick to go in a woman. I enjoyed a woman's mind, their attitude. The sex was just a plus for me. My pimp mentally made me that way.

The next morning, after Rebecca and I had breakfast from room service, I sent her on her way. I took a shower and then checked my emails. I saw that Paul Turner opened the email I sent him, but I didn't receive an email nor call from him. Him opening the file was good enough. Now all I had to do was wait.

Elijah, Solo, and I went out to The Mall of the Emirates to tear down the mall. It was the largest shopping mall in the world. They had every big-name brand that we had in the U.S.A. all in one building. We spent so much money that I lost count.

After we left the mall, we headed to the Gold Souk. There were 380 jewelry retailers there in that big market, with 10,000 pounds of gold present any given time. I bought me a bunch of gold jewelry as well as all my models a gold ring, and a gold-link chain with a big AM medallion, which stood for Advance Models.

While I was at the mall, I called my models to get all of their finger sizes. Although I didn't know Sunshine's ring size, I paid for her a ring anyway, hoping she could fit it. If she signed the contract with us while we were in Dubai, I was going to give it to her. After I purchased the rings, chains, and medallions, I took them to a diamond retailer to put princess cuts into them all. They were scheduled to pick up later on the next day.

Throughout that day, I saw all type of foreign whips on the highways and streets. I saw a Ferrari limo, a coined Range Rover, a Diamond Celestial Rolls Royce Phantom, a gold Nissan GTA, an Aston Martin One-77, Bentleys. What tripped me out the most was Dubai had a Bugatti taxi service. These fucking people were getting at some real money out here. The streets being clean had me surprised also. I mean, there was no litter on the streets like it was in the United States. I was falling in love with Dubai every single day we were here. I could become accustomed to this way of living.

I didn't hear from Paul Turner until two days later. It was 11:08 P.M. in Dubai when I got his call. I was still awake, surfing my Instagram.

"Did you read the script?" I asked eagerly after recording our call.

"I sent it to one of my readers, and she read it in less than three hours. She was excited about it and told me I should consider directing it. If Sally says it's good, then I'm rolling with it. I did read five pages of it before I sent it to Sally. I must admit, I'm impressed on what you found. So, here's what I'm going to do. After I'm finished reading the entire script, I will set a budget so we will know the budget and how much the screenwriter will get. Afterwards, we will set up a meeting with the writer first, and then we will go over everything else, okay?"

"Okay, sounds like a plan. Thanks."

"Oh, you're welcome. Thanks for finding something I needed. I will aim to complete reading it all and meeting with the writer by Friday and guarantee it by Sunday. I'll give you a call then."

"Alright, I'll be waiting."

Afterwards, I called Marilyn Sunshine and told her to meet me in the lobby alone in ten minutes if she wasn't busy. When she made it, we went to sit down on a white leather sofa in the lounge.

I let her listen to the recording of my phone conversation with Paul Turner. When the recording ended, she said, "I can't believe this, you really did it, Monopoly." She put her hands over her face because she started crying out of happiness.

"Sunshine, take your hands off your face and look at me." She did as she was told before wiping tears away from her face. "I wanna ask you some questions."

"What is it, Monopoly?"

"Since you been knowing Josh, Rose, and me, have we done nothing but help further your career?"

"Yes," she said, nodding her head.

"Do you believe that we can add on to your career far better than David can at Perfect Models?"

"Yes, I believe so. The video shoot and that recording is proof. You did something David couldn't do."

"Really, in essence, Josh is the root to you coming around us. To be honest, I didn't start wanting you around until a couple weeks ago, when I saw that it would boost my models' careers. Either way, my models are going to succeed. It's inevitable. Anyway, I'm really glad that I got Josh as a partner and friend. He's intelligent, experienced, a go-getter. I like that about him. I will never do anything to jeopardize the relationship I have with him. I have his back, and he has mine. I said that to say this, Josh really wants to be with you and he really loves you."

"I know he does," she said, looking down for a couple of seconds, and then looked up.

"Do you love him?" I asked to see her eyes and facial expression on her face to see if she really loved Josh or not.

She nodded her head, and said convincingly, "Of course, I do."

I badly wanted to ask her why the fuck were you messing with the enemy of your lover if you love him so much, but I didn't. I already knew her answer. It's because she chose her career over love. "If he asked you to sign with us, would you?"

She nodded her head. "Yes, I would if he wants me to. He's never brought it up."

I called Josh and told him I'd be up to his room in five minutes so we could discuss something. I excused myself, and then went upstairs.

I let Josh listen to the recorded call with Paul Turner, and then the conversation I had with Marilyn Sunshine just a few minutes ago. I did my best to always stay on point when dealing with people. I was a man that liked to have solid proof about things, and I was like that when I presented something to people. I just didn't go around recording the conversations I had with people. In these matters, it was caused for.

"Damn, you really did it, bro," he said unbelievably.

"I told you I'm good at what I do. Now, all you got to do is present her with the contract. Have her sign it and then call up David to serve that punk. When you call him, tell him you are going to have lawyers call him to get her dropped from her contract with Perfect Models."

"Man, he's not going to handle that too well."

"That's not our problem, Josh. He's going to deal with that, not us. This is strictly business. He has good things going at his business. He's not going to jeopardize that. I believe he will try his best to get her back, but that will be determined by how strong you two love each other and most importantly, the handling of her career. She's going to be with what's the best fit for her career. And that is us at the moment, right at Advance Models."

"Sounds good. I guess you're right."

When we walked into the lounge, I saw her reading the script on my laptop, and one of the jewelry boxes was open as well. I left the jewelry boxes and my laptop open showing the TV series script I had for her on purpose. I knew she would be curious to either read the script or look to see what was inside the jewelry boxes, even though she had money that she could buy a thousand of the same ring, medallion, and chain, if she wanted to. All I wanted her to do was reflect on the idea of her being with Advance Models.

She read the mission statement and two contracts, and then happily signed them. Afterwards, Marilyn Sunshine called David on her phone, and handed Josh the phone on speaker.

"Sunshine why aren't you returning my calls and texts?" David asked as soon as he answered.

"This isn't Sunshine. This is Josh. Long time no hear, how have you been, old friend?" Josh said sarcastically.

"Why are you calling me from Sunshine's phone? Where is she?"

"She's here with me. It's what I'm calling you for, David, so I can inform you that Sunshine just signed a deal with my new company, Advance Models."

"She can't do that. Nice try, but she's under contract with me," he said arrogantly.

"Well, soon she won't be anymore. Our attorneys will be in contact with you. I gotta go, David, you have a good one." David started to say something, but Josh hung up on him.

"Nice job, Josh," I said, smiling while we shook hands. I faced Marilyn Sunshine. "By the way, I know you have millions to buy you a thousand each of those." I pointed at the jewelry boxes. "But those are yours, Sunshine. Welcome to Advance Models, where your dreams get bigger. We're glad to have you."

"Thanks. I'm glad to be here also," she said with a huge smile on her face, showing her pearly whites.

I closed my laptop and told Sunshine, "I will shoot the script to your email when I get upstairs."

***

Two Days Later

I got a call from Tight Game at l0:16 A.M. I wondered what he wanted. Even though we stayed in the same hotel, we hadn't spoken to each other since Friday, which was six days ago. We'd both been doing us. "Look out, nephew."

"Wuz up, Unk?"

"Naa'ilah's father called me today wanting your number to give it to her. I didn't give it to him until I okayed it with you."

"It's okay, you can give it to him."

"Okay. What you and Naa'ilah got goin' on, nephew?"

I told him how I met her and a brief of what happened between her and I the times we were in each other's presence.

"All I'm gonna say is don't hurt that girl. I been knowing that girl since she was 13 years old. It seems like she really likes you for her to go through what she did with her father. I vouched for you, don't hurt that girl, Damion. Before you two decide on dating, you need to choose a side on whether you're going to be married on the square side or to the life. You can't do both, nephew. So, ponder on that. I got some business to attend to. I'll catch up with you later."

"Alright, Unk."

Fourteen minutes later, I got a call from a crazy looking Dubai number. I answered it, it was her.

"Hello, Damion," she spoke in the prettiest sounding accent I'd ever heard from a woman.

"Hey, how are you?"

"I'm great now, since I got my way through to you. How are you?"

"I'm good. Just handling business and enjoying my time in Dubai. I'm curious, how did you pull that off with your father?"

"I thought you were going to show up the next day, but you didn't. I even stayed there an extra three hours for you to jog up on me like you did those first two days you showed up. I did that for three days, Damion. When I saw that you weren't going to come, I took matters into my own hands to get in contact with you. I didn't know when I'd see you again. I asked my father to get your contact for me. He denied my request and disagreed with me being with you until I told him about himself."

"What did you tell him?" I asked, wanting to know what I was up against with her father when I talked to him.

"I let him know I knew about what he does on the weekends and what skyscraper is being used for their parties. I told him since he's enjoying himself at these parties doing forbidden things, why can't I enjoy myself with someone I'm interested in. I didn't have to threaten him, but I would've if I had to. When can I see you again?"

"Tonight. Meet me in front of the Mall of the Emirates. I want to see the Dubai Fountain while we sail in a boat, so we can talk and get to know one another. Be there at 6 P.M., okay?"

"Okay, I'll be there," she said, sounding like she was smiling.

"Call me when you get there. I'll see you then," I said, and then hung up.

I arrived at the mall at 5:47 P.M. Naa'ilah was already there sitting at a wooden bench. Haadee was about twenty feet away. She was zoned out in deep thought. I walked up on the side of her. She smiled at me and then stood up. We gave one another a hug.

"What were you thinkin' about before I walked up?"

She looked deep into my eyes, and said, "I was wondering if I did the right thing with my father and dating you, knowing that you're not part of my faith."

"You're wasting time worrying yourself with negative thoughts. That's your father, he's going to love you regardless. And me, I know what you want out of me. I wouldn't have accepted your request if I wasn't ready to take on that responsibility of being Muslim. If you hadn't accepted and respected where I am in life at this moment and were willing to intend to have patience with me, you wouldn't have called me today. Allah works in mysterious ways. I believe I was brought here to Dubai for you. Anyway, we'll never know if that's true until we experience time alone together. This is our first date amongst many more." I put my hand out palm up so she could put hers on top of mine. "Come on, let's enjoy ourselves."

She smiled and then put her hand in mine. We got into the long line of customers who were waiting to pay their admission fee on a cruise ride in the Burj Lake in a boat to see the Dubai Fountain show. The fountain show was the most beautiful thing I'd ever seen performed by water and lights. It was a beautifully choreographed visual spectacle. Naa'ilah told me it featured 6,000 lights, 25 colored projectors, and 22,000 gallons of airborne water. It was very animated. From where we were, we could see the fountain show, and in the short distance I could see the lights on the skyline of Dubai. It looked amazing.

***

When I wasn't with my hoes, I was with Naa'ilah. We spent time together every day going out somewhere I hadn't been yet. Naa'ilah might be one of the ones for me. Yes, I said one of the ones. A Muslim woman and a prostitute were the only women who could be in a relationship with me. They were the only women that I wanted, the ones who didn't mind their man having other wives, as long as he was who he said he was. Pinky and Shae would be my wives if they could get on the same page as me. The only thing they would be fucked up about was me marrying another woman first before one of them. I didn't give a fuck, though. They'd get over it sooner or later. They had to accept it if they wanted to be with me in that way. If not, I could live without them being my wives, and just being my baby mothers. But I did hope they accepted it, because I did want to marry them.

Coming to Dubai turned out to be great and profitable. As a whole, my stable made over $800,000. I had never made that much in 10 days pimpin'. These rich tricks in Dubai spent big money for women from America. I was only taking half of my hoes' earnings. Since I opened up my modeling agency, I'd been getting half of their prostitution earnings. I'd only been taking 35% off their legal money. I figured that would be a smart idea to put that in their contract. My pimpin' went a lot smoother, and plus, I was constantly teaching my hoes how to live a better life and be more prosperous with the game I supplied. Also, I was doing it because I'd be giving up the game soon. If a ho left me, I really didn't give a fuck. I couldn't care less. No matter what, a woman was going to leave me with proper game to live life and in better shape than she was when she came into my life.

Anyway, Josh and I knocked Marilyn Sunshine from David. That would open new opportunities for myself, my models, and the modeling agency.

I swear, being in Dubai made me think about where I came from. On some rags to riches type shit. I grew up in the projects, barely having shit, to now I was vacationing in Versace suites and living in mansions with two thriving businesses and a good record deal. Here in Dubai, I touched a higher level in the Game. I went from putting hoes on the track to a ho serving rich tricks. I couldn't call myself an International Pimp yet until I came out here, set up shop again, and knocked some women from this way. I had to come back to Dubai. I didn't want to leave this motherfucker, but I had a bunch of business in the states to tend to.

Smoove Dolla

Chapter 14
The Fashion Show in ATL
Monopoly

After leaving Dubai, we flew back to Dallas. I unpacked then re-packed some more of my things for ATL. The models that were going to participate in the fashion show and I flew out to Atlanta, GA for the dress rehearsal, promoting purposes, and I had three appearances to make on *Love & Football*.

Since Tiffany was engaged to Kevin Rodgers, who played wide receiver for the Atlanta Falcons, he got a deal to be on the reality show *Love & Football*. The producer thought it would be a good idea to put the fashion show and myself on the reality show since I was an R&B singer. I thought that would be a wonderful idea. The producer was a white man in his late 30s. I thought of him being a little crazy when he told me on a conference call a few weeks ago that he wanted to stage a fist fight between Kevin Rodgers and me at one of the rehearsals. Then he started talking about the ratings and how much exposure I would get if we did it. I let him know there was no deal if I had to do all that to be in a reality show. He had to accept me and pay me no matter what, because I was going to perform in and was part of the production of the fashion show.

I wasn't doing what he asked for no damn exposure nor a woman, even if it was all staged. I was a pimp and a man who accepted my BM's relationship. What would it look like on national television fighting over a woman who didn't want me? Hell no. Plus, Kevin really turned out to be an okay guy. He had two kids from a woman here in Atlanta. They were at Tiffany's house when Kevin and I met for the first time. He seemed like a family man to me, from seeing him interacting with everyone. I felt he would be good to Tiffany and the three kids she had. Her oldest son, who was nine years old, played football for my homeboy Black's pee-wee football team in South Dallas. That would be a good look for her son and mine.

I'd been around Kevin twice since then. Nothing had changed about him. I was glad Tiffany found her a good, successful man. She deserved that.

I paid for three rooms at the InterContinental Hotel in Buckhead for the hoes and myself. I left the others there while Elisha, Rose, Sarah, and I took Uber to a foreign dealer shop to rent the latest Hummer, Jaguar, Audi, and BMW for my hoes, and a Bugatti for myself. We headed back to the InterContinental Hotel. I spent a little over an hour giving them instructions on what to do. I let them know what escort sites to post on and what strip clubs to work in the ATL. Even though my models had their own bank accounts with thousands in them, I still gave them spending money for their pleasures. I didn't want them spending the money they had in their accounts for unimportant things. I was teaching them how to save their money. A couple of them had good credit, and a bunch of them had bad credit, some had no credit at all. So, I was showing them how to build their credit.

Rose, Sarah, Heather, and Claire followed behind me in the Hummer and Audi. I got two rooms at the Waldorf Astoria hotel in Bankhead.

Sarah and Claire wanted me to take them to the nail shop, so I took them to Diamond N the Rough nail salon on Fairburn. Claire went to sit at the booth to get her manicure. Sarah and I got escorted to the booth to get a pedicure. "I'll get with you both in a minute," a sexy black lady had said.

This was my first time ever in Atlanta, and my first time ever seeing black people working in a nail salon. Every nail shop I'd been in, there were Asians running them. Just when you think you've seen it all, you haven't. There was always something new to see in this world. Upon my arrival here, there were a lot of black people here in ATL. I'd heard stories of black people coming out here to pursue their dreams and getting put on, especially in the rap game. I didn't have to go around the city to see if that was true or not. I'd noticed that from the black people I saw at both hotels, at the international airport of Atlanta, and while driving and walking around the ATL.

I took off my own Balenciaga socks and shoes before the chick that ushered us here and another pretty young black chick came over to service us. "You looking at my feet as if you're surprised," I told her.

"I am. This ain't common for a man. Yo' feet better than some women I've seen."

"I love myself more than anything. I take care of myself very well, as well as my loved ones. You look like you know what you're doing with those pretty hands of yours, but before you start, I have to ask to make sure."

"What is it?" she asked me.

"Do you know how to treat a man of my caliber who knows how to take care of himself?"

She smiled and said, "Yes, I believe I can."

"Work your magic then," I said, smiling back.

"What do you do for a living?" There I go, getting that question again. "I'm a manager and R&B singer."

"Bitch, look at that nigga's pinky ring. That nigga a pimp, he ain't no R&B singer. Don't let that nigga fool you, girl," the chick that worked on Sarah's pedicure had said, being hostile.

The chick that was working on me looked at her co-worker, and then at me. From the look in her eyes, I could tell she had agreed with her. "I've never heard of you, nigga. If you can sing, sing something."

Both of my hoes looked at me, smiling like I was about to start singing. I could have sang for them, but it was the way she demanded it, so I didn't do it. I grabbed Sarah's purse to get the fliers for the fashion show out of it. I gave the two in front of me a business card and flyer. There were six other women in the salon also. "Claire, give each of these queens in here a flyer. For you two, as you can see, I'm on the flyer. I'll be performing at the Gateway Center Arena and it's being recorded to be on the reality show *Love & Football*, so come see me if you want to see me sing, or just look up Monopoly. You did guess right; pimpin' is my profession. I'm also a business owner of a clothing line and a modeling agency with over 30 models."

"You said Monopoly, right?" a woman in her mid-thirties had said, who was doing Claire's nails.

Both Claire and I told her 'yeah,' and I added, "Just like it's spelled in the board game."

The woman, who I found out was the owner, excused herself and started looking it up on her smart phone. When she found the nine videos I had on YouTube, she hooked it up to her stereo system in her salon. "Let us hear what you're talking about here, because I'm curious if you can sing or not. I'm a music lover." She tilted her head to the side a bit. "Uhhh, I wanna hear 'Certain Passion.'"

My song started blasting out the speakers. It had every woman in the building bobbing their heads, either slightly or heavily. "Girl, is it really him, though?" a young woman in her early twenties had asked. She was getting her nails done too, but she walked over to where the owner was to see for herself.

"Yeah, it's him, girl."

I had to laugh at them. This was funny. They were so used to niggas lying to them that they didn't believe me. I prided myself for being a real man.

"Sure is," the young chick had said when she looked at me then old girl's phone.

The six women in the salon, my women not included, all said they liked the song, and would find some time to come to the fashion show. When I mentioned there would be a woman's gift bag worth over $100 for every woman that attended, they said they were coming.

We talked while she worked on my feet. The one who was doing my feet name was Candance. She was 24 years of age. The aggressive friend's name was Toni, and she was 26 years old. She had a problem with men. What it was, though, a bunch of renegade hoes thought down on most men. They believed niggas couldn't do anything but pay them, and when the ho wanted it, get some head and get fucked how they wanted. From what I told them about myself, and the proof of it, added interest in me and value to me. I believed I had the one working on me. I knew that when she started being sweet on me. The aggressive one would follow her friend's lead.

She was going to choose because her friend did, and the curiosity to see how it was with my pimpin', really where it could take her. They both were from the south side of Atlanta and danced at two strip clubs. They worked at the nail salon part time.

They both were stallions with big asses. Toni's looked real, but Candance's ass was fake, which was cool with me. She still was a bad bitch. Candance had a pretty, dark-brown face with thin, blonde, long braids hanging down her back. She stood about at 5'8, flat stomach, and phat in all the right places. Toni, on the other hand, was tall and dark. She had a fat face with thick, juicy lips and a wide nose that looked cute on her. Both of them had a bunch of tattoos, but Toni had tattoos on her arms, breasts, back, ass cheeks, and legs. They were some bad, tall stallions that I wanted down on my team.

I bought lunch for everyone from a soul food joint a couple of streets down. I was a pimp nigga from Dallas in town, so I had to make myself seen and remembered. Plus, I did it because I wanted everyone in the salon to attend our event. Before we left, I told Candance don't call me unless she had a G to choose me.

She called me that same day at 6:06 P.M. "Hey, Monopoly, this Candance. What you doing?"

"At the room. Just got through picking up some of my models from the airport. What's up with you?"

"Chilling at the shop, we just got off. Anyway, me and Toni gon' choose with you. We have $2000 for you. Where do you want to meet up at?"

"I'm at InterContinental Hotel right now. You know where that's at?"

"Yeah, I know where it's at. We on our way. We'll be there in 10 minutes."

After hanging up with her, to be on the safe side, I told my homie, Lil' Kenny, to watch my back when these hoes came through. I was just being cautious since I was out of town in a city I'd never been in. I didn't know what these hoes were up to.

When they pulled up in the parking lot in a late-model Toyota Camry, I waved them over to get into my rented Bugatti. Toni sat in the passenger seat and Candance got behind Toni in the backseat.

I turned towards them. Toni tried to hand me my choosing fee, but I had her put it on the dashboard. I knew that wasn't all the money that they possessed, which was cool. It would be different if I had demanded for them to break themselves. Breaking themselves meant they had to give me all they had, but I didn't want it. Eventually, in a week or two, if they were still under my pimpin', they would be signing an Advance Model contract.

I didn't want them to be broke. That was a little funny to me to say that shit. Months ago, I wouldn't have dared said no shit like that. Back then, I would have told them I wanted every dime they had. Things were a little different since I opened this modeling agency. I wasn't the average pimp. I really wanted my hoes to accomplish something in life other than just prostituting. It wouldn't be in justice to the Game first and then my women to just take from them without giving back to them.

"If you haven't already, go open your own bank account and put the rest of the money y'all have stashed in it.

"Damn, you don't want all a bitch's money?" Toni asked.

"No, not the money you have saved. You can keep it. I want all the money you make from here on out after you get out this car. What I feel you should have will be given back to you. I'm at a part in the Game where it's about giving back to the ones who are giving to me. Every woman that works for me has over $50,000, a few have over $100,000 in their banks. I have one model whose net worth is 4 million dollars. Some have more than others. That depends on their level of productivity, gifts, and talents they possess. I'm about making dreams come true. After fucking with me for a couple years, a woman will be living her dream as a millionaire. What all do y'all do for money other than work at the nail shop and dance?"

"We sell pussy," Candance said.

"Am I the first pimp y'all been under?"

"Yeah, but not Toni."

"Toni, how long have you been working without guidance?"

"For about six years now."

"What happened?"

166

"He went to the feds for pimpin' an underage girl. You don't beat women, do you, Monopoly?" Toni asked.

"If I was blessed enough to attain you, I'll maintain you with manifestation of good game, which is what I'm about. I don't have to put a foot up your ass to get you to stay or be obedient, 'cause pimpin' is a non-contact sport. I will have your mind so occupied with nothing but greatness all the way around the Monopoly board that you wouldn't want to stray, disrespect, or betray me. Example, this is how a coward thinks, why challenge you intellectually when I can conquer you physically? When I can't get my way or I can't talk past go, I'll just go upside your head. I'm sure you are familiar with that type of coward. I will kick yo' ass if I have to, but not for the reasons you think it is. You can leave me any time you please without any consequences. Anyway, where are y'all living at?"

"In The Parke at Oakley apartments in South Fulton," Toni said.

"When do y'all find time to work outside of that nail shop?" I wanted to know because that was a waste of time unless they used it to cop hoes for me. Other than that, I didn't want them working there.

"We work at the nail salon for Tracy four days out of the week. The days we work at the nail shop, we normally get about three hours of sleep, and then hit the club," Candance mentioned.

"Alright, do that. Do y'all work at the shop tomorrow?"

"No," Toni said.

"Well, I'ma call y'all in the morning. We're spending the day together tomorrow. What time do y'all get off at the club?"

"At 3 A.M."

Tomorrow, I planned to spend the day with them to break down my game in a more relaxed environment, and so they could show me around the A.

The next day, Toni, Candance, Poppa, and I went to the Escobar Restaurant and Tapas for lunch. Next, we went to the Trap Music Museum on Travis Street. After that, we rode around the city for about two hours as I broke down my rules and instructions while Poppa followed behind us. Later on that evening, I worked them on two high-dollar escort services, and then had them work at the club for four hours.

Friday morning, the head of the Pink 4 Cancer Foundation, named Martha Lewis, Tiffany, her fiancé, Kevin Rodgers, Syn, and myself had three segments on Atlanta's Hot 107.9 morning show. Also, the chick Kimberly, the guard I met when I was in jail, was in attendance with us. Since she was getting her bachelor's degree in communication at TCU, I wanted her to see for herself how it was in this type of environment. From being in this studio, I felt like I was on my shit. Really, it was the fact that I was about to be on a reality show. There were two cameramen in the studio with us now recording for *Love & Football*. That was doing big things to me. I was glad I was part of it as well as my models.

First, they talked about Breast Cancer Awareness month, sharing facts with the radio audience, hoping to save a life and give support for someone who was fighting breast cancer. She also mentioned that they would be taking pictures in a photo booth at the event, and it would cost $1. The proceeds went to the foundation as a donation. That lasted the whole first segment. They played Usher's "Let It Burn" song after the commercial.

The second segment, they asked Tiffany what kind of clothes would be expected to be seen on the runway. Tiffany mentioned there would be bras, panties, and clothes by her, Forever21, and Gap, as well as the vendors that would be there. She added that free gift bags would be passed out.

In the same segment, they started talking about Kevin Rodgers and him being one of the cast members in *Love & Football*. They asked Kevin Rodgers and Tiffany questions about their relationship and being in the reality show before that segment ended.

After the commercial, the morning show played one of my songs, "Certain Passion," and then the duet with Syn. "That was music by singer/songwriter Monopoly and Syn, who's in the house this morning. Monopoly, what kind of music will we be getting tonight at this fashion show?"

"We're gonna have inspirational, motivational, loving, caring, strong, sexy music, all that a woman is and more. We will have a performance from your own Future and myself. And I can't forget from my modeling agency, Advance Models, singer Syn. There's 16 gifted, smart, and gorgeous women that will grace the stage tonight."

The director of the radio show held up ten fingers and mouthed 10 seconds to me. I nodded my head. "The whole show will be phenomenal. You gotta come see it. You won't be disappointed."

The male personality got back on the mic. "There you have it. Text Monopoly to 35139 to win $500. We'll be back with the morning mix."

I gave the radio station $10,000 for giveaways to the listeners. I can't lie. I did it for more reasons than to just help the people out. I did it so people would know who I was and attempt to listen to my music. Another reason I did it was so I could cop some of these ATL hoes. I knew by my name being said on the radio multiple times a day that it would get people familiar with my name and music.

Last night, before sending Toni and Candance out to Magic City, I told them to tell all the strippers about me and to listen to Hot 107.9 morning show, because their pimp would be on there. Later on that same day, after the radio appearance, my phone started ringing. I copped four more hoes just for being on the radio. Now I had 16 hoes under my pimpin', plus six of my models that flew out here four days ago.

Later on that night, backstage, I was absorbing everything that was going on around me while getting a fresh bald fade by one of the best male barbers. To the right of me, Rose and Heather were getting their hair-do up to par, talking amongst one another about how excited they were being a part of this fashion show.

I was just as excited as they were. This fashion show only would elevate Tiffany Designs & Collections and Advance Models on a bigger level. I'd been advertising this breast cancer awareness fashion show on multiple outlets, through social media, word of mouth from all that were involved, and commercial ads on Hot 107.9. Tiffany and Kevin Rodgers put it up on billboards throughout the city of Atlanta and posters in every mall in the city. They both used a couple of celebrities they knew in Atlanta to promote the event as well.

I only came out my pocket with 15 bands for some promotion, hairstylists, and make-up artists. Our sponsors, vendors, and *Love & Football* producers paid most of our expenses for the event. They helped out a great deal.

When the barber stepped to the right side of me to edge me up, I saw Jazz in a booth alone, looking at herself in the mirror. She had doubt all in her face. Her insecurities were getting the best of her at this moment. I guessed she sensed someone looking at her and looked right at me through the mirror.

"Bitch, come here, bring yo' ass over here," I said, smiling. She walked over in a slow pace. "Wuz wrong?"

"Ain't nothing wrong, I'm gucci."

I frowned up. "Bitch, you gon' stand there and lie to me in my face. Bitch, you know I'm a Game nigga. I can read yo' body language. Now, tell me wuz wrong."

"I don't know if I can do it," she said, not being too sure of herself.

I wanted to shake my head, but I didn't. I didn't want to discourage her more than she already was. So, all I asked was, "Tell me, what have I been stressing every day since I presented this event to y'all?"

She didn't answer, she just stood there looking dumbfounded.

"I'm not gon' ask you again. I wanna hear you tell me what I've been stressing to y'all."

"That we need to tighten up, workout, do whatever we need to prepare for the fashion show."

"And what did I offer?" I asked.

"Help," she replied.

"I've been a true leader and gave opportunities for y'all to workout with me or get y'all own personal trainer. I offered you to get plastic surgery, but you denied it. When I saw none of that didn't work, I still accepted you and continued to cherish and love yo' body since the first time I touched you. Am I lying?"

"No sir." She put her head down towards my feet.

"Bitch, I'm your pimp, give me some muthfuckin' respect. Pick yo' muthafuckin' head back up and look me in the eyes." She obeyed me. "I'm doing my best, making sure everything is right with my queens. You can't even get down with my program. What is it? Is my pimpin too big for you or something? You need to get with a nigga pimpin' that's lower than mine. Is that what it is? If so, we can make that happen right now," I said while picking up my new iPhone. "You can tear yo' ass, I don't need a non-confident ho on my team. I wanna go getter, a queen that wants better for herself. So, what are you gonna do, Jazz?"

"I guess I'ma do it. I gotta get myself together."

"Get yo' ass out my face. You have 30 minutes to make a decision. If you let me down, I'm breaching your contract and I'm sending you home for good. And I mean that shit. Now tear yo' ass."

The barber finished cutting my hair three minutes later. I called Josh over to me, who was talking to Erika, Heather, Sarah, and another model we had. When we met each other, I told him what was going on with Jazz, and then said, "I need you to go talk to her in about 25 minutes. See if she's gonna participate or not. I really want the ho to be a part of this fashion show. See if you can talk some sense into her. If not, I'm breaching her contract."

"Jazz is cool. I don't want her to lose out on this opportunity. This is all of our time to shine. I'm about to go talk to her right now."

After he left, I walked up on Shae, who was three booths down, doing Claire's hair. When she saw me, she started smiling. Naturally, I smiled too.

"Hey, baby," she said. It was good to see her in a good mood. She'd been a little cranky and mean since she'd been pregnant. I had four baby mothers, and I been around them enough to know and understand to not take it personal. Their entire being went through so much during pregnancy that they had to find a way to let out all the frustration.

Everything wasn't bad during their pregnancies. I loved the moments when they were the most sensitive and vulnerable. It made me show my love more, cherish them more, and take care of them. Even though it didn't make me change, it made me think about it.

"Hey, my queens. I'm just checking on you two. Y'all need anything?"

Claire said no. Shae wanted some water. Back stage, I had two big coolers, one with bottled waters and the other with sodas, tea, and orange juice. I brought her two bottles of water.

After talking with my daughter and son that were backstage with us, I went back to sit down and talk with the barber, from Atlanta's Trophy Room Barbers, that cut my hair for a few minutes, before I called Jazz back over to where we were. He heard me go off on Jazz, now I wanted him to hear me pimp at my ho in a smooth manner. I knew how the barber shop talk could be. I didn't want to be talked about being a gorilla pimp, because that I wasn't.

When she got in front of me, she put her head down. "Pick yo' head up."

She did.

"Look, Jazz, I want you to know, everything that's going on today, I'm not just doing for myself. I'm doing for the sole purpose of Advance Models. I'm doing it for my queens that's in my life. I really want y'all to succeed in life. I don't think you know how much I want the best for you, or do you, Jasmine?"

"I know you do, Monopoly."

"Truly, I can't believe that you think you are not fine because of this," I said, as I lightly pinched her baby fat on her belly. "You are one of my sexiest queens. You are in high demand every day and night you work. Even so, when we make love, don't I cherish and appreciate every inch of your body?"

She smiled at the thought. "Yes, you do."

"When I first started this modeling agency, didn't I tell you, you will be in magazines and doing events?"

"Yes, Daddy, you did."

"This fashion show is being recorded and will be aired on television one day. Just imagine the look on your daughter's face when she sees how beautiful you are when you walk down that stage and sees you achieve something positive. Yo' daughter and mother gon' be so proud of you. I'm so proud of you because you are here with me and your wives being a part of this fashion show." I grabbed both of her hands in mine. "Can you please participate in this event, Jazz?"

"I'ma participate, Daddy," she said while smiling hard.

"Then go take yo' sexy ass back over there and get ready to walk that runway," I said before smiling myself.

Out of nowhere, she hugged me while I was still sitting down. I got up out the chair to hug her and kiss her.

"Thanks for everything, Monopoly"

"You're welcome. And thank you." I swear, for me to be so young, I was a smart muthafucking pimp. I caught on fast. I didn't know if it was the pimp God putting the signs and the messages in front of my path to catch or not. I knew that conversation was a lot smoother than the one we had about twenty minutes ago. This second conversation really motivated her to do what I wanted her to do. With that second conversation with my ho, I made that barber give me my props for doing some real pimpin'.

***

Twenty-Five Minutes Later

Martha Lewis, the founder of the Pink 4 Cancer non-profit foundation, stood on a small stage right next to a big, long stage. She started stating facts of breast cancer.

"Did you know breast cancer is the most common cancer for women worldwide. It kills nearly 41,000 women each year. Did you know every 13 minutes, one woman will die of breast cancer. One in 1000 men will receive a breast cancer diagnosis. One in 8 women will receive a breast cancer diagnosis. Did you know alcohol beverages increase the risk of breast cancer? Only 5-10% of individuals diagnosed have a family history of breast cancer. Over 3.3 million breast cancer survivors are alive in the U.S. today. I want to honor and salute the fighters, the survivors, and the deceased. Enjoy the show."

After she ended her fact speech, the lights went off over her head. The lights came on over Syn and a cancer fighter on another small stage on the other side of the long one. Syn had dyed her hair hot pink. She had on a hot, pink-colored dress from Tiffany Designs with a pair of pink, six-inch high heels. The dark-skin breast cancer fighter was in her mid-forties. Even though her head was bald, she was a very attractive woman. She had a pink scarf around her neck, one pink ribbon around her wrist, and a white short-sleeved dress by my son's mother, Tiffany, with a pair of pink three-inch heels.

A slow tempo instrumental to "Strength In My Corner" came on the speakers. As Syn started humming, the first breast cancer survivor walked down the long stage with special lingerie on. She had on a matching pink bra and panties. Her bra was special made, also from Tiffany Designs. The woman only had one breast, so she had that one breast in the big cup in the bra and the other cup was tight-fitted where the other breast was supposed to be.

I made Syn's song "Strength In My Corner" more suitable for this event. Martha Lewis had given a breast cancer patient money from her organization. The patient asked Martha Lewis could she perform spoken word. Martha asked me, and I agreed.

Syn started singing the hook from the "Strength In My Corner" four times, and then the breast cancer fighter started reciting her poetry.

"Never underestimate their ambition or will
challenges faced to clear hurdles or hills
through trials and tribulations one care to bear
compassion and generosity much to spare
survivors stretching their arms farther
than their sleeve
self-sacrifice toward others constant need."

Syn started singing the hook again as another good-looking survivor came out strutting in a special lingerie made by Forever 21.

"Enduring diabetes, cancers, and heart disease

they never wavered through weary or need
Genuine hearts giving a hand to help
Even when I could not do for myself."

Syn started singing "Strength In My Corner" as the same survivor went backstage, and another woman walked on stage.

"With mouths to feed and bills to pay
working two jobs day after day
never for granted what one may not seethe
anxiety, frustration, and uncertainty
a sister, a daughter, a wife, or mother
it breaks my heart to see anyone suffer."

Syn sang the hook for the fourth time.

"Prayer goes up and blessings come down
tears of joy is abound
though some pass on it's not a goodbye
so please don't cry
determination and will to live
encourages everyone God heals
an inspiration yes indeed
never give up always believe
attain the zeal the overcome
for God's will shall be done
pure love and joy on display
that's the outcome
when we keep the faith."

Syn ended it with the hook.
After their performance, they both got a standing ovation. As the crowd gave them applause, Syn had her hands over her mouth in shock. I was backstage behind the curtain on the main stage. The breast cancer fighter and Syn walked backstage from the small one

with a huge smile on her pretty face. As soon as she saw me, she ran into my open arms. She hugged me tighter than I hugged her.

"How did I do, Daddy?" she asked, wanting approval from me.

"You did a splendid job. How do you feel right now?" I said after we quit hugging, and then we held each other.

"I don't know. I feel the best I have ever felt in my life. I appreciate you, Daddy."

The lights were off when I walked on stage. After I got into position in front of the mic, the lights came on around and over me. My momma started yelling my real name and clapping for me, until Shae calmed her down. I couldn't help but smile. It felt good to see my mom proud of me. Shit, I was proud of my damn self for being on stage performing.

When the slow tempo instrumental to my song "Caught Up" came on the speakers, Erika's fine ass stepped out on stage. She walked down the runway in a sexy stank walk. She wore a tight-fitted, long Tiffany Designs dress with a long slit on the side of it, and three-inch heels on her feet. Before she stopped to pose, she threw her big hips towards the crowd, and then turned her head quick so the long, big braid on the left side of her flew to the right side in front of her.

I started singing.

"Caught Up emotions and feelings
I wanna know if you're willing
Cause I'm willing, girl, let's give it a try
I was confused the last time
No longer that man girl understand
 what you came and you did to me
I was confused the last time
go do what I can,
long as it stands till the end,
that's you and me."

Heather switched and twisted off the stage like she was on the blade. She eyed the crowd with a big smile on her face, and then put her left hand on her waist after switching to put her weight on her other leg. Heather had on a tight, pink, short Forever 21 dress with white-netted, six-inch heels. She held the stance for three seconds and then walked off, with her big breasts bouncing all over the place.

I worked the stage as I sang the verse.

"My heart is in it
If want a new beginning
My heart was missing
But you came and love me
And know my heart is heart felt
Before I meet you I was heartless
Baby you came around the other I put 'em down
No longer I needed a lot of women out in public."

Rose came out strutting, wearing a long, white Gap dress that was tight fitted around the upper body without sleeves. It had big roses all over it with pink, six-inch heels. By the time she made it to the stage to pose, I was finished singing the second hook and going into the second verse.

Marilyn Sunshine looked drop-dead gorgeous in a pink, tight-fitted, sleeveless, short Tiffany Designs dress that was strapped around the neck.

It seemed like the photographers took over fifty photos of us the whole time I was on stage, because I saw nothing but flashes all around me during my performance.

The next segment featured Future performing "Trophy," while Jazz, Claire, Elisha, and two of my models walked the runway in sexy lingerie from Forever21 and Tiffany Designs.

The next segment featured Sarah, Bre, and four other women from Advance Models, displaying shirts and pants by Tiffany Designs and Gap to music by Raheem Devaughn.

The last segment featured Rose, Claire, Marilyn Sunshine, and Elisha displaying blouses and skirts by Gap and Forever21. They walked the runway to "Beautiful" by Snoop Dogg and Pharell.

When the breast cancer awareness reception came around, about 2,300 people gathered in a big hall to socialize, eat, and drink alcoholic and non-alcoholic beverages until a few women got on stage to recite their speeches.

After the speeches, I chopped it up with Future, telling him that I wanted to record a song with him tonight if he was free to, and that I had the money, just name a price.

He told me he was headed to the studio once he left here, and that he'd charge me $100,000. I agreed. I wasn't trippin', he was a platinum artist. I knew it was going to be a banger with whatever we came up with.

Chapter 15
Too Good to Be True
Rose

Tonight was so fucking lit. The fashion show went perfect, it couldn't have gone better. Since I'd been with Monopoly, he'd amazed me with every move he'd made. I was so happy when he started Advance Models. Home was with Monopoly. He created ways for us to make legal money other than prostituting. He had all his models open our bank accounts. For the model who didn't have transportation, he had them lease out new cars in their names as well as got apartments and houses for them. He really did upgrade us. He believed in our dreams. Even though he was hard on us all, he wished the best for us as well as did his best to make life better than it was yesterday.

Josh really did believe in us also. They had helped in every way. I was Monopoly's rider for sure.

After everyone left the Gateway Center Arena, some of us split up and went to the Blue Flame strip club. I had most of my girls with me. Sarah, Heather, Erika, Bre, Jazz, Alicia, and Pinky and Shae's pregnant asses. Marilyn Sunshine with her famous ass. There were over 15 other women who were signed with Advance Models. Monopoly wasn't here.

Syn, Kimberly, and Josh were with Monopoly. Monopoly was in the studio doing a song with Future. I was happy for him to make that kind of move for himself.

We had $10,000 in dollar bills wrapped up in 10 stacks in plastic. We were all acting a fool and showering dollar bills at Claire and two fine ass black chicks dancing in front of us to "No Hands" by Waka Flocka Flame feat. Wale and Roscoe Dash.

While Claire and Erika were dancing here tonight, I told them hoes that they didn't have to work tonight, but they just loved dancing. It was a celebration night. And this was our first time being in the ATL, so they wanted to see what all the hype was about in Atlanta's strip clubs. Even I was curious about it also, but I didn't want to dance tonight. Although, I did understand why a bunch of dancers

I'd known working in DFW clubs came out this way. It was turned up as fuck. Plus, there were a bunch of opportunities at every turn in Atlanta. If a woman had the looks, she could be discovered in the strip club to be a video vixen or whatever else she was into.

There were a bunch of celebrities, rappers, producers, and dope boys here on this Friday night. The dudes with the most money were sprinkled throughout the big VIP section upstairs where my girls and I were.

***

Thirty Minutes Later

Everyone was enjoying themselves until a hot song by Yung Thug cut off and the screams replaced it without the speakers. The DJ did his best to control the crowd without the influence of the music, but there was still a bunch of screaming. All the lights in the club came on.

Automatically, I ran to the balcony, because I was nosy, and some of my girls were downstairs. Following behind me were some of the people that were with me and other people that I didn't know.

"Wuz goin' on down there, shawty?"

Dam, that shit smelled good. His compelling cologne made me look to my left. I didn't know who this black man was, but I was sure I'd seen him before in a video or magazine somewhere. I thought he was a famous singer or producer or something. Before I could respond back to him and ask who he was, Sarah said my name, snapping me back to what I was over here for in the first place.

"That's Heather. She's bleeding bad."

While the other people were making comments about how much blood it was on the floor, I damn near jumped up over the balcony trying to get to my girl. Instead, I ran out the door and down the stairs.

I ran through the standing crowd, screaming Heather's name at the top of my lungs. My little ass was pushing and shoving people, doing my best to get to my friend. I heard a female call me a white bitch. I didn't care at this moment, but any other time I would have checked the bitch.

When I finally made it to her, Erika was down on her knees, holding Heather in her arms. Blood was all over her skin, even her white Gucci thong and bra were covered in blood in the front.

"What happened to her?" I asked.

"She was stabbed," Erika said.

I looked up from Heather and looked around to see if I saw a guilty face or anybody with their backs turned towards me leaving out the door. Nothing looked off to me. There were too many people around anyway to tell.

"Did you see who did it?"

"No," she said, still looking down at Heather.

"Y'all gonna have to get her to a hospital," some black man, who might be the manager, had said, sounding like he was trying to get us out of the club. I bet the only reason he said that was because if anybody got hurt or killed inside the club, there was a possibility they would close his club temporarily, probably for good, until someone changed the name of it. I knew because I'd been a dancer for a little over five years and had seen a bunch of bullshit in these strip clubs.

"Fuck you and your club, dude, my friend's dying here. Fuuuuuuuck." It took everything in me to get myself together in this place. Almost every girl that came with us was around me. Bre told someone to call 911.

"We can't wait on no damn ambulance. We got to take her to the hospital. Fuck! Heather, don't die on me, please," I said as tears started running down my face. "Come on Sunshine, Erika, Shae, Sarah, let's pick her up and get her in one of the Hummers."

Sunshine and I had one leg each. Erika held her shoulders. Shae and Sarah held her up with their arms and hands on the sides of her back. "Hold on, Heather, we going to the hospital," I told her.

Poppa was escorting us out with his gun in hand, looking side to side and forward for anybody with a suspicious look. I looked back while still walking and said, "One of y'all call Monopoly and tell him what happened."

We drove in one of the Hummers we rented. On the way to the hospital, all I could think about was my friend getting stabbed. The thought of Heather dying was killing me inside, as I had my foot down on the gas pedal, going 65 miles per hour on a 40-mph lane.

Monopoly wasn't answering the damn phone. Erika, Sarah, and Shae called Monopoly and Josh multiple times. Where the fuck were men when you really need their asses? I knew shit was too good to be true.

"Drive this fucking car, Rose. Heather just lost consciousness," Sarah yelled from the backseat.

While tears were streaming down my face harder than before, I pushed the accelerator down a little more, weaving through the little traffic they had at 11:16 P.M.

You know how you feel when something fucked up happens and you wish it was a nightmare? To better explain it, as she was dying, I felt like I was too, and that I could die if she did. I wanted to close my eyes and believe this was a bad dream, but I was speeding.

As soon as I pulled up into the emergency entrance, I parked, got out, and then rushed in between the gliding doors to get someone to wheel a stretcher outside to the Hummer.

"I need help! My friend just got stabbed." Everyone in the waiting room looked at me. I ran to the desk. "My friend just got stabbed! I need a doctor," I said it a notch under a scream to some white, geeky-looking young dude in scrubs.

He looked at all the blood on my white Dior dress and asked, "Where is she?"

"She's in the truck. You need to hurry up, she's dying!"

"Okay. Okay." He turned around yelled out that he had a woman bleeding outside. He speed walked into a room. He appeared again with a stretcher and PPE gear ten seconds later. Two black female nurses came out the same room he just walked out of.

All four of us rushed outside to the Hummer. The back door was wide open. Erika stood outside of the truck, looking provocative as ever in a white one-piece lingerie with blood smeared all over the front of it. When I got to the Hummer, my girl Heather was laid out in the backseat, unconscious.

"Come on, y'all, let's get her on the stretcher," the older black nurse had said, demanding help from us.

It took four of us to get her out onto the stretcher, doing our best to not hurt her more than she already was. We hurried inside right behind them, until a geeky male nurse stopped us in the lobby, telling us we couldn't go back there while they were operating.

After attempting to call Monopoly three more times with no answer, I put my head down in my lap. It was crazy how a wonderful day could turn into a fucking nightmare. Why did this have to happen to Heather? She didn't deserve that.

About 15 minutes later, the older black nurse approached us with fresh blood all over the white gown and bad news written on her face. I stood up first, my girls followed.

"Sorry to tell you all that your friend has passed away."

Instantly, my heart dropped. If you don't know what it feels like to lose a true friend, a woman you really loved and cared about, I felt heartbroken. I bust out crying. My girls tried to console me, but I waved their hands away. I didn't want that. I didn't want to talk to anybody. I didn't want to be around anybody. I wanted my friend back.

I stood up without saying anything to anybody and walked out the hospital to the Hummer. I cranked the car up and drove off with no destination.

***

Monopoly

I fell in love with the A from being out here 12 days. I'd touched almost every hotspot, every popular strip club, and a bunch of hoods. It was fun and a different vibe than what I was used to living in Dallas, Texas. I'd met a bunch of entrepreneurs, rappers, singers, and people with good careers who were loving what they did for a living. The people of Atlanta had mean hustle and a lot of success stories. At this very moment, I was doing a record with my favorite rapper from Atlanta, Future.

I had to spend that $100,000 he wanted for a song. I knew it was going to be well worth it. I brought Josh, Kimberly, and Syn with me just for the experience. We were at Patchwerk studio with Future, his producer, and three of Future's homeboys. After listening to seven instrumentals, we decided on a mid-tempo beat. We called it "That Life." The song was about living the good life, hustling, stunting, and fucking with hoes. Future was almost finished with his rap verse when I checked my phone for any calls or texts. When I got here, I put my phone on silent. I didn't want to be disturbed. I wanted no interruptions while I was recording. Especially when I had just paid all that money to record a song with Future.

When I took my phone off my phone clip, my screen lit up with a lot of missed calls and texts from mainly my hoes and a few models. I'm like, what the fuck is going on now?

I ignored the texts and calls from everybody else and called Rose since she was the captain. It rang once and then went straight to her voicemail. I called once more and got the same results. I called Erika, she answered on the third ring. "What's going on, Erika?"

"Heather died about twenty minutes ago," she said, sounding sad.

I wasn't sure that I heard her right, so I asked, "She what twenty minutes ago?"

"She died, Monopoly. She gone," she said, crying.

"What the fuck?" I said to myself. I closed my eyes, wishing that shit wasn't true. I even questioned God. "What happened, Erika?"

"We were all at the Blue Flame. They say she went to the restroom. Next thing you know, she's getting stabbed downstairs."

"Did anybody see who did it?" I asked.

"No, not none of us."

"Where is Rose at?"

"I don't know. As soon as the doctor told us she had passed away, she got up and left us. Poppa picked us up from the hospital."

"Put his ass on the phone."

"Yeah."

"Bro, where the fuck were you when that shit went down?"

"I was upstairs in the VIP with the girls, bro. That shit happened so fast. I'm sorry, bro."

"Alright, bro. This shit ain't over with. I'ma talk to you when I get to the room," I said and then hung up. I'd talk to them later. I had to find Rose.

After I talked with Josh, Kim, and Syn along with Future about what happened at the club, I left to go find Rose. As I was leaving, I thought about Heather. Just when things were getting better with Heather and me, this bullshit had to happen. I could have accepted her choosing another pimp or management team and lived with it, but it was hard accepting her death. I knew this tragedy was devastating Rose. That was why Rose forwarded my calls. She wanted to be alone during this loss. That's how she was. When she was feeling down, she would withdraw from everything and everybody. Even though I knew all that, I still wanted to mourn with my queen.

I paid the small fee to find where Rose was at. I put her cell number into thelocator.com They said she was at Four Seasons Hotel in Downtown Atlanta, so I made my way there.

I didn't want her to forward my call again nor turn her phone off. Instead of calling her, I text her.

"I'm outside of the Four Seasons, what room r u in?" Oct. 3, 2012, 11:26 P.M.

I waited a minute for a response, and when I didn't receive one, I sent her another text.

"I understand u want to be alone, but I'm dealing with this tragedy 2. There's 2 things I want in this world at this very moment. I want my Queen to be alive. Since I can't have that I want 2 B n ur arms. I apologize 4 not accepting ur calls. U know where I was. I didn't even finish the song. Fuck all that. I'm here. If you don't respond back within 2 minutes, you don't want to be with me no mo. That's how I'm gonna take it. I don't want us 2 leave each other. I'm damn near begging u 2 text me telling me what room u r n so I can B by ur side. I don't want 2 lose U 2"

Oct. 3, 2012, 11:28 P.M.
She text back 30 seconds later with the room number.
233
Oct. 3, 2012, 11:29 P.M.
Once I made it up to the front door, I saw that it was cracked open. I went inside without doubting her loyalty nor fear that she would try some dumb shit to hurt me in any way. I knew she was overwhelmed with emotional stress, but she wouldn't harm me because of what happened. She was still in love with a pimp. Love didn't have shit to do with it, but she still needed me in her life, so her wanting to cause me harm was slim.

After I walked in, I could see everything in view. I didn't see her, so I went to the room. She was there lying in bed, fully dressed, on top of the covers. I took my Yeezy's off and then got into bed and laid on the side of her, facing her. The room was gloomy, because the only light in the room was the bathroom light, but I could still see Rose. Some of the makeup on her face was smeared from falling tears. The supposed-to-be whiteness of her eyes were bloodshot red.

"Why, Daddy? Why this had to happen to my friend? Why?" she kept saying and hit me on my chest twice while crying.

I grabbed her chin softly, looked her right into her pupils, and told her, "I want you to know that I'm doing my best to protect you all. If you blame me, please forgive me, Rose. I apologize."

"She didn't deserve that."

"I know she didn't. Whoever did this shit will pay. I promise you that," I said that and then shut up. I let her vent out everything she wanted to say.

I didn't go back to the studio. I stayed with my queen the whole night. I didn't even call him letting him know I wasn't coming back. I probably lost the 100 racks I had paid him for the song with him. I was trippin' about it at first, and then I said fuck it. What mattered the most to me in this very moment was my ho, making sure she was okay in this state of mind she was in. I had sixteen hoes that could easily make 100 racks in five days at the max. I was positive that I had eight down hoes, that if they knew I lost that kind of money for this cause, they would easily make that 100 bands back for me.

Smoove Dolla

Chapter 16
Looking for Revenge
Monopoly

That next morning, when Rose and I woke up at 9:12 A.M., I called Future to apologize for what happened last night, and that it was an emergency. He was so much of a G that he told me if I was free, we could finish the song in two days. That's when his producer would be there again. All I had to do was lay my verse and part of the hook down to finish the song. Future did his part already.

"I'm about to go to y'all rooms at Waldorf Astoria, ask the girls did they see anything last night. You coming with me or do you still need time alone?" I asked when I got off the phone.

"I'm coming with you. I want to know who did this shit too. We in this together," she told me while getting out of bed.

When we got to their rooms, Rose and I took a shower together. She changed clothes, but I put the same outfit I had on yesterday. I didn't have any change of clothes in the car. Plus, I didn't give a fuck right now. All I cared about was finding the motherfucker who killed my ho.

When we got to the room Sarah and Claire stayed in, they were already up. Their eyes were bloodshot red from crying so much. I apologized to them both as well as told them to forgive me if they blamed me for Heather's death. Seeing them cry for something I could have prevented made me feel some kind of way. I didn't know how long I would be in Atlanta. What I did know was I was staying out here until I found Heather's killer and took care of him.

"So, what happened last night?" I asked.

"We don't know. All we know is that Heather went to the restroom to pee, next thing you know, she was downstairs getting stabbed," Rose said.

"Who was with her when it happened?"

"Nobody," Sarah answered. "Erika was downstairs, but she didn't see anything. She showed up after she heard a white girl was bleeding."

I called Lil' Kenny, Josh, and Marilyn Sunshine to the room since they had rooms here at this hotel. When they came up to the room, I asked Marilyn Sunshine about what she saw last night. Her answer was damn near identical to my hoes' story.

"I gotta find out who did this shit," I said out loud, not really talking to anyone in particular.

"How 'bout we get the video footage of the club last night. They have to have cameras," Josh suggested.

"I don't think that's gonna happen. I cussed him out, saying fuck him and his club. He fucking told me I needed to get Heather out his club," Rose said.

"I might have a way. The manager knows who I am. He told the DJ to give me a shout out last night. He begged me to host his club tonight. I'll talk to him if you want me to," Marilyn Sunshine offered.

That was good to hear, because I was thinking about paying him a few thousand to get the footage. If her offer didn't work, I would offer to pay him. I knew he wasn't going to turn down no bands.

It took about ten minutes for us to come up with the proper approach. Marilyn Sunshine googled the main phone line to Blue Flame and called the manager up, putting him on speaker. "May I speak with the manager."

"This is he. Who is this?"

"This is Marilyn Sunshine, you remember me?"

"Yeah, I remember you, shorty. Wuz going on?" he asked excitedly.

"I thought about what you asked me. I'll do it if you can do something for me. It'll be a favor for a favor."

"Okay, what you want me to do?"

"Can I come to the club to talk to you there instead and not over the phone?"

"That's okay with me. When are you coming?"

"Give me an hour. It's been a long night. I just woke up. Let me get myself together and I'll be up there in a bit."

While I waited on everyone to get ready, I called my hood nigga, 8 Ball.

"Wuz good, bro?" he asked when he answered.

I got straight to the point, no beating around the bush. "I know I don't be calling like that, bro, but I really need a favor." I hadn't talked to nor seen him since my birthday party, which was over a month ago.

"Bro, you know it's all good with me. You forever fam. Wuz the favor? Tell a nigga something."

"I'm in Atlanta. We had a fashion show yesterday. All the models went out to Blue Flame to celebrate and, bro, one of my hoes got stabbed and died. Poppa and Kenny with me, but if I need y'all to come out here and handle business, would you?"

"I got you, nigga. Just call me, I'll have some of the dawgs come with me out to the A."

"Aight, bro. 'Preciate it."

"Oh, it ain't shit, you fam."

Forty minutes later, Rose, Marilyn Sunshine, Lil' Kenny, Josh, and I were on our way to Blue Flame in the Hummer. It took a few minutes to get to Mid-Town from Buckhead. At 10:43 A.M, there were about six vehicles scattered throughout the parking lot.

When we walked into the club, Destiny's Child's "Soldier" was on almost two minutes into the song. Two black bouncers stood at the door after the entrance door. After we got searched, we stopped at a locked door. There was a clear window to its right side on the other wall.

Before Marilyn Sunshine could speak first, a pretty, exotic-looking, black, heavyset chick said, "It's $20 entry fee for each of you."

"Tell her you're here to see the manager."

After Marilyn Sunshine told her, the black chick picked up the phone and made the call for the manager.

Two minutes later, a short, bright-skinned man appeared out another door closer to the entrance. He mugged Rose as he approached us and then said, "I see you brought your whole crew. I don't want to see them, so you, Marilyn Sunshine, follow me to my office."

A second before I was about to say something to him, Marilyn Sunshine spoke up. "If they can't go with me, I'm not coming. We're here together." She turned towards us and said, "Come on, you all, I guess he doesn't want to do business." She took two steps away from him.

"Okay. You all come on, come to my office," he told us, and then told his bouncers to come also.

I liked Marilyn Sunshine. She had a little game. She knew her worth.

Once we were in the office, he sat down in his chair behind his desk. One bouncer stood behind the manager and the other stood by the door, both looking at us. Rose and Marilyn Sunshine sat in the two comfortable chairs in front of us. Kenny, Josh, and I stood behind them.

"So, tell me what you want in exchange for what I want."

"Well, I'm giving you one night to host at your club, tonight or whenever you need me to. I have millions of followers. I have been in Atlanta plenty of times, I have a large male and female following here in Atlanta, and I can get some of them here. In exchange for that, I want you to show us the footage of the stabbing that happened here last night. All we're trying to do is find out who's responsible. Can you do that for me, sir?"

Five seconds later, he raised himself up and slid his chair up closer to the desk. He pushed a key on his keyboard. "Look up at that screen right there," he said, as he pointed to a 58-inch flat screen television to the right of us on the wall. It had ten camera monitors on it. All those screens turned into a background with typed dates in the small boxes. He tapped in last night's date. That overhead camera had eight hours of footage on it. He went straight to the time before Heather got stabbed, like he had watched it before we came.

The camera wasn't a high-quality camera. This was a good looking and nice size club. The cameras should have matched the quality of the club.

From what I could see in the video, the club was in its normal functioning, until the murder started. A white girl whose face I could barely see crept up behind Heather. Once she got close enough, she poked Heather five times, like she was in prison or doing time. Then she fled the scene, leaving Heather walking slowly, holding her lower side, towards the back. It took her dropping to her knees for anyone to notice my queen bleeding. There were a couple of black females who started to scream and tried to console her until Erika showed up to aid Heather.

"Her figure looks familiar," Marilyn Sunshine said as she stood up to get closer to the big flat screen. She looked at the manager. "I need to see that girl's face. Is there a camera on the exit door facing the stages?"

"Yeah, hold up." He went back to all the cameras and then went back to the recorded videos of last night. A minute later, after rewinding the footage to the exact time the short white girl left out the exit door, "That's Khole," Marilyn Sunshine damn near shouted.

"Who is Khole?" I asked.

"She's a new model at Perfect Models."

"Wait a minute, wasn't she at the fashion show?" I asked Marilyn Sunshine. I recognized her too. I remembered seeing her in the crowd when I was performing.

"Yeah, she was there along with another girl that I don't know."

"Are you a friend of Khole's?" I asked her, hoping she was not.

"No, she's not a friend, but I know a bunch about her."

"Where does she live?" I asked.

"In Dallas. They're probably on their way back to Dallas or already there."

That was enough talking in front of the manager and the bouncers. We'd finish that conversation after we left this club. I walked up closer to the desk. "I really do appreciate this. Don't worry, this won't be getting out, not from us. I will make sure Marilyn Sunshine hosts for you when you want her to."

"'Preciate it, shorty."

***

In the meantime, while in search of Khole in every way, I stayed in Atlanta. Only Syn, Erika, Marilyn Sunshine, Josh, and Poppa stayed with me at the Waldorf Astoria hotel. Everybody else went back to their city and state they lived in. I gave all my hoes time off, except for Candance, Toni, and the two hoes I had in California, until the tension went down in my stable. I knew it was hard on them dealing with their sister dying. I had Rose and Sarah getting Heather's candlelight vigil as soon as I touched down in Dallas.

When it came time to do my track, I could have recorded at my studio and just sent it to him, but I wanted that experience of being in the studio with him in Atlanta. I thought that would motivate me to go harder on doing my part, but my head wasn't right. I was thinking about my ho and our revenge. The entire time I spent at Patchwerk studio for the three hours I was there, I must have fucked up about eight times. I couldn't get Heather out my mind.

After I was finished laying down my part, I told him the truth about what was going on with me. He understood, but I kind of got the vibe that he thought I was bad business when it came to recording. I probably was tripping though, because he did say we could record another song when I felt like it, if I had the money.

Marilyn Sunshine was a women of her word. Two days later, she hosted the Blue Flame for free for six hours. We left for Dallas on a plane the next morning.

We went all out for Heather's candlelight vigil and funeral. We had sympathy flowers, lit candles, displayed photos of Heather on a projector, pics of her on balloons, and an open mic session for the memory of Heather. There were a bunch of people from Arlington that came, her friends, most of my hoes, a few strippers who worked at Best Cabaret, some people she went to high school with.

I didn't go to Heather's funeral, but Rose, Sarah, Erika, Claire, Bre, Kimberly, Syn, Josh, Marilyn Sunshine, Jazz, and Elisha did. Her parents were fucked up at me, because word was out that she had a pimp for a while now, and that she was with me when she got killed. As Heather's man, I wished I had done better in protecting her. For that reason, and the possibility of it happening again, I paid professional bodyguards to be around my hoes and Marilyn Sunshine, just to make sure that David didn't do any more dumb shit. The ones that were in Cali and the Atl, I paid the bodyguards extra because they were still doing dates through my modeling agency and a high-dollar escort service.

It was hard getting everything back on track. After the funeral, it was the same as before. Heather's death put a damper on my closest hoes' hustle. The legal money was even coming in slow. Rose wasn't producing at all. Her whole drive was gone. She was sad all the time, didn't want to talk to anybody but me, her son, Pinky, and Sarah. I got her her own penthouse in the same building I had mine. Rose, Sarah, and their kids stayed there. I let them take a break from everything for a while to get their heads together and spend time with their children.

Syn, on the other hand, her music was blowing up in a major way. Her fan base had gotten bigger since we did the fashion show. Really, all my models who participated in the video and fashion show had gained hundreds of followers on Twitter and Instagram. Rose and Syn were the only ones who had gained thousands of followers on those outlets, as well as YouTube subscribers. I was really proud of all my models. I wished Heather could have been here to strive for her dreams and climb up the ladder with us.

Smoove Dolla

Chapter 17
Getting Our Revenge
Monopoly

It took me a whole two weeks to find the whereabouts of the bitch who stabbed Heather. The upcoming events that she posted on Instagram weren't good spots at all to get her knocked off at. Khole and a couple other models from Perfect Models lived with David in a gated, rich neighborhood. Although I could have snuck one of my hoes on the security guard at the gate to disarm him of us for the home evasion, I waited for another opportunity to present itself.

Days ago, Marilyn Sunshine told me about a spa named The Spa Castle that she got an endorsement from. I decided that this was the time to handle her. Lil' Kenny and Poppa waited in a stolen blue Honda Civic. I waited in a stolen white Maxima. I was here just overseeing that everything went down properly and looking after my lil' homies' backs.

As soon as Khole and her bodyguard pulled up in a gray, late-model Lincoln, I called Lil' Kenny to tell them their target was here, with whom, and what car they were in. Ten second later, Kenny and Poppa were out the car, creeping up on the Lincoln that was five cars down from them. They both were parked in the same row of cars. I was parked farther out in the parking lot, close to the main street, about 30 yards away from them. I could see everything.

Doing a quick count, there were four people walking in and out of The Spa Castle and about twenty automobiles in this big parking lot at 11:53 A.M. As long as there were no laws around, we were good.

Kenny went towards the driver's side, as her bodyguard pushed the door open to get out, before the bodyguard saw Kenny walking towards him, ski mask up with a 12-gauge shotgun pointed on his target. As soon as he put his foot out the car door, Kenny fired three slugs, hitting him. Right after Kenny's first shot, Poppa fired four dome shots from his Glock into the window of the Lincoln.

Kenny and Poppa peered inside the broken windows with their guns pointed, just in case they had to shoot again. There was an older white couple who were walking on the sidewalk of the building when the shots fired, and they ran into The Spa Castle. A couple more other customers ran for cover as well. I couldn't see anybody else now. They were either hiding in their cars or inside the spa.

Kenny ran behind the parked cars while Poppa ran in front of the cars in the street.

Out of nowhere, I saw a black Lincoln speed in front of my view, running right into Poppa. Before I thought about blowing the horn to warn him, it was too late. Poppa didn't know what hit him. He went over the hood, hitting the front windows, and went flying to the ground.

A young tall, muscular white guy got out the black Lincoln. Before he could get around to where Poppa was, I pulled the trigger four times. Two bullets hit an SUV, and the other two hit him in his left shoulder. He ducked low and got out of my eyesight.

I heard two gunshots. Poppa's Glock was a couple feet away from the driver's side of the Lincoln. My heart dropped. I knew that was Poppa who had gotten shot.

As soon as I questioned myself where the fuck was Lil' Kenny at, I saw him coming around a blue Suburban with the shotgun pointed. He released three shots at him. I saw a model I saw at the fashion show who coupled with Khole, in the backseat of the Lincoln. I didn't want to fuck with her, but I could tell she knew who I was. She looked me right in my eyes with fear in hers, and said, "Please, Monopoly, don't kill me."

I shot her twice in the head. My heart was pounding hard. I was scared to death of getting caught, and then I just said fuck it. It is what it is.

I picked up Poppa's Glock and then walked over to him. The bodyguard was laid on top of Poppa's head and shoulders. Once we rolled the big dead bodyguard off Poppa, we saw that he had two bullet holes in his head. I shook my head, and then grabbed the bodyguard's pistol. We hurried to pick up Poppa's lean, tall body, and then rushed him to the backseat of the car they were driving. Lil' Kenny got into the passenger's seat, and I drove.

The whole time I was driving back to South Dallas, I thought this took the cake on me being the scariest I'd ever been in my life. I did my best to drive the speed limit, but I kept catching myself going a little over the speed limit on Highway 181. Because of the blood all over me and the car being stolen, if I got stopped by the cops, I was a goner.

I could tell Lil' Kenny was ready to kill something else from the evil look on his face. I was fucked up too about Poppa being dead. I cared and had mad love for lil' homie. We'd become pretty close over these last couple of years. Poppa and Lil' Kenny were closer than he and I were. They'd been knowing each other since pre-school, and their mothers were like each other's mother.

Anyway, I knew Lil' Kenny was down for me, but what I didn't know was if Poppa's death would end our friendship and the loyalty he supposedly had for me. You never knew with these young niggas these days.

Three minutes later, I parked the car behind an abandoned building that used to be Truette Elementary School right beside Bonton Projects. After we got out and met up in front of the car, I told Lil' Kenny, "I'ma catch up with you in about 30 minutes. I'ma 'bout to change clothes and come right back."

"I ma 'bout to do the same. Get Poppa's blood off me," he said sadly.

"We going to Janet's house. We gotta tell her out of respect," I told him.

"I know."

We gave each other dap and we went our separate ways. He went to the projects while I walked to one of the three houses on Myrtle my first cousin Bobby owned. Two of them were five-dollar powder, wet, crack houses, and the other was a stash spot. My Rolls Royce was parked inside the stash spot in his garage.

I was spooked about leaving my car here because Bobby's traps were booming, and one of them got hit last week. Three niggas went to jail, so I decided to take a quick shower at a room. I went to a cheap ass motel on Martin Luther King Jr. Street and 175. I paid for two hours, a room that I was in for 15 minutes. I put on an outfit that I had in my trunk, put the old one in a plastic bag, and then headed back to the projects.

Halfway there, I got a call from Lil' Kenny. "Don't come back to the projects. 8 Ball said he gon' do you something if you do. I told him it was my fault, but he not trying to hear it."

I got fired up. "What! I don't care what he talking 'bout. I'm on my way, bro," I said as I hung up.

I didn't like assuming things, so the whole three-minute drive there, I thought about what I would do if he really started tripping. I knew one thing was guaranteed, he would bust his gun. And so would I, if I had to. I just hoped it didn't go that far. We were too cool for that, that wasn't for us.

After pulling up at the stop sign on Myrtle and Bexar, I saw a couple of patrol cars on the side of the building towards the back. I acted like everything was normal, making a left on Myrtle. I crossed the railroad tracks, and then made a right into the projects.

There were about eight big building units on each side. I went to the third building to the end. It was where Poppa's mother, Janet, and 8 Ball stayed but in two different apartments. I believed the main reason 8 Ball was tripping so hard was because he looked at Poppa as a son, even though 8 Ball and Janet weren't together. They were just fucking.

As soon as 8 Ball saw my Rolls Royce pull up, he stood and took some steps forward down the porch. The niggas behind him followed his lead. I knew all six niggas with him. One of them was Bobby, my first cousin. All of them were bloods, my hood niggas I was cool with, but they were going to ride with 8 Ball before they did me.

Since the parking lot was full, I parked in the street, right in the street behind some parked cars and trucks. 8 Ball pulled his strap out of his waist band. He told the dawgs something, and then he started walking towards my car as I was getting out of it.

"Nigga, you didn't get my message!" he said before stopping about 15 feet away from me in the dirt between the building and parking lot.

"Yeah, I got yo message. I didn't come for no trouble. I just came to talk to Janet, bro."

"Nigga, you think she want to talk to you after what happened? Get the fuck up outta here before you be next." He raised his .45 up at me. I raised my hands up in the air.

Lil' Kenny walked in front of me. "8 Ball, it wasn't his fault. It was my fault. I didn't make it to him in time."

I put my hands down and took two steps forward. "Fuck that, Kenny, this nigga's trippin'. Nigga, we done lost a bunch of niggas in war over blood, bro," I said as I threw the big B up in front of me, and I wasn't even a blood anymore. But I did it for effect. "Now you fucked up at me because of a young dawg getting killed for putting in work for me. Nigga, fuck you, you gon' have to kill me. I'ma go where I please. I was a G before I was a P."

A small crowd started to form close to us. "Watch out, Monopoly," Lil' Kenny yelled out, but it was too late. I felt a hard punch that connected to my right ear, and then another to the left jaw, making me fall to the ground.

That shit stung like a motherfucker. I did my best to shake the effects of the punches off. The blow that hit me on my upper jaw had me a little dizzy. By the time I got up, Lil' Kenny and Chris, the nigga who beefed for me, were in the mix. A nigga we called Budd ran up on me. We squared up, and seconds later, we went into a blend. He threw a right jab. I weaved it, and I swung a right hook, followed by a left jab, connecting both. He stumbled back wildly. I tripped him with my right leg, making him fall backwards on his ass. I looked back to see Chris about to stomp Lil' Kenny out, but before I could rush over towards him to help, there were two gunshots fired that stopped everybody in their tracks.

I looked at the direction the shots came from to see Black and Duke, Lil' Kenny's big brother and uncle, heading in our direction.

I was glad Black had come before it was blood shed out here. Black had more respect and credibility in our hood than 8 Ball did. Young niggas in our hood would put in work for Black before they would for 8 Ball, on the strength that Black did more for our hood. He put a lot of niggas out the hood on money. He supplied more than ten spots with dope, and only had niggas that we knew in them. He also had two barbershops in South Dallas, threw block parties quarterly, and owned a little league football team.

Black was the same nigga Bobby, my first cousin, and I tried to rob eight years ago. 8Ball, on the other hand, only fucked with a handful of dudes hard out our hood by putting them on in spots and using them as security when he did shows and parties. On the strength of 8Ball fucking with niggas outside the hood, he had a bunch of pull in other hoods in Dallas.

"Chris, if you kick my lil' brother, I'ma kill yo' young ass out here, boy. Get yo' ass up, Ken."

After Lil' Kenny got up, he dusted himself off, and then touched his swollen lips. Damn, my nigga helped me out. He wasn't about no punching, but he was about that pistol play for sure.

He turned to the young niggas that were riding with 8Ball. "Bet not nothing happen to my lil' brother or Monopoly. Or it's gon' be some shit, that's including you too, 8Ball. Whatever happened is dead. Come on, Ken."

Five young boys around the age of 8 to 11 came running from between the project buildings from the back of them, making police noises and yelling that the police were coming down the road into the projects.

Everybody that had something going on or didn't want to deal with the laws scattered out, not wanting to be seen by the laws. I got in my Double R and fled the scene, leaving out rom out the back of the projects. I wasn't worried about the laws pulling me over now. I was in my car now and I had my Masonic sticker on my bumper as well as my other identification information on me to get me out of a traffic stop. I didn't even talk to Janet about what had happened and give her money for the funeral. I'd just have to come back to-morrow or give her a call for her to meet me somewhere to talk to her. It was too hot around here. I would let the heat die down with the laws first.

***

I didn't have any problems out of 8Ball, Chris, nor Budd when I went to the jects to go talk to Janet and give her the money for the wake and funeral. Black told me that he had meet up with the three of them to squash everything after things calmed down.

Four days later, we had Poppa's wake in a Baptist Church in South Dallas. Erika, Bre, and I went to it that night. Two young females and a young dude I didn't know walked alongside of us with RIP shirts with a picture of Poppa on them.

There were about 200 people here that attended his wake. After talking with a few people, the girls and I got in a line of about 15 people to see Poppa's corpse.

It took us seventeen minutes to get to the expensive walnut casket. Poppa looked peaceful, as if he was sound asleep. I was surprised he didn't have a closed casket, knowing he had gotten shot twice in the head. The two places he got shot in were patched up with something different of the color of his skin. Other than that, he looked the same.

My hoes and I were fucked up to see the lil' homie like this. Most of my models had become close with Poppa and Lil' Kenny, because they were around us a lot as bodyguards. He was like a lil' brother to them. Erika dropped some tears for Poppa. I embraced her for a few seconds until I heard some commotion behind us.

I looked back to see Janet holding some young nigga back about 25 feet away, who was looking at me with tears streaming down his face.

"Janet, this nigga got my cousin killed, let me dust this nigga boots!"

Even though I didn't see a gun in his hands, I knew he had one on him. I didn't know him from Adam.

"Calm down, Dee! We don't need more bloodshed."

I turned and told my girls, "Y'all stay back. Let me straighten this shit out. Only use that if called for, Erika." I was referring to her pistol in her purse. I had my hoes register and buy a firearm for protection.

I walked over towards them. He started yelling at me. "Nigga, I'ma smoke yo' boots! I promise you that!"

"Look, man, I didn't come here for all that. I just came to show my respect to my lil' homie and leave."

"Nigga, I did, tho'. I came for some gunplay," said Dee.

"I told yo' ass to calm down. It's not gon' be none of that in here, Dee. If you keep on, you gon' be leaving yoself. I'm not playing."

Dee raised his shirt up. 8Ball jumped in front of Janet. He pushed Dee hard where he stepped back our feet. "Dee, you heard what yo' auntie said, nigga. It ain't gon' be none of that shit in here. You gon' show her some respect while I'm here, lil' nigga."

He still had his hand on his tool with a mug and tears streaming down his face. "Oh, Dee, you bucking a big dawg. You want some problems, nigga."

Niggas out my hood stepped up closer but stopped when Dee let go of his gun. "Yeah, that's what I thought. Nigga, give me this muthafuckin' gun," he said while taking it out his waistband.

Janet hugged Dee, comforting him and softly talking to him in his ear to calm him down. "I apologize to you both for what happened," I said, talking to Janet and 8Ball.

I had to show some respect. He was still my big dawg, even though we were going through some things. 8Ball really did that for Janet, but I saw he was for me also.

When I called my girls over and we were heading out, I heard 8Ball tell Dee, "Here. And nothing bet not happen to him when you leave. It's gon' be some shit you can't get yoself out of if you do."

That meant he still had love for me. I reminded myself to give him a call later on.

Chapter 18
Vote Christie Giddens for Mayor
Monopoly

Every day for a week, I'd been seeing advertisements about Christie's campaign on my Facebook page. Christie and a couple of her friends on Facebook were my friends also. They reposted her post almost as much as Christie did. Also, around the city, they had billboards up that read Vote Christie Giddens for Mayor, and a pretty photo of her. On the day she was to speak for her campaign, I tuned in, watching it on my projector in my theater room with Claire, Erika, Bre, and Elisha.

"I was born Christie Giddens at Park Land Hospital here in Dallas, Texas. As a child, I grew up with my younger sister in Mesquite, Texas. I graduated from Mesquite High then graduated from SMU Dedman school of Criminal Law with a Master's degree in Criminal Justice. Shortly after, I became a lawyer to fight for justice for the innocent and fight for fair sentencing for the guilty. With hard work and dedication, I became a high-priced attorney very quickly. Since my childhood, my father and mother have been entrepreneurs, who owned a few franchises. I took after them, and I now own four businesses. I have a bunch of leaders in my life. The main two are my father and fiancé."

Damn, I didn't know he asked her to marry him. That came as a surprise. I didn't notice the big ass diamond on her finger until she said that. I wondered what his plans were for Christie in the future.

"Through them, I have learned from observing their experiences, and the two embedded purpose, values, leadership, being business minded, and entrepreneurship in me. When I become mayor, I will lead this city with those characteristics. In criminal law, I've been the number one lawyer in Dallas-Fort Worth. I could have easily gone for judge, but I wanted a tougher challenge to overcome. I've been living in Dallas my whole life. I know what needs to be improved in Dallas. I know what needs to be done. I know what the people of Dallas want because I have those same needs and wants. The people of Dallas need more jobs created. The people want a freeze on property taxes and business taxes. The people want the improvement of recreational facilities. The people want the city's money to be spent wisely. The people want a better educational system."

The crowd started yelling out her name and raising the yellow and red signs that read Vote Christie Giddens for Mayor. That made her smile.

Seconds later, she started speaking again. "Calm down, calm down, please. My team and I have the ability, vision, and responsibility to contribute to a better, more successful Dallas. Also, upon being your mayor, I promise to run two foundations. A Community Fund and Annual Golf Classic. I have a long list of sponsors, and I can promise you all that every dollar from those foundations will be donated to this city. Dallas city dwellers will be in good hands."

After her speech, I started thinking about Christie's campaign to be the mayor of Dallas. Tight Game really knew what he was doing. Even though he was out the Game, having a ho that you'd actually pimped on become mayor was really a huge accomplishment for an ex-pimp. From this accomplishment, I didn't understand why he still wanted to kill her. I understood she deserved death for her actions, but I would have let her live, and punished her in a proper way. But this was Tight Game that I was talking about. He was very serious about loyalty and honor. If he didn't kill her, I would still look at him in the same light I always had. A man with Game tighter than a tick's asshole. He knew what was best for himself.

Chapter 19
The Masonic Meeting
Monopoly

Timothy told me before service that the brother needed to discuss something he did not know about. Damn near the whole time during our meeting, I was wondering what could it be. If the issue was associated with the Masons, I'd been doing everything I was supposed to be doing. I'd been paying my fees and I had been coming to our meetings every week unless I was out of town, and even then, I was checking in in those cities, so it couldn't be the absence. The only thing I could think of was the pimpin'. And sure enough as shit stinks, that was brought up after service, but in a more fucked up way than I thought.

"Damion, you have become a disappointment and disgrace to our lodge with the things you're getting yourself into. After giving you a chance to get yourself together, you still failed us, better yet, failed yourself. We can't tolerate your criminal activity anymore. Before we vote you out, Mark has something to tell you," Tony, our Worshippedful master, had said, referring to our brother who worked for the FBI.

"Damion, my department received an anonymous tip yesterday from a man saying that you're prostituting women out of your modeling agency." I was about to say something, but he cut me off and said, "Before you say anything, I'm not asking you if it's true or not. All of the men in this room know that call holds some kind of truth. Because I respect you, I believe you should know what was said so you can save yourself from a harsh sentencing when it comes cracking down on you. I'm informing you now, you need to clean up whatever you got going on, because we've started our investigation on Thursday on you and your modeling agency. If we don't find anything within a few months, we'll end the investigation. It might be sooner or it might be longer. Since you have a prior charge of relative activities, it might be longer."

This news wasn't a big deal, because the prostitution was covered up. However, it was bad news that I wished could go away.

This time, I definitely would be giving the life up for good. I had been taking too many losses. I had to give it up. I chuckled inside. This was what had to take place for me to leave the Game. Really, it was a lose/lose situation now. I was about to start getting investigated for pimpin', and today I would be expelled out the institution of Masonry. It was a sad day, because I would be giving up two things I loved being in life. I could still live a good life without being a Mason. The only problems I would have was most of my resources would be stripped away from me. That was the part I was going to hate. With the Game, at least Monopoly would be remembered as a stand-up pimp, and I did it in a major way like the Game should be played. I was really proud of myself for that. I wouldn't take it back for nothing in the world.

The Secretary, Tyler, Lodge Master, Grand Master, Most Worshipful Master, two deacons, and past master, all voting members, voted me out for the reason you already know.

I wasn't tripping about Tight Game, our grand Master, voting me out. I understand all of them. They were all tired of my mess and wanted no part of my situation to link back to them when the feds started their investigation. Everyone, except for Tight Game, Timothy, and two other masonic brothers, told me to delete their numbers out my phone. Timothy told me to call any time I needed something, that he was there for me. Tight Game told me after the meeting to head to his mansion in Highland Park because we needed to talk.

I walked out the lodge a non-active Mason. I would no longer be paying my dues to them anymore. It was a sad night, but, I had to move on with my life.

While driving, I called Tight Game, telling him that I was stopping for gas, and when I was done, I'd be on my way.

***

Tight Game

"I got a change of heart, Mr. Herbert," Elijah mentioned as I sat down at the table outside in the huge backyard.

"Change of heart in what, nephew?" Elijah looked to see if the glass patio door was shut, because he didn't want to be heard by Christie.

"In killing Christie. I don't care if she dies or not, but I don't want to be the one to do it." Elijah chuckled. "It's crazy what I did with that white girl. Even though I did it, I'm not into that weird stuff. I'm not my father, I'm not a murderer."

"I understand, nephew. It ain't for everybody." I was glad that he didn't want to seek revenge himself like he said he wanted to at first. That's what made me come up with the idea on the dominatrix shit. Anyway, he needed to focus on his future in football. He was a bright kid with a big future ahead of him. Killing someone would definitely fuck him up mentally and spiritually. He would never be the same afterwards.

***

Monopoly

When I got there, Christie opened the door and invited me in. "Are you here to tell Herbert what happened between us, are you? If so, I'm ready to tell him."

"Christie, that was months ago, I done moved on from that shit. If you want to let him know what happened, bitch, you tell him," I said before stepping into the big living room. "Where he at?"

"He's out back."

I knocked on the glass before sliding the patio door to the side and then going outside to the huge backyard. Tight Game uncrossed his legs when he saw me and took the cigar out his mouth. I grabbed a chair and turned it so I could sit facing the back of the chair and put my arms on top of it.

"You disappointed me, Tunke. After all the work and time I put into you, you still let me down."

I couldn't say nothing, because he was right. I fucked up.

"And what is this shit about you beefing with some white boy?"

I didn't have to ask him how he found out. He knew damn near everything that was going on with me. Plus, somebody put some crazy shit on YouTube talking about our beef. "Yeah, it's all over knocking Marilyn Sunshine from him."

"So, I heard. What part of the Game is it when you start killing women? Pimpin' don't get down like that."

"I know. He started the shit when he got his model to kill my ho. I wanted him to feel what I felt with my loss."

"He's not a pimp. He's not going to feel what you feel. You know better than that. Control your emotions, Tunke. Don't let that be your downfall. What you should have done was taken the sucker out first, which is the head, instead of them two women. Look, in two days, we'll go back to Dubai. While we're out there, the white boy will be taken care of. I want to bring you to the attention; I will not be killing Christie."

Why was I surprised right now? I didn't know. I guess because I believed him when he said she'd be next to die! From hearing her campaign speech, I would have changed my mind also. I would have never considered killing her in the first place, if I was planning on one of my queens becoming mayor. "Why did you change your mind?" I asked out of curiosity.

"Like I was telling Elijah, when I think about it, I was a little crazy to start thinking about killing her. Yeah, it's sad and fucked up in the manner of what she did. Although, that is what a true queen is supposed to do for her king. I've worked hard on coaching and helping Christie build her career. It's me who inspired her through every step of the way to become a lawyer and then a candidate for mayor. She'll be better off alive than dead. Through her as mayoress, we, as in the three of us, can control aspects and influence the people of Dallas. Christie and I have ties to many things and to every race in the city, so we're destined to be a success."

"Did she tell you everything that happened when you were in a coma yet?" I asked, trying to see if I was getting played in any way by Christie.

"No, not yet. She's still trying to hide it."

"On my way out here, she told me she's ready to tell you," I told him.

"Well, we can get that out the way now." He called her on his cell, telling her to step out to the backyard.

When she came out, she studied all three of our faces. Even though I was still fucked up with her, I looked at her with a blank face. I didn't want to make her uncomfortable. I wanted her to feel comfortable in my presence so she could reveal all that she did.

Elijah, on the other hand, looked at her in a disturbing way that didn't make the situation any better. I guess he felt the same way I felt about this bitch holding that secret this long without telling Tight Game.

Tight Game smiled in a loving way the moment he looked at her when she slid the door open. He knew what he was doing. He ushered her to a chair next to him with his hand. "Tunke, tells me you want to tell me something."

She looked at me unpleasantly. "I understand your motive for doing what you did, and I forgive you," I said half-heartly. "It's okay, you can tell him what happened. He will understand."

All the attention was on her. Seconds later, she started off with telling Tight Game our sexual escapade. She let him know how she paid Jennifer to set me up, onto how she had Big Country kidnap me, and then went into how that got Big Country killed. Then she said, "I didn't know what else to do. I did everything for you."

"Bitch, hold the fuck up. Do not give me that bullshit. You didn't do that disloyal shit for me. You did that for your own selfish reasons. Bitch, you didn't have any facts. Your emotions drove you to do that shit. You know I would have never approved of you doing that shit to someone I call family. Like my nephew said, I do understand, but you're gonna pay for what you did. Since you're my family, you owe these two young men a huge apology, love, loyalty, and you're gonna compensate them in favors for their losses that you caused, until they feel you have paid your dues. Bitch, apologize and get the fuck up out of here. We'll talk later."

She did as she was told, and then went inside their home.

"I know you've done nothing but give to me. There's one last thing I want from you," I told Tight Game.

"What's that, nephew?"

"Naa'ilah and I have been talking every day since we went to Klaaliq's restaurant after Jumi service. We've been talking about marriage, with Baaqir's wishes. Can you arrange for us to talk when we get in Dubai?"

He smiled. "You must really like Naa'ilah."

"I do, Unk."

"You know you have to be Muslim to marry her?"

"Yeah, I know. I'm ready now."

Tight Game chuckled. "That investigation got you spooked, uhh?"

"I ain't gon' lie, yeah, it spooked me. I'm done with the Game, big bro. It's over. I'm not going back to the pen."

"As long as you out, you don't have nothing to worry about. Just keep your nose clean, youngin'. Do you have anything else going on that we need to fix before we go to Dubai? Naa'ilah's family are powerful religious people. You don't need any trouble, nothing coming back to haunt you, if you want to build that future with Baaqir's daughter. That's what you will have to do."

"Nall, I have an alibi for the murders. Other than that, I have nothing else going on."

After we sat and chopped it up for about two hours, I decided on spending the night here. I took one of the guest rooms to sleep in. I called Josh to inform him that we needed to meet up and talk tomorrow, which he agreed. Afterwards, I Face Timed all my hoes that were out of state one by one, except for my two hoes in Atlanta, telling them what was going on with me.

After I was finished, I told Toni and Candance on Facetime, "You're either goin' to quit hoin' and sign on to my agency, allow me to elevate your life through it, or you can let me guide you in the direction towards another certified pimp." I was referring to Solo and Serious Jones. Those two pimps had the proper program I knew Toni and Candance could vibe to. "Now, don't tell me you done hoin' and you still gon' do it. I'ma find out. It has to stop if you want to continue to fuck with me. Which one are y'all going to choose?"

"I'm good where I'm at," said Candance before she looked at Toni.

"Yeah, we good where we at. We not leaving you, Monopoly. We can stop hoing, but shit, Daddy, can we still dance at the club?" Toni asked me.

"Of course. I'm just talking about the selling pussy part. Everything else is good. I'll have Rose email you both the contracts and explain everything that needs to be done so you two can get rolling in modeling and get y'all some clientele."

After I got Toni and Candance situated, I sent a group text to all my hoes to be at my house at 1 P.M. When I finished, I went to sleep.

Smoove Dolla

Chapter 20
Changing for the Greater Good
Monopoly

After I took my shahadah, the declaration of faith, three Muslims including Tight Game greeted me with the Muslim greeting and embraced me.

I guess this was the next phase in my life, because I was totally out the Game. I would do what I had to do to stay out of the pen. I couldn't waste my time being in prison for no amount of time for something that wasn't even worth it. I had all the qualities to be somebody wealthy and very successful. I would use all my talents and gifts to make that happen.

Since yesterday, I'd been thinking heavily about moving to Dubai for a while. It seemed like it would be a great move with what was going on here in the U.S. in my life at the moment. Every time I talked to Naa'ilah, I got peace. She was my peace.

Tight Game left while I sat in the parking lot of the mosque in North Dallas. I called Naa'ilah on Facetime. "Assalamu alaikum," I said, greeting her as soon as she answered.

"Wa alaikum salam wa rahmatullah," she said, smiling.

Her jet-black hair was hanging down her back. This was my first time seeing her like this without her wearing a hijab. She looked the best I had ever seen her. "Is this what I'm going to be unwrapping, appreciating, loving, and waking up to every day?" I said as I pointed at her towards my Galaxy phone with two fingers, as I went up and down a couple times.

She blushed like crazy. "You don't supposed to be seeing me like this."

"I believe I do. You believe it too, because you would have never let me see you in such a way. Matter of fact, I'm 100% sure you're going to be my first wife one day soon."

"What makes you so sure? You haven't become Muslim yet."

"That's the reason why I'm calling you now. I just took my shahadah a while ago at this mosque," I said and turned my phone around to show her the mosque that I just walked out of.

"Allahu Akbar," she said excitedly, out loud. It meant Allah is the Greatest. We both started smiling hard.

"I have to be honest with you on the reasons why I did it. You got the right to know."

"It doesn't matter why, as long as you are a Muslim. Your sins are washed away now. We'll get through it together, whatever it is."

Damn, I really liked that coming from her. She had to be one of the ones for me. "It does matter, but we'll talk when I get there."

"When are you coming?" she asked eagerly.

"Some time tomorrow we'll be on our way. I don't mean to let you go, but I really have to take care of some things before we come to Dubai. Call me later, before you go to sleep, okay."

"Okay, I'll call you later."

Josh decided to come to my house. My other hoes that didn't live with me that stayed in the DFW area came also. I talked with Josh in my study room before I held the meeting with my hoes.

After I told him my situation, he asked, "How do you know if it's true or not? Who told you?"

"I can't tell you who, but it came from a valuable source, from someone I trust."

"So, what are you gonna do?"

"I'm not pimpin' no more. I got you here to tell you that if shit falls down with our company, I will take the blame. I'm not letting you go down for something I did," I said with sincerity.

He gave me a handshake and said, "That's real, bro."

"You shouldn't expect nothing else but that. A real man takes responsibility for his actions."

"Let's just hope everything turns out fine with this investigation."

"Yeah, I hope so, in my favor." Then I told him that I would be in Dubai for a while.

"Let's go talk with the girls."

I gathered up all my hoes in the theater room. There were three other models visiting at my house, chilling with everyone that lived here. I didn't allow them to come into the room while I talked to my queens. My hoes were the only ones prostituting. The other models weren't, so they didn't need to hear what we discussed.

I started off with, "I have some bad news to present to you all. Starting tomorrow, the feds will be investigating me and our modeling company."

"Really?" responded one of them, while the others wanted to know why.

I looked in all nine of my queens' eyes and studied their facial expressions. I couldn't see any betrayal. I trusted my own judgement, being that no one in this room was the cause of me being investigated. I had seven cameras around my home, and never once did I detect anything out of the ordinary. It had to be David who lit the flame.

"Yeah, yeah, some muthafucker dropped a tip on me. It couldn't be nobody but that muthafuckin' David from Perfect Models. This muthafucker can't handle a knock. He caused all of this bullshit. But he's not a pimp, so what happened should have been expected. Now I'm being investigated. So, before all this comes to a head that I'm really, really pimpin', I'm getting out the Game for good as we speak.

"This is it for me. I have too much legal shit going on to fuck it off on some illegal shit. When something you really love doing hurts your future more than it uplifts it, then you gotta let it go. Anyway, as far as our modeling agency is concerned, nothing is going to change. All the hoeing has to end now. I want you to cut all ties to tricks. Each one of you should have over $300,000 in your bank accounts, am I right?"

The nine of them nodded their heads yes.

"By this time next year, all of you will be millionaires. If you don't have anything legal going on, I want you to start thinking about enrolling in college for something or start your own business. Let Josh or me know your decision so we can make it happen. If you can't get down with my program, you can pack your shit and leave now. Your contract with us will be torn up." I gave them seconds to make up their minds to give up the life as I did or continue to play the Game without me. "So, your decision is to follow me.

Oh, yeah, I want y'all to go to the polls and vote for Christie Giddens for mayor tomorrow, or y'all can go to today. It doesn't matter.
Just go vote for her. Some things about to be in the making with that
move. Alright then, this conversation stays between us."

After our meeting, Rose and I went to my room to talk. We sat
on the bed facing each other.

"How have y'all been holding up?" I asked, referring to her,
Sarah, and their kids.

I hadn't talked to Rose nor Sarah since I got them the condo.
The only communication we'd had was through text, and that was
only three times within the last week. I talked with Rose's son a few
times since then, and that's because he missed me and my son, but
he was with Tiffany.

"It's been okay. I just been taking it a day at a time. What about
you, other than the bad news?"

"These last couple of weeks have been hell. Nothing but fucked
up shit. But for sure, I'ma get through it. I really been missing y'all
being around," I said as I grabbed her hands and put them in between mine. "I want to apologize to you again for what happened.
If—"

"It's okay, Monopoly. I know if you could have prevented it,
you would have. It's not your fault. Can you promise me something?"

"What?"

"That you'll do something to David. Make him pay for what he
did."

"I promise you I will."

After that, I made love to my Rose for about an hour. We got
out of bed and took a quick shower.

A short while later, everyone in my house went to a bowling
alley in Garland so we could all spend time together.

Chapter 21
Getting Permission
Monopoly

After arriving in Dubai, Tight Game, Elijah, and I rode to the Palace Palazzo Versace Hotel in a rented limo. Being at this hotel room was a real luxury for me. I loved the scenery. I would be here until I found a penthouse I really liked, that was fit for me. Tight Game and I took a quick shower and then headed to Baaqir's estate, leaving Elijah at the room.

Baaqir and his family lived in a huge mansion with other properties on over 100 acres of land. Tight told me that Baaqir's mansion and the other buildings were built by Khaaliq Properties. There were six other houses, a farmhouse with cattle, camels, and large gardens around his estate. About ten big families could live on this land. It was that big.

Our limo stopped on the side of two guards in front of Baaqir's estate. Tight Game rolled the window down. When the two guards saw who it was, they waved to another guard to open the golden gates.

Baaqir was outside waiting on us before our driver stopped. Baaqir opened the door for Tight Game. Our driver opened the door for me. Baaqir excitedly greeted Tight Game with a smile and a firm hug. When he got to me, he looked at me suspiciously but still shook my hand and greeted me with the universal Islamic greeting. This guy had on a ten-thousand-dollar long-sleeve robe on. I knew the cost because I saw it at the Mall of the Emirates last time I was here. Seeing that one piece of clothing cost 10 Gs was throwed to me. A man had to be making some real muthafuckin' money to do it like that.

After we went into the mansion, Tight Game and I sat on the long, pearl-white sofa while Baaqir sat in the same color love seat in the big living room. Baaqir and Tight Game chopped it up for eight minutes before Tight Game said to us, "Well, I'ma let you two men talk while I check out your library."

"Alright, akhi. Check out that book I was telling you about."

After Tight Game left, Baaqir asked me, "How's a Muslim?"

"I'm great. How are you?"

He didn't answer me. Instead, he asked me a question. "How and when did you and my daughter meet?"

I was sure he had asked Naa'ilah how and when we met, but I figured he was testing me to see if I would lie or hold back from him. I didn't. I told him the truth.

"What do you want from my daughter?" he asked, as he leaned forward in the love seat with his hands on his knees.

"You're a man with great knowledge to know that every woman is the beginning to a man's path to enlightenment. I need what she knows. I need her to bring me closer to Islam. I want her love. I want her hand in marriage."

"Mr. Johnson, how long have you been Muslim?"

"In all honesty, I've only been Muslim for three days now." His eyes widened, and his eyebrows raised up in shock. "Before you say anything, may I please get this out? I'm alive today because of Herbert. I'd be dead right now if I hadn't meet him. It's because of Herbert that I became a Prince Hall Mason five years ago. It was him that put the idea in my head about being Muslim back in 2006, and that idea motivated me to study Islam. What I learned turned out to be beautiful. But the reason why I didn't become Muslim back then was because I wasn't ready. I wasn't ready to take on that challenge of changing. I did it three days ago because I'm ready now. Everything that I've said I am, I've truly lived as. And I am going to live as a Muslim now, and not go daalin," I said. Daalin meant a Muslim who went astray. "There are more things I would like to say. I know that I'm not what you pictured for Naa'ilah, so I understand if you don't like me or won't accept me. But I am begging you to give me a chance to be with your daughter. That's all I have to say. My actions will show and prove that I'm for Naa'ilah."

He leaned back in his seat. "You're right, you being with my daughter, isn't what I had in mind for her. I wanted Naa'ilah to marry a son from one of the royal families here in Dubai, but she doesn't want that. She wants you. I see you are an intelligent and driven young man. Herbert spoke highly of you. If Herbert vouches for you, I'll give you a chance," he said in a strong accent in English, and then stood up.

I stood because he did. He offered his hand to me. He squeezed my hand a little tighter than a normal handshake. "But I'm warning you now, don't hurt Naa'ilah."

I didn't respond to what he just said, all I asked was, "Where is she?"

"She's at Al Warsan Lake."

I smiled, because that was the place where she and I first met, at her favorite place. "I told Naa'ilah that I'll get a lake built here on our land with birds she likes, but she insists on going to that lake every morning."

"She really loves feeding the birds there. Excuse me, Baaqir, I know I just got here, but I really need to catch her before she leaves the lake. Baaqir, do you have a loaf of bread here?"

***

Jon Jon, Darius, and Lonny had been following David for forty minutes now. Lonny had been telling Jon Jon that he wanted to murk him thirty minutes ago, until Jon Jon got tired of hearing Lonny's mouth and said, "Fuck it." They were both driving on 114 in North Dallas traffic.

"Jon Jon, line up the van with the Mayback," said Lonny.

Right after Lonny raised the baby choppa towards the Mayback door, he nodded his head for Darius to slide the van's door to the side.

The driver saw the door slide open. Fear appeared in his eyes and shock masked his face when he saw the choppa pointed at him. David sat in the back seat, and he looked more afraid than his bodyguard.

David hit the driver's seat hard multiple times, telling him to speed off, but it was too late. Lonny fired shots into the driver's side door. Lonny worked the choppa side to side, back and forth, hitting the left front tire to both doors as well as the driver's window. The choppa's bullets hit the driver's face, fucking him all the way up.

David jumped out the car on the passenger side back door before it swerved off the freeway onto the service road in rapid speed, until it went up the steep hill up under the underpass, and then flipped over onto the service road upside down.

Lonny had noticed David running up the steep hill of grass. "Stop this van. The white boy jumped out the car, bro. I'm 'bout to walk 'em down."

The van's tires made a stretching sound when he stomped on the brakes on the service road. Lonny jumped out the van. He left one foot on the ground and put the other on the steep, grassy hill. He aimed the baby choppa at David, who was wildly running up the hill.

Lonny started letting rounds off at places in the grass where David's feet had been, until the bullets reached his legs. The bullets tore into his backside then up his back and ended at his head. The remainder of David's body landed sideways right on the side of Lonny.

After Lonny saw that he was dead, he hurried to get in the van. Jon Jon burned rubber and got into the thin traffic on 114.

***

It was a pretty, 78-degree, sunny morning. The last time I was out here, it was like this every day. I could get used to this every day.

Naa'ilah's bodyguard was in the same spot he was always in in the morning while watching her. I nodded my head to him, and he just looked at me.

I waited until a few runners passed by and walked over to Naa'ilah.

"Naa'ilah, baby, you mind if I join you?"

She was wrapped three-fourths in a hijab and expensive robe. She closed her eyes and smiled. She opened them after a couple seconds. "You know you can any time you want. I missed you, Damion," she said in a sexy Arabic accent.

I grabbed her hand to stand her up, and then we hugged each other. We gave each other a kiss. "I missed you too, Naa'ilah. How are you?"

After she sat down, she said, "I'm great now since you're here. How did you know I was here?"

I picked up the bread bag that had three pieces of bread inside of it, and I replaced it with a full loaf of bread in between us. I took three slices out of it. I tried to hurry up so we could start on the new loaf of bread. "This is where you are every morning. But your father told me you were here."

"Oh, you talked to him?" By the time she had asked that, I was tearing the second slice in four and then feeding it to the birds.

"Yeah, we had a good little conversation. I had asked him for your hand in marriage."

"What was his answer?" Naa'ilah asked.

I threw the last piece of bread that was in fours, and then I opened the new loaf to get the end bread out of it.

As I was telling her about what her father and I discussed, she reached inside the bread bag to retrieve a slice of bread, but instead, she grabbed two slices and her $300,000 engagement ring I had put in the bag on the ride here. I hoped it fit her finger.

"What is this?" she asked as she opened the ring box. I didn't know how they did it out here in Dubai and in Islam, but I hoped she accepted my ring and said yes.

When she looked at me, I said, "Naa'ilah, you're the main reason why I became Muslim. My second reason is because I got tired of the results I was getting in my past life. When you came into my life, something changed within me. I knew you were someone worth acquiring even before I knew the meaning of your name. You have this certain unique force that pulled me into you, and during the process of getting to know you, it inspired me to change and want to do better. I'm dealing with a bunch of things in the U.S., but that's not why I want to be with you for life. I promise you, from this moment on, every day I will cherish you, love all of you, respect you to the fullest. I will be nothing less than a man, nothing less than a good Muslim man, nothing less than a good husband.

Naa'ilah, may I have your hand in marriage?" I put my hand out, palm up.

She smiled, showing her deep dimples. "You can have all of me, Damion."

When she put her hand in mine, I put the ring on her finger, which was a little too tight, but it went on.

Chapter 22
A New Life
Five Months Later
Monopoly

Having Naa'ilah in my life was one of the best things that had ever happened to me. She had made life better for me. Being with her had brought me closer to Islam. It was her who introduced Islam to Shae and Pinky, and Naa'ilah who was teaching them how to be Muslim women. I had them move to Dubai with me until their eighth month of pregnancy, and then we went back to the states, leaving Naa'ilah in Dubai. Even though she was my wife now, I didn't want to disrespect Baaqir in any way, and plus, I didn't know what I was going back to when I touched down back in Dallas.

Anyway, when we went back to the states, I didn't hear too much about those murders nor the investigation. Josh, Marilyn Sunshine, and Rose had the same story, that they all had a couple cars following them for two months, but they never pulled them over. They probably were waiting on me to do the same thing too. After being in the U.S. for a month and a half, I didn't see anything out the ordinary. I started thinking I should have come here sooner so they could do the same to me and get it over with, instead of acting like I was running and hiding. If they would have fucked with me, I would have accepted my fate.

The court set my trial date twice since the last time I went to court to set my speedy trial. They were doing their best to find Jennifer but gave up and just dropped my charges a month ago.

As far as the movie with Paul Turner, the auditions were set for April 10th, which was 24 days away. Marilyn Sunshine had the role for sure, but I hoped Erika was good enough to make the role. She was supposed to graduate from performing arts school in August. But if she didn't, I would buy a good leading role in a short film script that was fit for her. She was going to make it under my management.

My baby, Syn, was blowing up quick. The video we did for her in Cali was the hottest video out. Record labels were calling me and

Josh for deals. We paid an entertainer lawyer to go over the contracts. She signed a 360 deal with Sony Records. She was mad at me because I gave the manager position to Josh. I told her I still love her and I'm there for her but Dubai is where I needed to be.

A couple of months after my son and daughter were born Shae, Pinky, our children, and I flew to Dubai. Shae left her shop to a friend to run that had a booth in her shop. I felt bad because I took her away frm living her dreams in life for me. I would think of something for her to do in Dubai with doing hair.

Since I wasn't helping Tiffany, my son's momma with our clothing business. I let her buy my shares for 1.5 million dollars. As far as the clothing line she wanted me out her hair. It was the best thing to do, I've did what I needed to do to help her business thrive.

As far as my career went, I bought a whole studio so I could make as many songs that I could and finished my record contract with Forever Records.

Nowadays, majority of my time went to my family. Nothing else mattered to me. After Shae and Pinky converted to Islam, I married them both separately at the same mosque

I married Naa'ilah. It was a beautiful thing having three wives who all loved me, cared for me and was loyal to me. Allah has truly blessed me.

I was curious about what Tight Game had planned for us and the city of Dallas. He was making some boss moves like always.

Whenever I get back to the States, I'm definitely going to use my favors from Christie.

She definitely owed me that.

To Be Continued…
Money Game 3
Coming Soon

Lock Down Publications and Ca$h Presents assisted
publishing packages.

BASIC PACKAGE $499
Editing
Cover Design
Formatting

UPGRADED PACKAGE $800
Typing
Editing
Cover Design
Formatting

ADVANCE PACKAGE $1,200
Typing
Editing
Cover Design
Formatting
Copyright registration
Proofreading
Upload book to Amazon

LDP SUPREME PACKAGE $1,500
Typing
Editing
Cover Design
Formatting
Copyright registration
Proofreading
Set up Amazon account
Upload book to Amazon
Advertise on LDP Amazon and Facebook page

***Other services available upon request. Additional charges may apply
Lock Down Publications
P.O. Box 944
Stockbridge, GA 30281-9998
Phone # 470 303-9761

Submission Guideline

Submit the first three chapters of your completed manuscript to ldpsubmissions@gmail.com, subject line: Your book's title. The manuscript must be in a .doc file and sent as an attachment. Document should be in Times New Roman, double spaced and in size 12 font. Also, provide your synopsis and full contact information. If sending multiple submissions, they must each be in a separate email.

Have a story but no way to send it electronically? You can still submit to LDP/Ca$h Presents. Send in the first three chapters, written or typed, of your completed manuscript to:

LDP: Submissions Dept
Po Box 944
Stockbridge, Ga 30281

DO NOT send original manuscript. Must be a duplicate.

Provide your synopsis and a cover letter containing your full contact information.

Thanks for considering LDP and Ca$h Presents.

<u>NEW RELEASES</u>

QUEEN OF THE ZOO by BLACK MIGO
MOB TIES 4 by SAYNOMORE
THE BRICK MAN by KING RIO
KINGZ OF THE GAME by PLAYA RAY
VICIOUS LOYALTY by KINGPEN
STRAIGHT BEAST MODE by DEKARI
COKE KINGS 5 by T.J. EDWARDS
MONEY GAME 2 by SMOOVE DOLLA

<u>Coming Soon from Lock Down Publications/Ca$h Presents</u>

BLOOD OF A BOSS **VI**

SHADOWS OF THE GAME II

TRAP BASTARD II

By **Askari**

LOYAL TO THE GAME **IV**

By **T.J. & Jelissa**

IF TRUE SAVAGE **VIII**

MIDNIGHT CARTEL IV

DOPE BOY MAGIC IV

CITY OF KINGZ III

NIGHTMARE ON SILENT AVE II

By **Chris Green**

BLAST FOR ME **III**

A SAVAGE DOPEBOY III

CUTTHROAT MAFIA III

DUFFLE BAG CARTEL VII

HEARTLESS GOON VI

By **Ghost**

A HUSTLER'S DECEIT III

KILL ZONE II

BAE BELONGS TO ME III

By **Aryanna**

KING OF THE TRAP III

By **T.J. Edwards**

GORILLAZ IN THE BAY V

3X KRAZY III

STRAIGHT BEAST MODE II

De'Kari

KINGPIN KILLAZ IV

STREET KINGS III

PAID IN BLOOD III

CARTEL KILLAZ IV

DOPE GODS III

Hood Rich

SINS OF A HUSTLA II

ASAD

RICH $AVAGE II

By Troublesome

YAYO V

Bred In The Game 2

S. Allen

CREAM III

By Yolanda Moore

SON OF A DOPE FIEND III

HEAVEN GOT A GHETTO II

By Renta

LOYALTY AIN'T PROMISED III

By Keith Williams

I'M NOTHING WITHOUT HIS LOVE II

SINS OF A THUG II

TO THE THUG I LOVED BEFORE II

By Monet Dragun

QUIET MONEY IV

EXTENDED CLIP III

THUG LIFE IV

By **Trai'Quan**

THE STREETS MADE ME IV

By **Larry D. Wright**

IF YOU CROSS ME ONCE II

By **Anthony Fields**

THE STREETS WILL NEVER CLOSE II

By K'ajji

HARD AND RUTHLESS III

THE BILLIONAIRE BENTLEYS II

Von Diesel

KILLA KOUNTY II

By Khufu

MONEY GAME III

By Smoove Dolla

A GANGSTA'S KARMA II

By FLAME

JACK BOYZ VERSUS DOPE BOYZ

A DOPEBOY'S DREAM III

By Romell Tukes

MURDA WAS THE CASE II

Elijah R. Freeman

THE STREETS NEVER LET GO II

By Robert Baptiste

AN UNFORESEEN LOVE III

By **Meesha**

KING OF THE TRENCHES II
by **GHOST & TRANAY ADAMS**

MONEY MAFIA

By **Jibril Williams**

QUEEN OF THE ZOO II

By **Black Migo**

THE BRICK MAN II

By King Rio

VICIOUS LOYALTY II

By Kingpen

Available Now

RESTRAINING ORDER **I & II**

By **CA$H & Coffee**

LOVE KNOWS NO BOUNDARIES **I II & III**

By **Coffee**

RAISED AS A GOON I, II, III & IV

BRED BY THE SLUMS I, II, III

BLAST FOR ME I & II

ROTTEN TO THE CORE I II III

A BRONX TALE I, II, III

DUFFLE BAG CARTEL I II III IV V VI

HEARTLESS GOON I II III IV V

A SAVAGE DOPEBOY I II

DRUG LORDS I II III

CUTTHROAT MAFIA I II

KING OF THE TRENCHES

By **Ghost**

LAY IT DOWN **I & II**

LAST OF A DYING BREED I II

BLOOD STAINS OF A SHOTTA I & II III

By **Jamaica**

LOYAL TO THE GAME I II III

LIFE OF SIN I, II III

By **TJ & Jelissa**

BLOODY COMMAS I & II

SKI MASK CARTEL I II & III

KING OF NEW YORK I II,III IV V

RISE TO POWER I II III

COKE KINGS I II III IV V

BORN HEARTLESS I II III IV

KING OF THE TRAP I II

By **T.J. Edwards**

IF LOVING HIM IS WRONG…I & II

LOVE ME EVEN WHEN IT HURTS I II III

By **Jelissa**

WHEN THE STREETS CLAP BACK I & II III

THE HEART OF A SAVAGE I II III

MONEY MAFIA

By **Jibril Williams**

A DISTINGUISHED THUG STOLE MY HEART I II & III

LOVE SHOULDN'T HURT I II III IV

RENEGADE BOYS I II III IV

PAID IN KARMA I II III

SAVAGE STORMS I II

AN UNFORESEEN LOVE I II

By **Meesha**

A GANGSTER'S CODE I &, II III

A GANGSTER'S SYN I II III

THE SAVAGE LIFE I II III

CHAINED TO THE STREETS I II III

BLOOD ON THE MONEY I II III

By J-Blunt

PUSH IT TO THE LIMIT

By **Bre' Hayes**

BLOOD OF A BOSS **I, II, III, IV, V**

SHADOWS OF THE GAME

TRAP BASTARD

By **Askari**

THE STREETS BLEED MURDER **I, II & III**

THE HEART OF A GANGSTA I II& III

By **Jerry Jackson**

CUM FOR ME I II III IV V VI VII

An **LDP Erotica Collaboration**

BRIDE OF A HUSTLA **I II & II**

THE FETTI GIRLS **I, II& III**

CORRUPTED BY A GANGSTA I, II III, IV

BLINDED BY HIS LOVE

THE PRICE YOU PAY FOR LOVE I, II ,III

DOPE GIRL MAGIC I II III

By **Destiny Skai**

WHEN A GOOD GIRL GOES BAD

By **Adrienne**

THE COST OF LOYALTY I II III

By Kweli

A GANGSTER'S REVENGE **I II III & IV**

THE BOSS MAN'S DAUGHTERS I II III IV V

A SAVAGE LOVE **I & II**

BAE BELONGS TO ME I II

A HUSTLER'S DECEIT I, II, III

WHAT BAD BITCHES DO I, II, III

SOUL OF A MONSTER I II III

KILL ZONE

A DOPE BOY'S QUEEN I II III

By **Aryanna**

A KINGPIN'S AMBITON

A KINGPIN'S AMBITION **II**

I MURDER FOR THE DOUGH

By **Ambitious**

TRUE SAVAGE I II III IV V VI VII

DOPE BOY MAGIC I, II, III

MIDNIGHT CARTEL I II III

CITY OF KINGZ I II

NIGHTMARE ON SILENT AVE

By **Chris Green**

A DOPEBOY'S PRAYER

By **Eddie "Wolf" Lee**

THE KING CARTEL **I, II & III**

By **Frank Gresham**

THESE NIGGAS AIN'T LOYAL **I, II & III**

By **Nikki Tee**

GANGSTA SHYT **I II &III**

By **CATO**

THE ULTIMATE BETRAYAL

By **Phoenix**

BOSS'N UP **I , II & III**

By **Royal Nicole**

I LOVE YOU TO DEATH

By **Destiny J**

I RIDE FOR MY HITTA

I STILL RIDE FOR MY HITTA

By **Misty Holt**

LOVE & CHASIN' PAPER

By **Qay Crockett**

TO DIE IN VAIN

SINS OF A HUSTLA

By **ASAD**

BROOKLYN HUSTLAZ

By **Boogsy Morina**

BROOKLYN ON LOCK I & II

By **Sonovia**

GANGSTA CITY

By **Teddy Duke**

A DRUG KING AND HIS DIAMOND I & II III

A DOPEMAN'S RICHES

HER MAN, MINE'S TOO I, II

CASH MONEY HO'S

THE WIFEY I USED TO BE I II

By **Nicole Goosby**

TRAPHOUSE KING **I II & III**

KINGPIN KILLAZ I II III

STREET KINGS I II

PAID IN BLOOD **I II**

CARTEL KILLAZ I II III

DOPE GODS I II

By **Hood Rich**

LIPSTICK KILLAH **I, II, III**

CRIME OF PASSION I II & III

FRIEND OR FOE I II III

By **Mimi**

STEADY MOBBN' **I, II, III**

THE STREETS STAINED MY SOUL I II

By **Marcellus Allen**

WHO SHOT YA **I, II, III**

SON OF A DOPE FIEND I II

HEAVEN GOT A GHETTO

Renta

GORILLAZ IN THE BAY **I II III IV**

TEARS OF A GANGSTA I II

3X KRAZY I II

STRAIGHT BEAST MODE

DE'KARI

TRIGGADALE I II III

MURDAROBER WAS THE CASE

Elijah R. Freeman

GOD BLESS THE TRAPPERS I, II, III

THESE SCANDALOUS STREETS I, II, III

FEAR MY GANGSTA I, II, III IV, V

THESE STREETS DON'T LOVE NOBODY I, II

BURY ME A G I, II, III, IV, V

A GANGSTA'S EMPIRE I, II, III, IV

THE DOPEMAN'S BODYGAURD I II

THE REALEST KILLAZ I II III

THE LAST OF THE OGS I II III

Tranay Adams

THE STREETS ARE CALLING

Duquie Wilson

MARRIED TO A BOSS I II III

By Destiny Skai & Chris Green

KINGZ OF THE GAME I II III IV V VI

Playa Ray

SLAUGHTER GANG I II III

RUTHLESS HEART I II III

By Willie Slaughter

FUK SHYT

By Blakk Diamond

DON'T F#CK WITH MY HEART I II

By Linnea

ADDICTED TO THE DRAMA I II III

IN THE ARM OF HIS BOSS II

By Jamila

YAYO I II III IV

A SHOOTER'S AMBITION I II

BRED IN THE GAME

By S. Allen

TRAP GOD I II III

RICH $AVAGE

By Troublesome

FOREVER GANGSTA

GLOCKS ON SATIN SHEETS I II

By Adrian Dulan

TOE TAGZ I II III

LEVELS TO THIS SHYT I II

By Ah'Million

KINGPIN DREAMS I II III

By Paper Boi Rari

CONFESSIONS OF A GANGSTA I II III IV

By Nicholas Lock

I'M NOTHING WITHOUT HIS LOVE

SINS OF A THUG

TO THE THUG I LOVED BEFORE

By Monet Dragun

CAUGHT UP IN THE LIFE I II III

THE STREETS NEVER LET GO

By Robert Baptiste

NEW TO THE GAME I II III

MONEY, MURDER & MEMORIES I II III

By **Malik D. Rice**

LIFE OF A SAVAGE I II III

A GANGSTA'S QUR'AN I II III

MURDA SEASON I II III

GANGLAND CARTEL I II III

CHI'RAQ GANGSTAS I II III

KILLERS ON ELM STREET I II III

JACK BOYZ N DA BRONX I II III

A DOPEBOY'S DREAM I II

By **Romell Tukes**

LOYALTY AIN'T PROMISED I II

By Keith Williams

QUIET MONEY I II III

THUG LIFE I II III

EXTENDED CLIP I II

By **Trai'Quan**

THE STREETS MADE ME I II III

By **Larry D. Wright**

THE ULTIMATE SACRIFICE I, II, III, IV, V, VI

KHADIFI

IF YOU CROSS ME ONCE

ANGEL I II

IN THE BLINK OF AN EYE

By **Anthony Fields**

THE LIFE OF A HOOD STAR

By Ca$h & Rashia Wilson

THE STREETS WILL NEVER CLOSE

By K'ajji

CREAM I II

By Yolanda Moore

NIGHTMARES OF A HUSTLA I II III

By King Dream

CONCRETE KILLA I II

VICIOUS LOYALTY

By Kingpen

HARD AND RUTHLESS I II

MOB TOWN 251

THE BILLIONAIRE BENTLEYS

By Von Diesel

GHOST MOB

Stilloan Robinson

MOB TIES I II III IV

By SayNoMore

BODYMORE MURDERLAND I II III

By Delmont Player

FOR THE LOVE OF A BOSS

By C. D. Blue

MOBBED UP I II III IV

THE BRICK MAN

By King Rio

KILLA KOUNTY

By Khufu

MONEY GAME I II

By Smoove Dolla

A GANGSTA'S KARMA

By FLAME

KING OF THE TRENCHES II

by **GHOST & TRANAY ADAMS**

QUEEN OF THE ZOO
By **Black Migo**

BOOKS BY LDP'S CEO, CA$H

TRUST IN NO MAN

TRUST IN NO MAN 2

TRUST IN NO MAN 3

BONDED BY BLOOD

SHORTY GOT A THUG

THUGS CRY

THUGS CRY 2

THUGS CRY 3

TRUST NO BITCH

TRUST NO BITCH 2

TRUST NO BITCH 3

TIL MY CASKET DROPS

RESTRAINING ORDER

RESTRAINING ORDER 2

IN LOVE WITH A CONVICT

LIFE OF A HOOD STAR

Smoove Dolla